W9-BBO-917

The Killing Kind

Books by Elliot West

Man Running
The Night Is a Time for Listening
These Lonely Victories
The Killing Kind

The Killing Kind

ELLIOT WEST

Houghton Mifflin Company Boston

Library of Congress Cataloging in Publication Data
West, Elliot. The killing kind. I. Title.
PZ4.W517Ki [PS3573.E817] 813'.5'4 75-34111
ISBN 0-395-24078-6

Printed in the United States of America

C 10 9 8 7 6 5 4 3 2

The Killing Kind

1

ONE NIGHT about six months ago Bedelia and I were coming out of a movie on Ventura Boulevard just as two narcotics dealers got the drop on two narcotics cops in the adjoining parking lot and shot them both. I shot both dealers as they were getting away, killing one of them. It was the first time I had ever fired a gun at anyone in all my years as a private investigator. It was ironic because the situation had nothing to do with me and only a one-in-a-thousand chance placed me at the scene.

The cops were trying to make a purchase and the two dealers got wise. My .38 revolver is always braced inside the glove compartment and I had a chance to get to it as the two hoods were jumping into their car after leaving the two cops bleeding on the ground. Bedelia gave sort of a scream and I told her to get down in the back seat. It wasn't hard for me to get a shot at their tires as they came down the open aisle past the row of cars in which I was parked. They were gunning it hard and their tires screeched. I was crouched alongside my right front fender and with two hands on the stock I easily shot out their right front tire. The car careered and slammed into the wall of the coffee shop on the opposite side of the parking lot and they were stopped dead as far as escaping in that car was concerned.

They weren't hurt and were getting out of the car. I couldn't back out of it now, and I yelled, "Freeze, you bastards," just the way cops do both on and off television. I had the .38 gripped tightly in both hands, my arms extended stiffly in front of me, my knees just a little bent and rigid. My heart was pounding and I was afraid they would shoot, which they did. They missed but I didn't, and both of them went down. It was so fast I didn't take it all in, and to this day I can't quite recall the exact details. But the difference was that they fired their guns while they were on the dead run and I fired mine standing still and aiming carefully. I fired quickly but steadily and I was lucky. I wanted to stop them from killing Bedelia and me and getting away. I must have been at least a little scared but I didn't know it until later. It is not easy to stand and exchange gunfire out in the open with scum like that.

Nobody seemed to know what to do immediately. Nobody came out of the coffee shop and I just stood there for what seemed like a long time. It was only a few seconds and I kept looking down at the two bodies. I knew right away that one was dead. I learned the other two men were cops when one of them told me as much in a strained voice from where he lay on the ground. Bedelia came running up to me, excited and frightened, naturally, and her voice was choked. "Sweetheart, are you all right?" she said. I had never seen her when she wasn't calm and poised. She grabbed my arm to be sure I was still alive.

"I'm absolutely all right," I said.

And then the crowd started to gather, coming out of the coffee shop and from other places, and in a minute or two a couple of black-and-whites swung in off Ventura Boulevard. The cops got out and began to take charge, two of them going to the aid of the wounded fellow-officers, one of them radioing for an ambulance and the other pushing people back. In a few seconds one of them was talking to me and I told him what had happened, who I was and what I had seen. He didn't say anything and walked over to where the two dealers were lying on the ground in their own blood. The color had come back into Bedlia's face as she looked at the two men I had shot, almost as if drawn to look in spite of herself. I took her arm and guided her a few feet away and said, "They'll want a statement, so we'll have to hang around for a few minutes. You okay?"

"Yes, I'm all right." But she was still shaken and it was easy to see why. I could feel the gun weighing down my jacket pocket where I had put it for the moment.

Inside of five minutes the area was swarming with policemen, ambulance people, a couple of police department doctors, and two news-camera crews and sound trucks. Homicide Lieutenant John Wagner went through the whole thing with me while one of his men made notes. The bodies were whisked away in two ambulances. The two cops were still alive but evidently critical. The surviving thug was hit only in the hip.

"Pretty tough babies," Wagner said. "Sorry you didn't get here a few seconds earlier."

"I wouldn't have known what was going on anyway until somebody shot somebody and started to run. The four of them looked like hippies; I couldn't tell them apart until one man said he was a police officer. And then it was too late."

"There'll be an inquest," Wagner said. "Probably next week, so stay in town. This your business address?" He was looking at my ID.

"Yes. I've been there for seven years."

"Your license clean?"

"Yes, it is."

"You'll be okay, I'm sure. The young woman saw what happened, didn't she?"

"Only partly. She was down in the back seat."

"You tried to make a citizen's arrest. The two men who shot the police officers resisted and tried to shoot you. You won't have any trouble. But maybe you should talk to your lawyer, just in case. You never know who takes it into his head to raise a stink on something like this. Some hotshot in the ACLU or a relative with a smart radical lawyer."

I didn't say anything and two reporters with microphones started to converge on me, a couple of guys with strap-on cameras following them. I said, "Get lost, I have no statements."

"You'd better give them something," Wagner advised. "That way they know everything is on the up-and-up."

I pushed Bedelia toward the car and walked a few feet away to be sure she was off camera. I told them what had happened, who I was and how it happened that I had a gun with me. No, I had absolutely no connection with the case. The two men fired their guns at me and I fired mine in self-defense. I said as much as quickly as possible and then excused myself. By then the crowd had thinned out considerably because the bodies were gone. Bedelia and I drove back toward her place.

"Darling, I can't believe it," she said. "I'm scared absolutely to death even now, but I can't help feeling that you're something to behold."

"You sound surprised," I said.

"I'm not, no, no," she said.

"Well, you should be. Because I am."

"I actually screamed," she went on. "I never thought I would do anything like that. I thought I was Lady Cool. I'd better look for some other image."

We got back to her apartment in a four-unit building on an uphill street off Laurel Terrace, and we had ourselves a couple of stiff shots of the Scotch I had bought a few nights before. "Strange, it should be you and me at just that moment," she said with a faraway look in her eyes. "We never have anything like that happen in our business, not even remotely like that. My God, what a weird feeling it is."

"Get to sleep, sweetheart," I said.

"Yes. You too, Jim."

Neither of us wanted to do anything more than say good night right then. At the door she said, "I know what it was that choked the sound out of me. In just those few seconds I felt my life fly out of me, Jim . . . Because I thought you were going to be dead when it was all over . . ." She held me tightly for a moment. I kissed her cheek lingeringly and then left her.

THERE WAS A LOT of publicity for the next two days, pictures at the scene of the shooting and long, detailed stories on the background of the two narcotics pushers and how the police had gotten onto them. And then a big dose about me and my "quick-triggered response" to the guns of the two criminals, about how I had acted with a cool head and "steel nerves in a hot spot." That kind of thing. Maybe it would be good for business but I would have been just as glad if it hadn't happened because I don't like that kind of spotlight when it comes right down to it. I must have received twenty-five calls from people who wanted to interview me either on television or in the papers, and I turned down every one of them. The following week the inquest, held in the Van Nuys Municipal Court Building, reached a verdict of justifiable homicide due to an act of self-defense on my part, and that was the end of it. Until the trial of the survivor. I would be a witness for the city, of course. But that probably wouldn't come up for quite some time. Bedelia said, "I wonder if you ever get away from something like this, Jim?"

"How do you mean?" I said.

"Does it keep coming back into your life in one form or another?" she said in that voice of hers that was like velvet with a little crimp in it. She was wise, especially for a kid of not quite twenty-five, and that was part of what had attracted me to her. She was half-standing, half-sitting, her buttocks braced against the edge of my desk, her arms folded beneath the splurge of her strong young breasts. She looked at me with blue eyes that were just as wide and almost as round as silver quarters. "I mean in ways that we can't even foresee," she said wonderingly.

"Maybe," I said. "But that's everything, sweetheart."

"Was it smart?"

"Maybe not. But I didn't go looking for it. And somebody else might have gotten shot dead or just crawled under his car."

She shook her head. "No, it wasn't smart. But you were larger than life, darling. I can't get over that, not even if I wanted to."

"Don't make more of me than I am, sweetheart. I was plenty scared at the time. And if it happened again I might just crawl under the car at that."

"It wouldn't matter because I'd be there with you."

"Let's drop the whole thing and get some work done around here before we're arrested for loitering."

But both Bedelia and the other member of the company were looking at me in a different light because of the incident. They were different relationships, of course. Don Price was my legs and muscle, a kind of junior partner who had been with me for two years before Bedelia arrived, and was a bang-up sleuth and never said no to anything I would hand him. He was very tall, quietly tough, but an extremely pleasant, almost shy kid of twenty-seven when he first joined me, and he talked with a slightly nasal drawl. It was a western accent that was smoothed out by contact with city people and by Stanford where he played a sticky-fingered pass-receiver for a couple of seasons while he was getting ready for graduate school to study law. Something he never did, by the way. He climbed walls and got away from punches a lot better than I could at that point in my life, and even took one or two on a couple of occasions with no ill-effects. I wasn't suited to too much of that kind of thing any longer. He said, "The penalties are too soft. Those two guys were in on narcotics charges twice before and right back on the street because of so-called improper police procedure. Result: one cop dead and one being fed through a tube. Shit. I'm glad you got one of them, Jim. Too bad it wasn't both of them."

He said all of that without raising his voice and he meant it. He was that way. He hated violent criminals and thought the law protected them far too much, which isn't exactly a unique opinion. A great many people feel that way. But Don had an old-time frontier outlook on justice. I guess I shared it to some extent but I had no regrets about not killing the other dealer.

Anyhow, the three of us were sitting around doing very little when the Colby case fell into our laps. A man named Simon Brooks telephoned for an appointment and then arrived at the office an hour later, acting as a go-between for Mr. John Colby, who was to be the client. By then Don was out of the office on a skip-tracing job we were working on for one of the big hotels in Beverly Hills.

Brooks was a perfect right-hand man to a hard-fisted millionaire — about fifty, well turned-out, neat, gray, closely shaved, his eyes steady but not challenging, an air of injury in them, everything he did or said in behalf of someone else — another person through whom he had to exist almost exclusively. He was here, it turned out, merely to set up an appointment for me to meet privately with Mr. Colby at a place and time of Mr. Colby's choosing, and not to give me any more information than that. "You'll have to go along with Mr. Colby's — uh — passion for privacy and security — understandable in his position, of course."

"Maybe I will and maybe I won't," I said brightly. "What does he need to have done for him?"

"That's for him to tell you. I'm only here to authenticate everything and see if you agree to the simple conditions, that's all. And to make sure you know who he is."

"Are you being funny now? Who doesn't know who he is? But why did he choose me for whatever it is?"

"Now who's being funny? Or is it just coy? You're a private detective, aren't you? Or do you prefer investigator?"

"Either one."

"The power of — what shall we call it? — instant replay? You must be the best-known private detective in the business. For the moment."

He stopped. His face was a bit fleshy but even-featured, his voice the product of good schooling had long ago, but too clipped and self-conscious. You needed a front, an air of importance when you did someone else's petty errands or dirty work, so you could cover up for yourself, to distract attention from what you really were. "Now," he said. "Do I leave a small retainer with you or don't I?"

"You do," I said. "As long as there's nothing queer about it. If there is, you get it back. Fast."

"Five hundred do? I know that's not your normal charge, but don't let it bother you."

"Yes, that will do nicely," I said, and he took out a certified check made out to me and put it directly under my nose on the desk. I looked at it, picked it up, and said, "You were pretty sure you'd get me, I can see."

"You *are* in business, aren't you?"

"That's right."

He made a little gesture to certify the conclusion. "You will receive your instructions very shortly. Directly from Mr. Colby. By phone."

That was about the size of it, and after a couple of back-and-forths concerning the details of what happened if I missed the phone call, Brooks walked out. He passed by Bedelia's desk and nodded at her with gentlemanly restraint as he departed. She and I were separated by glass partitioning, and I stood in the connecting doorway looking toward the office entrance even after Brooks was out of sight. "Not just window-shopping, was he?" Bedelia said.

"No," I said, folding the check and putting it in my wallet. "Call our answering service and tell them to refer any calls from a party named John Conrad to my home phone." That was the code name Colby had chosen.

"Are you going to sit next to the phone for this?" she said.

"Don't you think it's the least I can do for five hundred dollars?"

"Could have made an appointment call out of it," she said. "Or would that have been too intelligent?"

"Never argue with five percent of the GNP, sweetheart," I said. "At least not about anything trivial."

"I'll try to remember that," she said. "What do you think he wants?"

"Maybe he lost a gold-plated yo-yo. Who knows? He's kind of a nut and he makes everything more important than it is, from what I've heard of him."

"I've a theory that money and brains seldom go together," Bedelia said, propping a pocket mirror against the base of the phone on her desk and then beginning to redo her lips with that almost unnoticeable, faint orange color. "It's all a matter of cunning . . ." She tapered off as she grew more absorbed with what she was doing, touching up her lips and then pressing them together the way dames do.

"Think so?" I said, enjoying watching her.

"Sure. Look at us. What's being brainy done for us? Nothing. We *still* have to work for a living." She looked up at me and said, "And the big question is — should we pick up Chinese and take it home, or should I cook something?"

"It's up to you. Do you want Chinese?"

"You don't sound too wild about the idea."

"It doesn't matter to me. Turkey and ham sandwiches would be all right too."

We were like that. Silly talk, good moods, bad moods, and ordinary, everyday details came in for their due all the time, just as if we were married or related. Nearly three years together can do that to people, and it's nothing to complain about, as a matter of fact. Not if a lot more goes on underneath it. Anyhow, in a little while we were waiting together at my apartment in Sherman Oaks for John Colby's call.

I don't know if that was the beginning of this story, or whether it was when I shot the two dealers that night in the parking lot. It somehow all goes together. The whole thing centers on John Colby and his dropout wife. Without that there might have been another story. But I'm inclined to think it began at the beginning on that day nearly three years before when Bedelia walked into the office in answer to the ad I had placed in the L. A. *Times*.

She had studied acting at UCLA but knew shorthand and typing too. I needed someone who was willing to stick, so I didn't think I would take her on and I offered to call a couple of movie agents I knew — straight ones — to see if she could get started in TV. With that kisser, why not? No strings, I assured her. And I could tell she knew it and could have smelled a setup very fast. But she convinced me, to my surprise, that she really had little enthusiasm for that whole business and didn't want any part of it — at least not in the immediate future. She wanted the job as a private detective's secretary, that was why she was here. It was fine with me and I said, okay, she could take the front desk, a hundred and ten bucks a week the starting salary. It wouldn't have mattered to her if it had been half of that. Because before the week was out we had gone to bed together, something of which I hadn't the slightest thought, not even a wild dream, until the very instant she said, "I want you to make love to me." And yet when she said it it seemed okay — right, natural, not even surprising. It took my breath away and I couldn't conceive of anyone to whom I had a more perfect right, and, more than that, to whom I had a greater obligation. She was past twenty-one and she was a virgin. Why she had picked me to do what at least a hundred others must have wanted to do for the previous five years or more I didn't know. And it quickly didn't matter. All that mattered was that I had done it and it had both pained her and pleased her exactly as she had wanted it to. I know that because she said it in so many words at the time.

"Did you know we would come this far together, Jim?" she said as we now sat drinking coffee after eating the take-home Chinese dinner, and listening to a recording of Oscar Peterson I had put on.

"I never thought you would want to," I answered, looking at her, never having stopped appreciating those terrific good looks in which she herself took frank satisfaction but without being too vain.

"Shows you how much you know."

"Listen, sweetheart, five minutes before you walked in on me that day nobody could have put an idea like this in my head."

"It must have been there somewhere, Jim," she said sweetly. "Just kind of waiting. I think I knew that. That was part of everything for me."

"And I figured you were going to use me as a stopgap until you could become a movie star."

"That was all dear mother's fantasy, not mine. I lived with it for twenty bloody years."

"I know."

"I was in a hundred-mile-an-hour slide and I didn't know where it was headed or where it would end . . ."

"I know."

"And I knew I had to get away from her. But Jim, darling, if you think I knew what was coming next until I walked in that day, think again."

"I know, honey," I said. "That father of yours didn't help any, did he, walking out . . ."

"You know my mother. Can you hold it against him?"

"Sure I can. There should have been a man in that house to slap her down."

"He wasn't that kind," she said with a wistful look. "But there were others here and there," she added, and it was obvious what had made her head as old as it was that early in life. "You know her," she went on. "Vain, self-centered, impatient with everyone except people stronger than herself . . . convinced she's ten times smarter than she actually is, ten times better-looking, more deserving, less well-rewarded than she should have been . . ."

"Yeah, yeah, I know."

"She keeps telling me I'll be back with her someday."

"You've fooled her already; you'll never be back with her."

"Jim, you're wonderful."

"Thanks, sweetheart. I'm glad you think so. Someday you won't, but right now you do, and that's good enough."

The phone rang just as she was opening her mouth to answer me and it turned out to be the man I was waiting for. In a raspy tough voice he gave me the address of a skid-row hotel and a room number and told me he would be waiting for me at midnight. I almost told him to take his business elsewhere, but I didn't. Bedelia and I talked some more about ourselves, and the detective business, about her mother, about my ex-wife and my two daughters. And before we parted I made love to her for the first time since before the inquest. It's all luck, all chance, and love is something mysteriously trumped up between the two parties for reasons neither of them can really put a finger on.

3

IT WAS A RUNDOWN DIVE just off Spring Street, and I parked my car in the darkened lot across the street. Mr. Colby had picked this as a meeting place because he was as normal as a talking snake. He was old, around sixty-five, but big and tough and craggy-looking like the former steel-worker he was, sure everyone was out to get him and his hard-won millions, and not really completely unjustified in thinking so. But this kind of a meeting was an example of the overkill people like John Colby use in every situation. Their gates are higher, their locks heavier, their caution greater than anyone else's.

He was sitting at the edge of a box-spring bed, a small table in front of him, a cigar smoldering in an ashtray, his hat unremoved, and he gave me the once-over with hard eyes, his expression slightly screwed up in skepticism. I just stood there and gestured politely. "Go right ahead and tell me all about it, Mr. Colby," I said, looking right back at him in the dim light coming from the wall brackets in back of him.

"I won't beat around the bush with you," he said with that gravelly voice. "My wife has run out on me, and for reasons of my own I want her tracked down. Here's a photograph of her to start with." He pushed an envelope toward me along the top of the table as if it wasn't important enough to be picked up and handed over. "She disappeared about a week ago without a word."

"Take all her clothes?"

"Most. I'll give you whatever details you need if I think they're necessary. All I want you to do is find out where she went and where she is living right now. Then report to me. Nothing else."

"Naturally," I said and looked at the picture. It was cut off at the waist and I could see just well enough in the inadequate lighting to tell that Mrs. Colby had the kind of ex-chorine good looks it might take to make a monkey out of an old hard-ass like John Colby. "I'll need a description in addition to this," I said, putting the picture back in its envelope. "Height, weight, age, coloring, distinguishing birthmarks or scars, when last seen and by whom . . ."

"Birthmarks and scars?" he scoffed. "Do you want her brassiere-size too?"

"How do I answer that, Mr. Colby?"

"Don't. Just answer a couple of other questions for me, Mr. Blaney."

"Like what?"

"Like what kind of background you have to qualify you for this work?"

"I thought you knew why you were hiring me, Mr. Colby."

"I'm just interviewing you, Mr. Blaney. And I'm paying five hundred dollars to do it."

"I'll tell you anything you want to know within reason," I said.

"Go ahead. I want to know as much as possible about a man who's going to be trusted with my wife's distinguishing birthmarks and scars."

I looked at him. He was someone incapable of give and take unless it was part of a fight. That was what made him what he was and I spotted it immediately. The gaucherie he mistook for slashing wit came out of the kind of dumbness Bedelia had talked about in connection with the very rich. It didn't take much to spot that too. I said again, "I'll tell you anything you want to know within reason, Mr. Colby. Where do I start?"

"Are you old enough for World War Two?"

"Yes."

"Start there."

I shrugged modestly and paced a few feet and said, "All right. Seized by a patriotic impulse I enlisted in the army the day I turned eighteen in nineteen forty-two. I'll skip everything except that I was given a battlefield second lieutenant's commission during the Normandy Invasion. By then I was twenty. That should impress even you."

"It does, if it's not bullshit."

I stopped. "Want me to go on?"

"Sure, I do. What's the matter? Can't you take it?"

"If I can give it back, yes."

"Go ahead, go ahead. I'm fascinated," he said in the gravelly voice.

I paced back toward him and said, "I came out a captain and for two years I attended Claremont Men's College on the GI Bill with nothing much in mind. Quit, and went to work as an insurance investigator. Then as a Burns man. Then as a legman in the L.A. County D.A.'s office. And finally as my own man in my own business where I have been for the past fifteen years. I have a fine staff and all the experience and knowledge necessary to take care of the kind of problem you're stuck with right now. But no kid gloves, if you want me to do the job — no baby questions or tiptoeing through your ego, Mr. Colby. If I ask for details I want them whether *you* think they're necessary or not. Otherwise it's no-go."

He didn't flinch. "Anything else?" he said.

"I'll have to snoop through whatever belongings Mrs. Colby has left behind, maybe dig up some things you won't like. And my associates will be doing the same — questioning friends, relatives, neighbors, servants, the whole thing. The question is, can *you* take it?"

"Think you're tough, do you? Think you're going to take me apart just for the hell of it, do you?"

I was ready to ignore stuff like that. He had been bluffing and pretending for so long that he couldn't be any other way but tough and one-up on you in everything, even if he really wasn't. I said, "Is that what I said sounded like to you, Mr. Colby?"

"Okay, okay," he said. And dumb or not, he made surrender look like contemptuous withdrawal from a battle too small to fight. "I haven't given you any argument, have I, Mr. Blaney?" he said.

"When can I come to your house?" I said.

"I'll give you the number. Call the housekeeper for an appointment tomorrow morning."

I didn't mention it but he could have had me do that right off the bat, of course, and skipped all the voodoo. "How about a few facts right now just between us?" I said looking right at him.

It amounted to very little beyond the usual situation of its kind. There had been no spectacular fights, after all, no walkouts up till that time and no hints ahead of time of what finally happened. The idea of foul play was almost nonexistent because Mrs. Colby had methodically removed certain of her belongings and got off the premises in such a way as to suggest a carefully and long-considered move, one she had kept completely secret from her husband. I knew he was leveling with me, and in a few days I began to get to know some of the ins and outs of John Colby's world, the boundary lines and who stood where both inside and outside of them. Seven brothers and two sisters, to go over it fast, hated his guts in various degrees, and since there wasn't one of them who lived in anything better than a second-rate apartment or a broken-down house in a seedy neighborhood, it was easy to accept the fact on its face.

Actually only three of these relatives were located in Los Angeles, and the others, scattered throughout the rest of the country, I learned of through various sources including daughter Merrilee who was married to someone named Craig Smith. These two were aspiring rock'n'roll promoters in their twenties and were not inclined to talk much about anything. I visited them briefly in their rented house above Sunset Strip and I could see that they looked upon me as a natural enemy, their aloofness and cool bare tolerance of my presence very plain.

But they did steer me to brother Haggard Colby, a massive, bull-necked man of sixty, much like his brother John, and he tried with near success to throw me down a flight of stairs outside of his apartment door in the Crenshaw district. He had nothing against me, as he explained. It was just his way of sending a message to John. I kicked his shinbone raw as he began pushing me with his hands on my throat toward a downward plunge I didn't need. He let go and gave up on the idea and I said goodbye. I was sure he didn't have any relevant information anyhow.

I made a few other probes here and there, but in the long run my efforts didn't matter. Because within a week's time Don had actually done the job. He had worked it out by talking to Brooks at some length and getting a line on who some of Mrs. Colby's contacts may have been, and by then staying in close touch with those contacts, and finally glomming onto a return Las Vegas address on the envelope of a letter from Mrs. Colby, using the name Lois Wilson, to one of her two sisters in West Covina. It may not sound like much, but boiling it down to that particular party was not that simple a matter, and Don passed for more than just a fair big-league detective handling it the way he did. It took a good deal of checking and cross-checking and a couple of very tricky conversations with people who weren't in the mood for talk or for giving out information, and no client of any private investigator ever got better service.

THAT PARTICULAR MORNING I was in the office just five minutes when Don called from Vegas and passed the information about Mrs. Colby along to me. We talked for about fifteen minutes. I then got in touch with Colby's office and told Brooks that I had information of a confidential nature for Mr. Colby. He said he would come by and tell me how to handle it.

My office was situated in North Hollywood in a patio of various offices and business firms — an insurance company, a hairdresser, an ice-cream parlor, a neat little dress shop, an art-supply store, a camera mart, and a few other things. We were on the second floor in a row bordered by a balcony and reached by the outside staircase, an old Spanish-Hawaiian air to the place.

Bedelia and I had some coffee, went over a couple of accounts, remained very businesslike for the moment, almost too familiar with each other by now, and she looked at me in a funny way, as if to say, what now, my love? It was three full years since she had walked through the front door wearing the brightly flowered summery cotton dress just above the knees, the flat-heeled shoes, the polka-dot hairband, and something was happening to us I couldn't quite grab hold of, but I could feel it and was starting to be uneasy about it. I was hoping she would be the one to steer things and tell me what it was, and I was glad at the same time when she didn't. Brooks arrived just before lunch, sat down, and said to me, "Do you know Mariposa Canyon in Mariposa Beach?" He seemed somewhat more tense than when I had last seen him and he even glanced over his shoulder. Now that I had met Colby and had a load of his charm and refinement, Brooks seemed a very special expression of Colby's need to lord it over someone who was better than he was. I couldn't figure the association any other way, and I supposed Brooks was getting very good dough for being a part of it.

"I know the place," I said. "And you don't have to worry. There's no one here but my secretary."

He stiffened because I had caught him in a nervous mannerism. "I'm not worried, I assure you. Just doing a job as we all do."

"Sure. I take it Mr. Colby wants me to meet him in Mariposa Canyon this time and not a skid-row hotel room."

He pretended not to notice my small jibe and said, "At midnight tonight. I assume there's nothing to prevent you from doing so."

"I can be there."

"It's a very good place to have a meeting in perfect privacy," Brooks said, a hint of apology in his voice. "It may seem a bit extreme to others, but it's his — call it style."

"I would resent it if I were his haberdasher, but in my line things are always a little extreme," I said. I could have given Colby the whole thing on the phone in a minute or less, but that was of no importance. "I'll be there."

"Drive in five miles from the highway entrance and park," he said, ignoring my observation. "Be there at midnight. He'll join you."

I said I would do as instructed and he said goodbye and walked out, again nodding in that reserved way to Bedelia.

"It's all so baroque," Bedelia said. "Midnight meetings, the go-between who looks like a capon, the dropout wife whose clothes everyone wants to tear off."

"Do they? How do you know? And who is *every*one?"

"I've seen her picture and that's the only reason Colby ever married her. Because every sailor in port would go for her like a shot. It's his taste. It's the only thing he couldn't hang onto. And that's what attracted him in the first place. It's part of his basically low mentality."

"You're quite the smart-ass, aren't you?"

She sucked in her cheeks. "I've learned from a master."

"If he's got such a low mentality how can we part him from some of that stupid money of his?"

"We can't. His mentality is not that low."

"I didn't think so."

"There's always an answer."

"But do you really think a man starts out knowing he can't hang on to a woman?"

"Oh, God, honey, that's one of life's little commonplaces."

"It is, huh?"

"Go through Stekel," she said with a shrug.

"Is it as good as 'Believe It Or Not'?"

"It goes *both* ways. Look at *us*. I knew right from the start I couldn't get as much as I wanted with you. But was I smart enough to quit and walk away?" She shook her head with that smile she had, as if the joke was on her. "I'm still here — three years later."

"Hey, what is this?" I said and I went toward her. I put my hands on her shoulders and she came to her feet automatically and looked at me as if she was now too embarrassed or too hurt to discuss it. "You want to talk about anything?"

"Are you tired of me, Jim?"

"Tired of you? Sweetheart, I'm crazy about you. When I was away last summer settling my mother's estate, I walked around for days up there in Frisco like a lost dog."

"Did you?"

"You're the best girl I've ever known."

"Better than Rita?"

"That was different. I was no judge of girls at the time and we got married."

"But you loved her. I think sometimes you still love her."

"Not a chance. She's the mother of my two girls and she's not a bad character now that we're divorced, but I don't love her. I love you. I'll take you to lunch and prove it. I'll even pick up the check."

She said, "I know something better than that. My place."

"Oh, you're available, are you?" She hadn't been for several days, and one of the signs of uneasiness in my outlook was the fact that I hadn't realized it.

"Does it appeal to you?"

"Whatever you're offering, I'll take it," I said.

"I'm sorry about the graceless exhibition of nagging I just put on, darling . . ."

"Come on."

"It's just that I would hate to have you be bored with me and not know how to get out of things."

"That could work the other way around more likely, sweetheart. Ask any odds-maker."

"Not if we moved in together," she said. "There, I've said it. No pride at all."

"Darling, I love you. And you know it. Otherwise you wouldn't be as open with me about something like this as you are. But you don't want that. You might right now, but you wouldn't ten or fifteen years from now."

"Why don't you let me take the chance?"

"Because you're too sweet to be allowed to make that kind of mistake."

"Sweet? . . ."

"Sure you are. And you'd stick with it long enough to ruin yourself permanently."

She frowned at me. "You're down, Jim. I can hear it in your voice all of a sudden."

"No, I'm not. I'm just remembering that eight months from now I'll be fifty. That's all. And you remember it too. You see, baby, I'm not going to be the last man in your life."

"What a ray of sunshine you are today," she said, and was obviously upset with what I was saying. "All right. I had it coming. Something made me twitchy and I bombed out. Pardon me while I turn a couple of colors."

"Come on, cut that out," I said taking her face between my fingers. "What we need is a vacation. That trip on one of those P. and O. ships down through the Fiji Islands and Samoa and all the rest of those places."

She looked at me with renewed interest because we had talked about it before. "You're serious about that, aren't you?" she said.

I smiled and kissed her hand. "Why not?" I said. "About six months of drifting through the lotus blossoms and the blue lagoons."

"Gorgeous. And expensive."

"I never dream small, darling. Now if only my income were as big as my dreams."

The phone rang and Bedelia picked it up. "James Blaney Investigations," she announced in the cool, tony way she had, every syllable and sound like well-struck piano notes in the middle register. The slightest hint of disappointment crept into her voice as she said, "Just one moment," and handed the receiver to me.

"Daddy," the caller said, my daughter Jan having no need to announce herself. "Are you busy?"

"What's up, sweetheart?" I said. "We haven't talked in weeks."

"Could we get together?" she asked.

I looked at Bedelia who was now standing at the door, her face blank all of a sudden as if she didn't care what came next. But I knew she did and I was almost afraid to ask Jan if something was wrong. I did anyhow and all she said was, "Can you get away? I'd rather not come up there. Can we meet for lunch?"

I looked at Bedelia as I said to Jan, "Yes, honey, of course, if there's something you want to talk about."

Jan said, "I'm at fourteen-eleven Tennis Trail, apartment three. It's just above Franklin a few blocks east of Highland."

It meant nothing to me and was even puzzling. Bedelia read the message in my eyes and the tone of my voice, and she knew without being told that our little matinee, to put it frivolously, was being called off. She gave me a look of farewell. There was something else in her eyes I was sorry to see there and couldn't quite figure out. "You go ahead," she said, walking out. "I've some shopping to do anyhow."

Alone in the office and torn in two directions, I asked Jan again if everything was all right. "I can't talk on the phone, Daddy," she replied.

Which meant that everything wasn't all right. I said, "I'll be there as soon as possible."

I walked out to the long balcony overlooking the patio just in time to see Bedelia disappearing through the Spanish arch leading to an arcade of more shops of various kinds. She had been walking rapidly and I had a sense of longing for her greater than it had been a few minutes before. That was life, wasn't it?

My car, a '70 Ford Galaxie just about paid for, was parked in the blacktop lot across the street on a monthly basis, and I got to it as fast as I could.

IT WAS A SCROFULOUS FRONT ROOM reeking with trouble and anxiety, the walls sickish green, the furniture grimy, the carpet punished by a million passing feet. It was all the more of a jolt to me because it had been my impression that Jan was still at home with her mother and her mother's husband in Hollywood, where they lived in one of those old houses north of Franklin and west of La Brea, along with Loretta, my other daughter who was only seventeen. I wasn't in constant contact, needless to say.

"It's just a temporary situation, Daddy," Jan assured me and then hustled me out of the place and back to where the car was parked. "I'll tell you all about it."

She was now twenty-two and she seemed less babyish than when I had last seen her, but a bit thin and fatigued. I drove toward the Farmer's Market for lunch and learned the whole story of her walkout, and the fact that she wanted me to do her a favor, something she couldn't do for herself because it meant she would need to see her mother and she wanted to avoid that. She wanted me to get the key to a safe-deposit vault containing certain of her belongings. And then she gave me the four-star punchline.

Simply put she was living with someone. A man. Not acceptable to Rita and Steve. She told me as much with the disdain and intolerance of the very young, and I said, "Jan, you can't expect parents to be thrilled when their daughter winds up that way, I don't care how much times have changed. Now I'm not saying what's right and what's wrong. But I *am* saying that you can't expect your mother to love the idea."

At that point we were still driving toward the Market along La Brea. "Daddy, will you do as I ask?" she said.

"Why don't *you?* It's simple enough. Or have you disowned your mother?"

"No. But I can't see her . . ."

"Who is this person?"

"His name is Richard Strelli."

"Strelli?"

"Italian, yes," she said. "But not a member of the Mafia."

"So he's Italian and not a member of the Mafia," I said, admittedly irritated by something in her voice. "What else is there to recommend him?"

"You'd have to know him."

"And you're living with him. And your mother is unhappy."

"But angry too. She loathes Richard . . ."

"Now wait a minute. Maybe she just loathes, as you put it, the idea that you're not married, whether you think it's outdated and all the rest of it or not."

"Oh, Daddy, are you that naive? Mother and Steve don't want what they consider a radical for a son-in-law any more than they want me to live in sin with him." She laughed with unexpected gaiety.

"I might not relish the idea myself," I said.

"You might or might not, but you're not hung up with the kind of conventions and standards that other people are . . ."

"What do you mean by that?" I said defensively.

"Only that you live as you see fit, don't you? You're not observing the totems and taboos, are you?"

"Do you mean Bedelia and me?" I said, feeling caught because I wasn't sure how I would be able to get out of the argument alive. "That's different."

"Oh come on, Daddy, how is it in the least bit different? You're not married. And I don't mean to be rude or disrespectful, but you don't exactly hold hands, and why should you?"

"Look, I'm forty-nine years old, and I've already gone through the expected and conventional things."

"And she's twenty-four, so where does that leave *her?*"

"Ah, but we've separate domiciles," I came back at her. "You and this man are under the same roof."

It sounded okay to me but Jan said, "Oh, Daddy, how can you rationalize like that?"

"There is a difference," I insisted. "She means a great deal to me, I'll be open with you about that, and we see each other constantly. But she's a person on her own, not bound to me by the appearances of a marriage that just isn't there."

"That's double-talk, Daddy. I wouldn't have expected it of you."

It went around and around like that and by the time we were halfway through lunch at the Farmer's Market I had agreed to act in the capacity she wished me to. We were sitting there with a little breeze flapping the awning fringes in the patio with its round dining-tables within the perimeter of the various food concessions — the coffee and donuts, the barbecued sandwiches, the pizza, the ice cream, the chow mein, — all clean and confident-looking places, lots of basically contented people lunching all around us. "I know you're having a hard time with the idea, but you'll understand it eventually," she said.

"I understand it now, Jan. It's your life. I'll give your mother a call sometime this week about the vault key."

By the time I got back to the Valley Bedelia was back at her desk and I could see that something was gnawing inside of her. But she managed to give me a soft smile. "Have a nice lunch?" she asked.

"Not too good," I said, and came over to sit on her desk. "I'm sorry about our date. I couldn't get out of this other thing. Jan needed to see me. Not that I don't think that being with you is important. It *is*. To me. You know that."

"Jim, if your daughter needs you, of course you have to go to her. I don't want you to think I'm competing."

But I wasn't satisfied. I felt like one of those guys who couldn't help *any*body out no matter what he did or said. "I just hope you really understand. The last thing I want is to have you get any wrong ideas about how things stand."

She gave me a smile that was a little too wise. "Jim, darling, I've done my silly act once already today. I'm not going to do it all over again with childish tantrums and jealousy. I've got to be a bigger girl than that."

"Then you *are* upset. You think you got a bad deal today. And if *you* didn't, Jan would. There's no way a man can do the right thing."

"Darling, have I complained?"

"Not in so many words. But I never had a chance to talk to you before you left. I got the feeling you felt you were being pushed aside."

She smiled. "Somebody has to be."

"Now that's just a little bitchy," I said without raising my voice or showing any anger.

"Darling, you raised the point. I was sitting here minding my own business when you walked in and started being guilty all over the place. You don't have to. You can only be so many things at one time."

"The thing is there's always tonight."

"That's true. But what if there weren't?"

"I try not to play games like that."

"Why not? You can learn a lot from games. I'm just supposing. What if there were no tonight or tomorrow? What if there had been just lunchtime today? You know. Like a soldier with just two hours before train time. Would it have made a difference?"

I just looked at her for a few seconds because I was so taken off balance and didn't have an answer. And then I said, "Which one of us are you trying to hurt with that question? Me or you?"

The expression of her face slackened, and I looked away from her and walked back toward my own area. I felt lousy and when I reached my desk I turned toward her and said, "Do you have Don's number in Vegas?"

"Do you want me to call him now?" she said, always the accommodating secretary, quick and efficient.

"Please. See if he's there, and if not leave a message asking him to call us back."

She began to take care of it, her face turned away from my momentary gaze toward her. I began to fiddle around with things on the desk and knew there was no way I could come out being anything but a ninny in a situation like the one that had come up, because I couldn't do much about it. I figured she had had to do something to offset her feelings, whatever they were. And if beating me up a little bit did anything for her, it was okay with me. I could take that much all right.

"Don is on the line," she announced after a minute.

"Hi, Jim," he said. "I'm still on the lady and nothing has changed. What do you want me to do?"

"Check in with me up till eleven o'clock tonight if anything does change," I said. "I don't know where I'll be, so leave your call with the service and I'll call you back."

"Okay. This is a roaring place, this Vegas."

He had never been there before. "Watch yourself, Don. The women up there bite."

"Shit," he drawled, and Bedelia laughed faintly. Don heard her voice and apologized. "Didn't know you were on the line, Bedelia."

"It's all right, Don," she said. "I have to find out about life sometime."

"Yeah," he said with a chuckle.

"Listen, Don," I said. "Stay put until I check with you tomorrow — that is, assuming we don't talk later today."

"Okay."

"I'm reporting to the client tonight. That will probably finish the thing and bring you back to L.A. tomorrow."

"Right."

"You did a damned good job, Don. I'm impressed."

"Well, thanks, Jim, gee that's swell."

"My lower lip isn't quivering and there are no tears in my eyes," I said. "But you qualify for a Puffed Wheat detective badge and a secret-code ring."

"Gee, thanks Jim," he said. "What about the whistle?"

"The whistle too, Don," I said. Then: "Okay. I guess that's about it."

"Does she look like her picture, Don?" Bedelia asked.

"It's a pretty good likeness, as a matter of fact."

"Well, okay, Don. Stay with it," I said.

"See you later, Jim. So long, Bedelia."

I walked back to Bedelia's cubicle. "Can I come by at the cocktail hour?" I said.

She looked at me fondly. "Sure," she said, nodding her head.

I followed her back to her apartment at about five-thirty. She put on Ella Fitzgerald singing Gershwin songs and a Teddy Wilson album with cuts of "Night and Day" and "East of the Sun" among others. Those were the upper-middlebrow and ancient tastes she had gotten from me. We listened and talked while we drank a couple of Bloody Marys, and the cares of the day vanished like feathers caught in a strong updraft. In a little while she was caught in the crook of my arm, her head on my shoulder as we sat on the sofa. "Want to make love to me?" she asked softly.

We didn't go out to dinner until eight-thirty. But when she asked me if I would come back after my midnight meeting, I said I thought it would probably be too late. She didn't reveal any disappointment if she felt any.

6

THERE WERE STARS in the sky but the night was nearly pitch black because the neighborhood was wild and unpopulated and no developer had done anything about it. Just a canyon connecting the main highway and the town of Mariposa Beach, hillsides filled with scrub and dried brush to left and right of the paved two-lane road. I gave Colby the rundown on his troubles as we sat side by side in the 1962 Ford he had chosen to drive to the rendezvous.

"Mrs. Colby is in Las Vegas," I informed him. "My operative has a full report on the situation. Basically, she is living with a man named Max Ganner. He's a known hood, though not high up. She knew him before she married you. Maybe you're aware of that. Maybe you're not."

I don't know whether he was expecting it or not but he didn't say anything.

"I'll give you the address," I said. "We can either continue the surveillance or call it off; that's up to you."

He looked toward me in the dark. "You think you've come to the end of the central issue," he said with triumph in his voice that seemed fake. "But you haven't."

"I don't think anything in particular. You hired me to trace your missing wife. I've given you the results."

"It's not her I'm interested in," he said. "That surprises you, doesn't it?"

"You could say that. Especially since my services will run you something over fifteen hundred dollars."

As if I hadn't said anything he went on. "A woman is one thing. Nearly a million dollars' worth of diamonds is something else. That's what I've been talking about from the beginning, though I wouldn't expect you to know it. I've been saying one thing and meaning another."

"Some people do that all the time."

"With a reason, Mr. Blaney. Never give too much information all at once. People can't handle it."

I didn't say anything, because I knew he had to save some face. His wife took a powder on him with a two-bit hoodlum, and he had to let you know it wasn't worth a Bronx cheer to him. He had been one up on you all the time and had decoyed you into looking the wrong way until he was sure you were ready to be set straight. But the funny thing was, it was all true. "We're talking about the better part of a million dollars in diamonds mostly — jewelry of different types, brooches, bracelets, rings, and a tiara she never wore — all bought for her but not her legal property. The ownership is mine only, not hers. She skipped out with it. And that's where you come in. If you've got what it takes."

"I'm in the dark in more ways than one, Mr. Colby," I said.

"I want the jewelry back without publicity, no scandal, no police. Otherwise I could report it and just bring charges against her. But she's not going to get that much satisfaction. So your job is to get it back without making a sound about it. Let her wake up and find it gone and with nothing to do about it, the slut. Now don't worry, I can produce bills of sale, so you've got the law on your side. No matter how you get it back, there won't be legal consequences because no one will have grounds to bring charges against you. See how it works?"

"I think you've got the wrong idea about me, Mr. Colby."

"Who's the millionaire? You or me? I don't get wrong ideas."

"Well, you did this time. I'm an investigator and I don't hire out as anything else."

And then that woeful funnybone of his hit me on the head again. "Oh, I'm so sorry. I didn't know you were one of the Rover Boys. Wait a minute while I get you your good-conduct medal."

"Well, it's better than a shroud. Look, your wife might have planned for a long time to steal off in the night with that jewelry for Max Ganner's benefit. She was evidently his sweetheart before she married you and now she's gone back to him, worth a lot more than when she left him."

He was burning like one of those blast furnaces he had worked at so many years before, because of what I was saying to him. "You're just too yellow to take it on. Admit it," he said, with the viciousness that must have helped him to climb up that ladder from the forge.

"I'm not trying to hurt your feelings," I said, still reasonable in tone. I didn't get steamed at the suggestion I was yellow and I wouldn't have from the time I was eleven. I liked adventure and I wouldn't have been a private eye at the age of forty-nine had my brain developed along with the rest of me — I wouldn't have lost a good wife and two daughters to another man. I knew what I was. But I was prudent about facing guns in the hands of people who meant to use them, despite what had happened a couple of weeks before. "If your wife took that stuff to Ganner for him to share or put to some personal use, it's not your wife that has to be faced, it's Ganner. A bad man with other bad men around him. Try getting it back from him without the help of two or three court-appointed marshals." I shook my head. "I don't do that kind of work, and I don't know a private investigator who does."

"I know that. And I thought you might be the exception."

"I never said anything to lead you to believe that."

"How about the shoot-out in the movie-house parking lot?" he said.

I said, "Oh."

"But maybe that was just an accident. Sometimes people get heroic when their minds aren't clear enough to know what they're doing. Sometimes they act out of fear."

"That's right. If I had stopped to think that whole thing through, Mr. Colby, I'd have stayed out of it. But I can see where your false impression of me came from." I started to open the door. "If there's anything else, you let me know, Mr. Colby. But keep it small."

"Blaney." He paused, and I stopped in the middle of opening the door to get out of the car with one foot on the ground. He said, "There could be a lot of money in this for you." He paused again and then said, "I'll make it fifteen percent of the face value of everything recovered . . ." His voice was suddenly wheedling and sly. "That could be as much as . . . a hundred and fifty thousand dollars."

I didn't say anything and he went on. "All you have to do is figure a way in and a way out — something that might take just a matter of minutes once you got it worked out . . ."

I got out of the car and shut the door and looked in at him. "I appreciate the offer."

"Disrespect for money is one of the greatest stupidities. You think about that."

I didn't say anything.

"I'll give you twenty-four hours. And a piece of advice to go with it. There's a difference between acting quick and acting hasty. Once you know what it is, you've got a head start on success."

He turned over the engine as I looked in at his dim figure hunched at the wheel and his deeply enshadowed face. "Anything else?" I said, and I didn't know why.

"Yes," he grumbled. "Don't ever get mixed up with a woman twenty-five years younger than you are." He added, "But she's not going to declare any dividends in this, you can bet on it. Twenty-four hours, Blaney. Not ten seconds more."

He began to accelerate and I backed away from the car. He drove away and left me standing there, his words ringing in my ears more than he knew. I went back to my car twenty feet away, got in and started driving back toward L.A. I felt the impact of what he had said a minute or two later. And then I was unable to get the idea of a hundred and fifty thousand dollars out of my head no matter how hard I tried. It made me a little dizzy, and I was glad he had given me time to think it over. Of course, I was a dead pigeon as soon as he did the arithmetic for me.

IT WAS DON who was ready to take the thing on right from the start. It was up to me to say the word and he made it hard for me to say no. "We can handle it between the two of us, Jim; I'm damned sure of that," he said. "Why shouldn't you get a shot at that kind of dough?"

"You'd come in for a fourth, Don, as far as that goes," I said.

"You don't have to give me a fourth, Jim," he said.

"Don't be General Custer, kid," I told him. "Nobody'll care when you're gone. Someone says take a fourth, take a fourth."

"I'm not exactly needy," he drawled good-naturedly.

"That's why it's only a fourth, dummy," I said.

We were driving back from the Burbank Airport where I had picked him up from his flight back from Las Vegas. He laughed and then squinted and said in that quiet, Wyatt Earp way he sometimes had, "We could take them if we had to."

"But you can't afford to be wrong," I said, keeping my eyes straight ahead as we moved at sixty-five toward the Van Nuys Boulevard off-ramp. "Guys like Ganner act funny when someone tries to hijack them. They put acid in people's eyes or pour cleaning fluid down somebody's throat. We're not selling that kind of service."

"Life is full of chances. And you're the boss, Jim. But I've seen Ganner and his boys and they're shit, if I can put it that way." Don was six feet four and he tapered down from a forty-four shoulder to a thirty-two waist, and he could put it any way he wanted to and make you believe it. "But hell, I don't want to push it."

I grinned a little and said, "Sure you do."

It was Bedelia's idea that the way to get a line on the jewelry was through Mrs. Colby herself. "I could get to know her easily and never be in any danger," she said, as she, Don, and I discussed it in the office immediately after we got back from the airport. "I could pretend to be a secretary on vacation, all alone and looking for action. There are girls like that at every watering hole in the country. If Mrs. Colby isn't on the prowl for men for herself, she'll take on a temporary girl friend sitting at poolside or somewhere else around the hotel. I can try anyhow. They hang around the Tremayne, you say, Don . . ."

"Ganner has friends there."

"Then that's where we should check in."

"What do you think, Jim?"

I saw there behind my desk, leaned back in the swivel chair like a tired Fagin who knew less about everything than the two pupils did. "I was afraid you'd ask me that."

"It gets us down on their level, no matter how you look at it," Bedelia said. "It's dirty work at the crossroads. But it's one hell of a lot of money. You'd be rich, Jim. Not filthy-rich but rich enough . . ."

She tailed off and I said, "You can't be dragged into it, honey."

"Don't be quaint," she said. "All I'll have to do is set things up if they *can* be set up. You could never do it any other way. It would be crazy to try rough stuff with people like that."

"I just want to say," Don said, "that there's nothing illegal in it. It's just not orthodox. We have to keep that in mind . . . I mean, we're not hurting anyone innocent. I've seen Ganner and Mrs. Colby, and I don't like to cast aspersions on other folks. And it's something I try never to do. But take it from me, those two are pure-bred scum. And I could say more but I'll leave it at that."

Bedelia and I both laughed because Don was deadly earnest about it. And then I stopped laughing and said to her, "I'd have to be a four-star rat to let you do anything like this . . . And I've got a sinking feeling that's just what I'm going to wind up being."

Don was standing near the window on his side of our area, tall, handsome, his features straight, his eyes blue and unflinching but at the moment looking away from us. "I'm going to have an ice-cream soda," he said. "I'll be back in fifteen minutes, okay?"

"Sure," I said.

When he got to the door he said, "Whatever shot you call, Jim, is okay with me. It's only money."

When he had gone Bedelia said, "It must be nice to be able to afford to say that and mean it."

I nodded. "I've got that sinking feeling," I said.

"Darling," she said coming over and sitting herself in my lap. "No mea culpas. If you want to do it, go ahead, and then don't look back and never feel like a four-star rat . . ."

"I'd probably get accustomed to it," I said, my arms around her.

"Sure you would," she said. "And if you want to turn it down, okay, do that, and then forget about it. If you think you can . . ."

I didn't answer and she kissed me on the mouth, not long and hard but sweetly. Then she looked into my face and I could see all that youth and life and passion in those eyes and I smiled softly. She said, "Do you think you could?"

I thought about it for a few seconds, and then said, "Not easily."

She said, "Neither could I."

The three of us were in Vegas by five o'clock that afternoon. Before leaving L.A. I talked on the phone to Brooks and told him to let Colby know that what we had talked about was acceptable to me, just that, nothing more. Bedelia, Don, and I each checked into the Tremayne (I'm just calling it that because I can't call it or its associates by their right names, and it doesn't matter anyway) from a separate direction and at a different time. The place is enormous and is jammed with guests even on weekdays and no one notices anyone unless he or she is a name or for some reason a target. So the three of us were in no danger of being connected to each other, and Don and I could keep an eye on Bedelia at fairly close range without any risk of being unmasked. That night she made a preliminary contact with Mrs. Colby in the ladies' room of the hotel lounge where one of the lesser comics and a flamenco trio, two dancers and a guitar, were being featured. And by the following afternoon she consolidated the gain at poolside.

I watched from the bar across the pool area. It was sunny and dry and the place was full of life. I couldn't tell what was being said, but Bedelia was seated side by side with Mrs. Colby, both of them wearing swimsuits and having a conversation. Bedelia seemed to be doing most of the talking and was doing it easily and pleasantly and Mrs. Colby appeared to be listening with interest. They both smiled from time to time and gave the impression of either being in agreement on something or exchanging a mutually appreciated joke, maybe risque or worse. Bedelia looked smooth and tawny and was wearing a cool-blue one-piece suit. Mrs. Colby was about thirty-five, a glittery and hard-boiled number with dark-blond hair, carefully streaked, her body pneumatic and smooth and sleek as the skin of a wet seal because it was coated with oil. She had all the obvious enticements of a high-class stripper, the prettiness she had started out with by now pretty well toughened.

Bedelia was walking a very tight line and from what I could tell probably walking it well. The idea was to worm into Clare Colby's confidence to enough of a point where the resting place of the jewels could somehow be calculated. Maybe Mrs. Colby would even shoot her mouth off about such prized possessions in an unguarded moment or an outburst of vanity. It was up to Bedelia to produce the unguarded moment or find that vain spot if she could. Talk among girls. That was the device.

She told Mrs. Colby she was up from L.A. on a two-week vacation from her job in an attorney's office. She indicated very strongly that she was out for a good time, and used flattery very carefully to soften up the target. She told Don and me about it that night when we met in my room.

The following afternoon I was sitting right next to them in almost the very same spot on Bedelia's right. I was stretched out as if I were after a suntan, my glasses covering my eyes and acting almost like a concealment. A guy lying out there taking the sun was just part of the scenery. My hand was inches away from Bedelia's firm and lightly tanned thigh, a faint dusting of golden hair-follicles along the surface of her skin. I felt slight stirrings of desire, the sun hitting me in just the right dose, a straightforward and honest erection on the rise and about to give me away. It didn't, thanks to the exercise of my will. I had a tough time stifling a laugh. And through it all I was straining to pick up their conversation in the yammer of other voices in the area and splashing of water and the occasional escape of piano music coming from the bar.

For a few minutes the talk centered on the merits of the floor shows at several of the different hotels along the Strip — Dean Martin at the Sands, Totie Fields at the Sahara, Diana Ross at the Tropicana — and then shifted to the psychology behind the joint viewing by husbands and wives of the almost totally naked and voluptuous women in the show at the Tremayne. "I think the women are just as aroused as the men because they're sitting there with them at the same time," Mrs. Colby said in her slightly high pitched voice touched with a midwestern twang. "They know what's going on in their husband's mind and it gets them jealous but it turns them on too."

"It's a form of voyeurism," Bedelia said. "Everyone has a touch of it."

"You sound as if you've had a very good education, honey. Were you to college?"

"Just secretarial school."

"You must have been paying attention to everything that was said. I never went beyond second-year high. I had no aptitude."

"You didn't need it with your looks."

"Men like a woman with some brains and nice ways, don't fool youself. That's why I've tried to elevate myself whenever I could. It's not just what's between one's thighs. It's what kind of a personality have you got."

"I think you've hit on a basic truth," Bedelia said.

"There's no doubt of it. Otherwise it's bang-bang and out. And you're like something dropped down a laundry chute."

The conversation seemed to be running downhill and I felt like a guy watching the ivory ball keep missing his number spin after spin. And then finally Mrs. Colby livened things up. "Ever hear of a man named Sal Bancanno?" she said.

"I don't think so," Bedelia said.

But I had heard of him.

"He's a friend of Max's and mine. Max is my fiancé. Anyhow Sal is a close friend, a bachelor and a charming guy really. I think he'd like to meet you if you have no other plans. I just happened to think of him because he's in town and unattached. He's taken out a couple of the girls from the shows but I don't think he was too interested."

"Who is he?"

Mrs. Colby's eyes drifted and landed on me. "He's a businessman," she answered.

"Oh."

I looked away as casually and innocently as possible and Mrs. Colby said, "Good-looking. Dark, but not too dark. The Latin type. Only about thirty-eight or forty. A nice man really. I think you'd bowl him over. And *you* might even like *him*. But I know how you might be reluctant."

"I'm no snob," Bedelia said with a laugh.

"I didn't think so. No one comes here by herself if she is. Unless she's a gambler."

"Not with money."

Mrs. Colby said appreciatively, "I like that. What's your room number?"

"One thirty-two."

"I'll give you a call. Maybe even tonight. That okay?"

"Don't hesitate. And thank you."

"What for? You're not just another Las Vegas bimbo, and I like that."

When we all met in my room later in the day I said, "I'm not crazy about this Bancanno thing."

"You're not going to get squeamish now, Jim, after all this trouble," she said, looking me in the eye with a flicker of real disappointment in her expression. "She's on the brink of opening up with me; I can feel it. She has no friends up here because she's new to the place. But she still needs to feel more intimate with me. Partying with her at night is the way to do it."

"Yes, I know all that," I said. "What happens if this creep begins to grope you?"

"Jim, I can handle it," she said earnestly.

"Can you?"

Don said, "Maybe Jim's right, Bedelia. Maybe we ought to try something else."

"Like what? Go in shooting?" she said.

"Or not go in at all," I said.

"I await your pleasure, sir," she said with a little shrug. "I'm just one of the crew."

Don said, "Look, guys, I'm going to go back to my room and get out of this and get into a shower."

All of us were still wearing poolside and tennis-court togs, and so Don's departure had some kind of a motivation to hide the fact he wanted to leave us to ourselves. Once alone Bedelia said to me, "I'll back out of it if you want me to, darling. But if you think it's worth losing a hundred and fifty thousand dollars just to keep my left tit from being violated even fleetingly . . . well, I don't."

"Depends on how you look at things," I said.

"Think about it, darling. And then you tell me what you want me to do."

"Let's pack it in."

"You don't mean that."

"No, I guess I don't."

"Not a damned thing will happen anyway," she said, coming close to me and putting her arms around my neck. "Bancanno isn't going to be stupid enough to get rough with any woman who doesn't invite it. Besides he's looking for re*feen*ment."

I looked down into her eyes and her closeness stirred me again. "You know, I suddenly got a terrific yen for you when we were sitting out at the pool before. I sent it away but it's back again."

Her eyelids dipped and her lips parted and she said, "Yes, darling, I've already noticed it."

I DROPPED a hundred dollars at the crap table and walked away and began to wander around the casino, entertaining myself as much as possible by looking at the gamblers. The roulette, the blackjack, the dice, and the baccarat were all busy and the din was immense. I tried to keep my mind on the rollers and the card players so I could keep my mind off Bedelia, but it was no use. She was out with Mrs. Colby and Ganner and some of those other creeps they hung around with, and her escort for the evening was Sal Bancanno. A very recognizable undesirable. Two more days had gone by after all by the time all of this was arranged.

After a while Don, who had watched the floorshow at the Sahara, met me in one of the downtown pokerino parlors where it was easy to loiter and drink coffee. It had an open front onto the sidewalk and was lit up like a display window: guys with boots and string ties, henna-haired, heavily rouged old ladies, long-haired teen-age boys, loose-swinging teen-age girls, and hookers everywhere, back and forth. We were sitting at a table with two a.m. hamburgers and coffee. "If the stuff is in a vault," Don speculated, "we'll need to find out in which bank and let Colby know about it. He might be able to work something out with the bank manager directly. That's if the rocks aren't in the house."

It made me irritable to hear him say as much and I said, "Come on, you're not talking like the bright young feller I know you are. If the rocks are not in that house of Ganner's we're out of business. Colby wouldn't for a moment consider such a move. He'd have to get a court order and for that he doesn't need us. That's just what he doesn't want. Remember?"

"Yeah, I remember," he said. "What the hell made me say that?"

"Another thing: Ganner himself isn't in a million years going to stash hot goods in a bank vault where the Justice Department or the IRS or even the local police can pounce on it. Hot goods or anything else." I shook my head. "They might be buried under the ninth tee of the Desert Inn golf course, but they're not in a bank."

"Then they're in the house for sure. That *is* what makes the most sense when you think it through."

"Sure, they're in the house. Unless they're not."

"Jesus, you can go on and on with that game until you start talking to yourself."

"Until you either find out where they are or give up trying."

"They're in the house," Don said, quietly convinced all of a sudden. "That's the only thing that makes sense."

"Okay. Then all we have to do is find a way to get our hands on them without winding up in shallow graves somewhere between here and Reno."

"We're not winding up in shallow graves. My mother wouldn't like it."

"I wouldn't like it either, kid."

He grinned faintly and took a bite of his hamburger and a sip of coffee. I sat there in a sour mood. It was too late to be sitting in a place like this waiting for what we were waiting for. "The trouble is we're suddenly not detectives exactly, but three desperate characters trying to locate the Maltese Falcon. But it's all ad lib. We don't have a plan from minute to minute." I took a sip of my coffee, my eyes on two hookers making contact with two blue-suited sailors. "We have no move to make until someone gives us an opening."

"Just one fumble, Jim, is all it takes," Don said with the quiet, square-jawed confidence. "You just have to be ready for it."

Just as he said it, Bedelia appeared, out of a cab and walking briskly across the sidewalk to where we both got up to greet her. As we all sat down she said with controlled excitement, "I saw them. I saw the goodies."

"The rocks?" Don said under his breath and with scarcely moving lips.

"The rocks." Her eyes were glistening. "She just showed them to me, just like that," she said, and her lips curled in a smile of satisfaction and also disbelief at the simple good fortune she had had. "It's crazy. You're looking for the hard way, and then this." She shook her head.

"Why would she do that?" Don asked, screwing up his eyes.

"Very simple. Because to her they're rightfully her own. As far as she's concerned all she's done is run out on a husband who got his money's worth for five years. And I'm just someone she can show off to, and for some reason trusts."

"Where are they kept?" Don said.

"In the bedroom. They're locked in a strongbox and the box is in a vanity-table drawer."

"How was Bancanno?" I said.

"The dream of his life is that you'll mistake him for Ronald Colman."

"Where was he when this was happening?" I said.

"Shooting pool with Ganner in the game room. We had all gone back to the house — Clare, Max, Sal, and I, a couple of other intellectuals and somebody's son from Chicago and a tootsy they had fixed him up with. This was after the show at the Tropicana and a couple of hours in the casino. I won *eleven hundred dollars* at the crap table, by the way, all with Bancanno's money. You'd have been very impressed, even proud of me . . ."

"Jim dropped a hundred," Don told her.

"Should I give it back?" Bedelia asked.

"Hell, no," Don said.

"What happened?" I said.

"She was wearing a ring and I admired it," Bedelia said. "That was all it took. She said, 'I'll show you things that'll make you go blind when we get back to the house. But just you, not those two whores with us.' Oh, yes, and 'Don't tell Max.' "

"She knows what she's talking about when she says that," I said. "Let me ask you — when she removed the strongbox from the drawer, did you get a look at the drawer itself or see her actually put her hands into it?"

She frowned a little and looked thoughtful. "Gee, I don't

remember specifically. She put the box — which is actually a large jewel case — on the table and opened it with a little key on a gold ring with other keys she carries in her purse. She never moves without it, I've noticed that."

"Yeah. And then what?"

"She said, 'This is for outstanding service, honey, above and beyond the call of duty.' Undoubtedly referring to our client."

"Anything else? Do you recall anything that happened before she took the case out of the drawer? She push any buttons or do anything that looked like she was shutting off a locking device or an alarm system?"

"She went to the bathroom," Bedelia recalled. "I waited in the bedroom. I remember it didn't take her terribly long and she was back in the room. She asked me if I had to go and I said no."

"The bathroom connects to the bedroom, of course."

"Yes. Why?"

Don said, "You think there's an alarm system, Jim, that's hooked into that dressing-table drawer?"

"If there isn't then Mrs. Colby and Ganner are the two most naïve and careless hardcases in history. You can bet she shut off an alarm system in the bathroom before she took that case out of the drawer. What triggers it? Who knows? The drawer itself? The removal of the case? Or it could be the turning of the little key in the lock."

Bedelia said, "Anyhow, the little trinkets *can* be reached by human hands."

"Which can then get chopped off," I said.

"I can get into that bathroom easily, if I go to the house again," Bedelia said. "If I knew what to look for."

"That part is easy," I said. "It's a small metal plate that contains a male lock for a female key, if the system is the one I think it is. But that's not enough. First you'd need the key. Maybe it's somewhere in the bathroom. I know people who have it on a hook, believe it or not, right next to the shutoff. But then you'd have to know how to turn it. And that part is tricky. Chances are you'd turn it the wrong way, and if you did they'd hear the thing go off in Brooklyn."

Bedelia gave a slight shudder and said, "From just the way those people act and talk about even the most casual things, you know how easy it is for them to kill. You just know it in your bones. Even when they're smiling and being perfect little gentlemen."

"If they get the chance," Don said. "Only if they get the chance."

"Let it simmer," I said, looking at my watch. "I'm catching a seven-o'clock plane back to L.A., because there are a couple of things I have to take care of that won't wait. But I'll be back around four in the afternoon.

"We have to be as tough as they are in a way to pull off a thing like this," Bedelia said. "I'm not sure we are. I mean we may have guts. But I don't think we could kill — not in cold blood. If we were reasonable, sensible grownups, we'd forget the whole thing and go home."

"Maybe you're right," Don said. "But you've got all that information and it would be a damn shame to let it go to waste."

"I said *if* we were reasonable, sensible grownups," she said.

"Let's get some sleep now," I said. And we all went our separate ways back to the Tremayne.

ONE OF THE FIRST THINGS I did when I got into Los Angeles was to call Rita from the empty office. And I wasn't looking forward to the conversation.

"Rita, this is Jim," I needlessly informed her.

"Oh, Jim, how are you?" she said pleasantly, just as if we were genuinely good friends — and I suppose we were to some extent.

"Okay, and you?"

"Fine."

"And Loretta?"

"Wonderful. She graduates in June."

"Wow. That tells the story, doesn't it?"

"Can you come?"

"What would stop me?"

She said nothing and I said, "Why didn't you let me know that Jan had skipped out on you and Steve?"

"How did you know? Have you seen her?"

"Yes. She got in touch with me."

"Where is she?"

"Don't ask me to tell you because she made me promise not to. And she *is* twenty-two years old. She wants me to get the key to her safe-deposit vault from you. I guess she was afraid to talk to you or see you."

"Oh, no, she wasn't. Don't you see what a ploy this is? My God, Jim, she can pull the wool over your eyes, can't she?"

"Oh, come on, Rita, she's not pulling the wool over anybody's eyes. She's right out in the open. And I'm not that dumb."

"Listen, Jim, she's no more afraid to ask me directly for that key or let me know where she's living than the man in the moon. She's just trying to line you up on her side of the issue, don't you see? Just by getting you to keep something from me and using you as a go-between, she makes an ally out of you, can't you see that?"

"You don't really think Jan is that cunning and devious, do you?"

There was a slight pause and then a faint laugh of pity and contempt for how slow-witted some people could be. "You know, Jim, you've had a lot of youthful influence in your life in the last couple of years, and it may have affected your way of looking at things without your even realizing it, more than you know."

I was determined not to argue with her. "Rita, there may be a sobering experience in the cards for our daughter. In the meantime . . ."

"I'll put the key in the mail to you and you can do what you like with it."

"Okay."

"You've been used, no matter what you say."

"Maybe I have. What's the difference if she's so insecure she has to pretend she has somebody on her side?"

"I've got to hang up now."

"Okay. Goodbye, Rita."

I was glad that was out of the way. I didn't relish juggling all these emotions. It was interesting that both my daughter and her mother, my former wife, made direct references to my relationship with Bedelia. Each to prove a point, neither of which had any connection with the other.

As I hung up, the morning mail came through the slot in the front door and the item I had been waiting for was with it: Colby's contract. It hadn't been among the three days' accumulation of bills and letters that greeted me when I first walked in. But here were the two copies of what was a simple two-paragraph arrangement between us, both to be returned in an enclosed self-addressed envelope with my signature. An unsigned typewritten note assured me a copy would be returned to me with John Colby's signature immediately. The return envelope bore Colby's home address in the very old, very aloof Los Feliz section of the city. I figured this was part of playing it all very close to the vest, and there was every chance that not even Brooks knew exactly what was going on between us.

I took care of the requirement and sealed both copies in the stamped envelope. I made a couple of phone calls — one to a man who owed us a thousand dollars for services and had promised to pay it by today, the other to my tax consultant in regard to a seven-hundred-and-fifty-dollar overpayment I had made to the IRS back in March now due for rebate. The first didn't answer; the second got me the assurance that it wouldn't be long now. I left the office, mailed the contracts, and drove to my apartment on Hazeltine. I was not in the best of spirits. That seventeen hundred and fifty dollars would have come in very handy right then. Also I was uneasy about Jan and irritated by the conversation with Rita. And my head was going around and around about what we had to do in Vegas and the fact that we didn't know quite how we were going to do it yet. But all of that took a back seat momentarily when I opened my mailbox before going upstairs to my apartment. There was a little typewritten message waiting for me. Not the kind you get very often, if at all, and certainly one you were not apt to throw away with the junk mail. It said: *Kill and be killed. Your days are numbered, fink.* Signed *Slow Death.* That was all.

I stood there at the letterboxes and examined the envelope it came in. It had been mailed in Los Angeles the day Bedelia, Don, and I had gone to Vegas. Naturally only my name and address, neatly typed, were affixed to it. It was obviously from friends of the two dealers I had shot, maybe from a relative of the one I had killed.

I looked around me and then quickly got upstairs to my apartment door, where I hesitated before entering. And when I had entered I walked carefully through the three rooms I occupied, opened the closet doors, looked in corners, and under the bed and various other pieces of furniture, and in all the places someone might have left something nasty — like a pipe bomb.

As soon as I was certain no one had, I shaved — something I had neglected to do before leaving Vegas on the seven a.m. flight — and then got into a shower. Fifteen minutes later I was walking toward the service station where I had left the car with the owner, whom I knew rather well. Nobody would have had time to set a charge on the starter between then and now — not in broad daylight. And nothing had happened, of course, after I had landed and picked up the car at Burbank. I now drove back toward Burbank for my return flight. It was by then one p.m. I'd be getting back to Vegas much earlier than I had thought I would.

I got on the plane and in a hour and a half I was back in my room at the Tremayne from where I called Don. He wasn't in so I called Bedelia. She didn't know where Don was but said she would meet me in a certain coffee shop at the south end of the Strip, almost surely safe from accidental discovery. She seemed a little bit keyed up. I knew she had something to tell me.

She sat in the little booth opposite me and said, "We have the key to the jewel case."

"I think you're ready to go into business on your own. How did you do it?"

"Don had a duplicate made. It was one of those things from the blue — fumbles, as Don calls them. Clare, believe it or not, plays a fair game of tennis. She called me this morning. And while she and I were running our behinds off for about an hour just before lunch, Don got it done."

"You lifted her key ring?"

"There was nothing to it. When we came off the court I simply dropped it back where it had come from in her drawstring purse."

"I'm impressed, sweetheart."

"We're all turning out to be as crooked as hell, aren't we?"

"With bigger crooks than we are or ever could be," I said and sipped some ice water. "It doesn't bother you, does it?"

"It might — a little. But not enough."

"Forget it. As long as we get away in one piece. I've got no qualms about anything else and I never had them. Only that. And neither should you."

"I seem to remember, darling, I was the one who was doing the persuading a few days ago," she said with a sweetly superior little smile.

"That was different. That was about something else. Not guilt about playing dirty with bums like this."

"She's not too bad. Just amoral." Bedelia looked toward the door. "Here's Don. I left a message for him at the desk."

He looked cool and tanned and was smiling softly and I didn't say anything about the threatening note that was still in my pocket. There wasn't time. We began to talk about the key. "There's only the matter of getting the chance to use it," I said. "That break will almost positively come our way."

"I think so too," Bedelia said.

"Did she say anything about getting together with you again?" I asked.

"Nothing specific," Bedelia said. "She asked me what I thought of Bancanno. I said he was a good dancer."

"Is he?"

"Terrific," she assured me. "And he doesn't try to wrestle."

"All right. I think you and Don should meet out in the open right away, and, the first chance you get, introduce him as an old friend who just happens to be in Vegas on his own. See where it gets us. If Bancanno asks you out again, tell him you're busy but be friendly. If he's really out to polish up his image he'll take it and be willing to try again."

"I've picked up something on Ganner from one of the local newspapermen," Don said. "He's been anxious to buy into the casino of the Tremayne for a long time."

I shook my head as if I were a lot wiser than I really was. "That's where those diamonds are supposed to come in, I'll bet."

"You mean he'll use her jewelry?" Bedelia said. "And she'll let him?"

"Well, what's going on between them, would you say?" I asked.

"Oh, she's hooked on him," Bedelia said. "And she's told me in very graphic terms all about it. Even though she always avoids the basic words. She's very elegant that way."

"She and those diamonds are at the man's disposal," I said.

"Then he's got to be waiting right now to sell them at the best price," Don said. "And that means a fence for *that* stuff."

"I want Don with you the next time you get into that house," I said to Bedelia, looking right at her. "You'll be invited again, no doubt about that. The thing that bothers me is how *I* can get in on it."

"Maybe you don't have to, Jim," Don said. "What's the difference as long as we can get in and out with the stuff?"

"What if you don't? It could make all the difference in the world."

Don nodded. "It should be you and me by ourselves anyway," he said, looking at Bedelia almost wistfully. "Bedelia shouldn't even be there." He looked at me. "If it all falls apart and there's any shooting . . ."

"That's always been hanging over us, hasn't it?" I said.

"It should be just us," he said.

"Look, you can't even get through the front gate without me," she said. "So what's the point of talking about it? We knew all of this right from the start, didn't we?"

"Honey, it's just that you *can* be hurt," Don said. "We'd hate that to happen."

"Don, I love you for that," she said. "But this is the way it is. And why are we dwelling on the worst?"

"Because it can happen," I said. "And we can still call it off."

"Two minutes ago you were gung ho, sweetheart," she said.

"I wasn't gung ho. I was saying there was no reason to have pangs of conscience about what we were doing. I've never been gung ho. Not with you in it."

"This is very unconstructive," she said.

"I'll tell you what I still like the best of all," Don said. "Jim and I getting in there and taking them by surprise while they're asleep or playing cards and grabbing the stuff and putting them under with a spray of chloroform."

"My God, that's ridiculous," Bedelia said irritably. Her movements were suddenly a little bit tense and impatient. "Even if that would work, have you figured out how you would get through the compound gate? If we start spreading out beyond what we are equipped to do we're *really* going to get our heads handed to us."

"That's never been an option and Don knows it," I said. "He's just having his druthers."

"The point is," Bedelia said, "we've got a very narrow situation to operate in. But it can work for us if we just make the most of it. In and out. Nothing complicated, nothing fancy." She gave a little snort with an ironic smile. "Hell, darling, I'd love to sit home and do nothing and see us make a hundred and fifty thousand dollars. But there's no way I can do that this time, is there?"

A few days later it was all academic anyway. Ganner gave a

cocktail party for just about everybody in sight because he and Mrs. Colby, or Miss Wilson as she was called, were hungry for social contacts. Everyone was there, including Don and Bedelia and me. I just slipped in with them because there were no limitations on any of the individual invitations. That part of it was a cinch.

10

THE THREE OF US were sitting in the front seat of the car we had rented from Hertz, Bedelia between Don and me, and I was driving. The five-o'clock sun was still high above the desert and it was hot enough for the air conditioning. Nobody had been talking for nearly the last two minutes as we approached the enclave of quarter-of-a-million-dollar homes, and there had been practically no conversation all the way from the Tremayne. And then Bedelia said, "What if I can locate the key to the shutoff?"

"Let it alone," I said, keeping my eyes straight ahead.

"Jim's right, Bedelia," Don said. "I know how those systems work and each one has a different key-setting. There are probably three different ways you can make a mistake and only one that turns it off."

"As long as you know it's there," I said, still not looking at either of them. "That box with the jewelry in it must weigh about twelve pounds. I think there's more than a fifty-fifty chance that the bottom of the drawer has a hair-trigger spring-panel which is held down by the weight of the case — probably a two or three-pound pressure is all it needs. If I'm right, lifting the jewel case out of the drawer sets it off."

"That's my guess too," Don said. "They work on the

assumption that somebody just might get into the drawer itself somehow and not trip an alarm, but that they wouldn't be looking for the alarm to go off just by lifting the box. Because that's what most people would do if they got to the box — lift it and stash the whole thing in a bag or something and run. They're not going to stop to jimmy it open. And the chances of anyone having the key are pretty slim. Isn't that about the way you're thinking, Jim?"

"Something like that. But there's one thing."

"What's that?" Don said.

"I could be all wrong."

We kept driving and nobody said anything for a while once again. As soon as we got to about a hundred yards from the security gate, I said, "I think we'll be all right with the key. Just don't move the box itself at all, don't even nudge it. Just stick your hand into the drawer and unlock it — lift the lid, take out the stuff, and put it away."

"What if there's no space between the front panel of the drawer and the lock, Jim?" Don asked.

I didn't answer for a couple of seconds. "Let's hope there is."

"Should we take a chance and move the box back?" Don said.

"If it looks safe. You'll be in a position to judge that; I couldn't guess at it from here. But you may run into that. And again there *is* a fifty-fifty chance the key will set off the alarm. That's better than the one-chance-in-four you take with the shutoff. But if it does go off, I don't have to tell you to get out of there as fast as you can without the jewel case and get lost in the crowd."

Bedelia said nothing and we had reached the fence that surrounds the area and the gate where they check you through, if you're not a recognized resident or a well-known visitor. The uniformed security guard had been checking a great number of cars into the area for the past half hour and now ours was one of them.

The house was low-slung and very big and surrounded by rocky formations and plenty of cactus, a tennis court to the right of it, a swimming pool to the left. A crew of red-jacketed boys were on hand to park cars, and that's what one of them did for us after we drove up and got out in front of a wide shalestone staircase leading toward the front door, set back considerably from the top of it. The sounds of the party were coming from within and from various outside areas.

A butler admitted us in a cluster of other arrivals all making noisy conversation, a couple of shouts of recognition ringing out and a terrific hub-bub going on all over the wide-open front room. It was made to order for us. "Miss Dean, Mr. Peabody, and Mr. Weinberg," Bedelia said to the butler. Her voice sounded steady and clear.

I immediately spotted a couple of torpedoes off to one side in the spacious entry-area, big, young, beautifully suited, their eyes steady and watchful. They threatened no one; they were just there. We drifted past them. Everywhere people were standing around or moving in and out, drinking, talking, gesticulating, laughter occasionally coming through, either rippling or explosive, music I couldn't quite identify being piped in from overhead.

"Clare, this is Don Peabody," Bedelia said, as she came up to Mrs. Colby. "I told you about him. He and my brother were roommates at college."

I was moving away at that point, wondering why she had picked that as a background story. And I quickly realized it was probably the best one she could have used, because I'm damned if I could think up a better one.

I got a drink from the bar, where two white-jacketed black guys were filling people's orders. I walked slowly around the place with a drink in my hand and was paid no attention to by anyone there. Bedelia and Don were standing with Clare Colby and two other people. I strolled outside to the pool area, where I got a good look at Max Ganner for the first time. He was in conversation with three men and a woman and I heard one of the servants address him by name, though I think I would have known him anyway. Tall, trim, a dark-eyed man with a well-fitting burgundy blazer and a quick scowling smile that might easily charm a great many people who didn't care what was behind it. I studied him briefly and then walked away and made a point of getting into conversation with an old dame about my age who was sitting on a reclining chair on the other side of the pool, a cigarette in a holder between her fingers. Bedelia and Don weren't ready to go to work yet and I could keep an eye on them from this vantage point. When they disappeared I would know the job had begun. Three to five minutes after that this large gathering of noisy gin-guzzling people would either have passed through a crisis unknowingly or been shaken up by some unexpected entertainment. Maybe people would be searching them. Maybe guns would go off.

"I'm Jim Weinberg," I said simply and pleasantly.

"I'm Sylvia Gertz," she answered, her brown eyes like those of a lynx, and I could tell she liked me well enough to give me some cover and concealment for a little while. She was not pretty and was a little too sharp, like certain kinds of cheese that are nevertheless interesting and tasty. "Weinberg, huh? Are you a friend or part of the window trimming?" she said, as I sat down next to her in an upright canvas chair.

"That's an interesting question," I said. "What about you?"

"I'm a bystander."

"I guess that describes me too."

"You're looking for excitement," she said. "I could tell from the way you were walking around, eyes open but a little skeptical of finding anything interesting."

"Is that how I looked to you?" I said, able to look at her and still keep tabs on Bedelia and Don. "Then you must have been watching me. That's very flattering."

She shrugged faintly and gave me a wry smile. "These things are always boring, aren't they?"

"Who are you, Sylvia Gertz? I mean, who is the real Sylvia Gertz?"

"The wife of Irving Gertz. We do all the plumbing fixtures at most of the best places, in case you hadn't heard."

"I see. And what are you doing here, Mrs. Gertz? I mean, besides being a bystander."

"Letting life run its course," she said, with a superior little smile. "Trying to keep from dying of utter boredom. Do you have an antidote for boredom, Jim? It is Jim, isn't it?"

"Yes. If you don't want to be bored, Sylvia, you have to find something to do with yourself that interests you."

"Did you think that up on the spur of the moment?"

I shrugged modestly.

"You're not bad-looking, but I'm beginning to doubt that you're a genius."

"I get better after a while," I said.

"I'll bet you do," she said. "And am I wrong? Or wouldn't you like to let that hateful blonde know it? The one standing by the living-room entrance."

"What?"

"Come on. You can't take your eyes off her."

"I thought I knew her."

"In another life." She added good-naturedly, "I think you sat down with me because the angle was good."

"You're doing me an injustice."

"Jewish men have always gone for that type."

I laughed. "Oh, I don't know," I said. "If you weren't a married lady I might have asked you out to dinner by now."

"Then you're the last of the red-hot gentlemen. Since when does marriage stop anyone these days? Not that I'm that type."

"It stops me."

"Who are you really, Jim Weinberg?"

"There's not much to tell you, Sylvia. Like a lot of people, I'm always hoping."

"You're giving me a routine."

"I'm looking for a moment of madness. A trip to the moon."

"They've already been there. It's not like Cole Porter says." She laughed.

"A walk along the stars I'd always remember then."

"If I knew you better I'd tell you what you're full of. No, I'm just kidding. I wouldn't want you to think I'm crude."

"Never."

It went around like that for a while and I finally got up and got her an old-fashioned at the poolside portable bar just a few feet away. Bedelia and Don hadn't yet gotten away from the people they were with and of course weren't going to make any sudden or suspicious moves. By then Sylvia's husband, Irving, had joined us. He was a barrel-chested guy of about fifty-five with curly but thinned-out gray hair, prosperous, and not as smart as his wife. He held a cigar in his hand and wore a corking diamond pinkie ring. One of his big *bon mots* was, "Sylvia been chewing your ear off here?"

And then suddenly Don and Bedelia were nowhere to be seen. In just a couple of minutes they would be lifting the rocks and putting them into Bedelia's smart leather-and-canvas bag, just right for late afternoon-early evening, semiformal cocktail parties in the desert, nice and roomy, enough to handle ten pounds of diamond jewelry without sagging. Either that or the three of us were in for some very hard times. I don't remember anything of what passed between Mr. and Mrs. Gertz and me for the next ten long minutes. By the end of fifteen I was getting ready to begin moseying toward the bedroom at the back of that sprawling house.

"Just what is it you do, Jim?" Irving was saying to me, as he sat on the footrest of Sylvia's recliner.

I was looking over his shoulder right past him and I said, "I'm with the IRS, Irving."

He smiled in a sickish way. "Yeah?" he said.

And then I saw Bedelia. She stood momentarily in the wide opening leading to the living room. The canvas-and-leather bag was slung on her shoulder and she looked as cool and casual as the queen reviewing the troops. Then she moved into the garden beyond the pool as if she had nothing more on her mind than the dress she would wear that night. I saw her come together with Don who had evidently arrived on that particular spot from another direction. They were not inconspicuous, even in that mob scene. But no one would ever have dreamed that they had just managed to steal, however legally, a million dollars' worth of diamond jewelry. But I could tell that they had done just that.

"I'm going to have to tear myself away from you," I said, standing up.

Irving managed to get to his feet also and said, "Oh, that's too bad. That's life. First it's hello, then it's goodbye."

Sylvia said, "Tell the truth, Jim. Who are you after? Bancanno or Ganner or both?"

I grinned and shook my head. "It's love I'm after, Sylvia."

I felt like an idiot talking that way but there had been no other way to talk. And now I was headed out of this place, my hand on the car claim-check inside my jacket pocket. I reached the front staircase and all those smart moves and clever calculations and lucky breaks of the past few days suddenly crumbled into dust. I found myself blocked by the two torpedoes who were both dressed to the nines, scarlet hankies stuck in their breast pockets, one of them sharp-eyed, the other giving off a dull but nasty glow. And they had no intention of letting me move down that staircase to where the stewards were waiting to park cars and to retrieve those belonging to departing guests.

"Excuse us," the blondish one said. "Aren't you the guy who shot two guys in L.A. a few weeks ago and was on TV and in all the papers and everything?"

I looked at him and then at the darker guy who was missing a neck and waiting to destroy on command. My .38 was tucked under my arm, something for which I was grateful as I said, "Not that I remember. You must have me mixed up with someone else."

"Ah, come on, don't be modest. That was you. And aren't you a private dick too, and that was how you happened to have a piece on you?"

I shrugged. "Okay. That was me. Just one of those things. Nice talking to you."

"Wait a minute," the spokesman said. "You're not going to run away just like that, are you?"

"What do you want? An autograph?" I said, resorting to big talk. "Why don't you be a nice boy and let me go about my business? It was a swell party."

The sun had just about disappeared and everything was beginning to grow a little bit purple, voices from the house becoming vague and distant. The darker, no-necked, guy looked as if he was ready to make some kind of a move. The .38 came out in my hand and went right into his belly. "Freeze," I snapped. "Or you'll never walk again."

But someone was digging a gun into my back and that was the end of that. The blond, whose name turned out to be Al, took my gun away and said, "The point is, sport, what are you doing here? Who do you know and how did you get in?"

I said, "I don't know anybody, to tell the truth. I got swept up in a crowd of people that was headed this way."

"Well now you're going to get swept a little bit further," he said. "Move."

And we began to walk around to the rear of the house past the empty tennis court and under an overhang of date palms, music and voices filtering out into the dusk. I was being detained and no mistake about it.

11

"A PRIVATE DICK out of L.A., who only a couple of weeks ago shot up two drug pushers. And he just happens to be here out of the blue — a half-assed gatecrasher, huh?" It was Max Ganner talking as if he was getting to the punch line of a very funny story.

"Why not go along with a simple explanation?" I said. "Sometimes things are that way."

"Sure. When you're three years old and you're playing with blocks on the floor."

I had been led to a large one-room building about a hundred and fifty feet from the main house. It contained a regulation-size pool table, a television set, some canvas chairs, and it was appended by a small pantry. Ganner stood at one end of the table and I at the other, and the two boys, Terry and Al, sat against opposite walls, Al in an elevated shoeshine-parlor chair, from which he looked down at me with suddenly phlegmatic eyes. Terry sized me up with a dull glare. The third guy who had held the gun on me had tailed off, back to his flexible duties elsewhere. Ganner's wide mouth revealed a jagged smile of doubt and even contempt. "You're going to stick to that story?" he said.

"It's the only one I have," I said. "I saw the cars drive into the compound and I drove in with them just on a lark. I never had any idea of where I was headed or whose house this was until one of the guests told me. Why get upset?"

"You're lying, Blaney," Ganner saic in his faintly accented voice, whose origin I couldn't quite place. "No one gets through that gate without perfect papers. How did you do it? Who gave you the ticket?"

"People can slip up," I said. "Even the guards at that gate of yours."

"That's for bedbugs. You're not a bedbug. You're here for damned good reasons. Big Joe and Augie the Knife'll do anything to keep me out of the Tremayne. It's connected with that, isn't it, Blaney? They sent you, didn't they? Didn't they?" The mouth got tighter now as he said, "I'm going to find out anyhow. And I'm telling you, I'm not the most patient man in the world, Blaney."

I started to open my mouth when the door opened and partway into the room came a thin, sallow-faced guy who looked like either an old-time knife-thrower or a disbarred lawyer. "Max," he said, looking at the other with important information in his eyes.

Ganner glanced at me and then went to the door and was guided gently outside by the other man. The door remained ajar as they conferred privately, obviously not wanting to be overheard or even seen. Al turned his attention toward the door momentarily, and Terry, the silent one, just kept looking at me. Maybe his mind was a blank and he didn't even see me.

Ganner came back into the room and he looked as if he had found whatever it was he had been told of more than routine interest. His eyes were full of lights, his hands gripping each other and flexing together, and he said, "Hang on to this guy. I've got something to take care of. I'll be back in about an hour."

"Just sit here with him for an hour?" Al asked.

"Shoot some pool," Ganner said and walked out.

Maybe at that very instant Bedelia and Don were standing on the sidewalk. I could see them with blank and puzzled faces, tension pulling Bedelia's mouth at the corners, Don's lips thinned-out. There wasn't a damned thing I could do about it.

"How about a game of rotation?" Al said.

I looked at him, a tin-pot blackshirt underneath the jazzy threads and the wise-guy talk, something right out of a sewer. But I said, "Sure, why not?" It was better than standing there and sweating out all the nasty prospects.

I walked to the cue rack and selected a stick. Terry stood up and placed himself near the door. "Shoot for break," Al said, taking off his jacket and revealing a gat in a shoulder holster. If I could just have gotten my hands on it.

I looked away and won the break. Then I began to shoot. The balls clicked in the silence as I ran a string of fourteen. "You shoot like a hustler," Al said. "Ever do this for bread?"

I didn't answer, first sizing up a shot and then glancing toward Terry who stood there as if he had never done anything in his life but stand guard or beat people up. He watched the table without visible interest and I began to aim the cue in the bridge of my fingers. But I never made the shot.

The door opened and Ganner was back in the room only five

minutes after he had left us. His face was full of murder. "So *that* was it," he said, with tightly clenched teeth, and looking right at me.

"So *what* was it?" I said.

"The diamonds, Blaney, the diamonds, as you fucking well know," he snarled furiously. "And if Eisenberg hadn't come in from L.A. just now and asked for a look at the stuff you might've got away with it. He was ready to handle it and the price was my ticket to the Tremayne, the whole thing oiled and ready to go . . ."

"Now wait a minute, Ganner — "

He whacked me across the face with his cupped palm and the blow sounded like a gunshot and my head went spinning. "Shut your mouth with the lies, Blaney," he said with that quick fury. "The stuff is missing and you were in on it because somehow those rats Joe and Augie found out about it. And somewhere in my house among that crowd out there there's one or two people, maybe a couple more, who are carrying a million dollars' worth of diamond jewelry on them. You know who they are because you were in it together and you better talk about it right now or you're a dead man."

Al's head jerked. This was news to him. "A million?" he repeated. "Jesus Christ, right here in this house?"

Ganner jammed a revolver up under my chin into the soft flesh of the V formed by the jawbones. "No one except the bums who sent you would ever know what might have happened to you," he promised me. "You can bet I'll do it, Blaney."

"I know, Ganner, I know."

"Then talk or the top of your head goes off when I count to three."

Of course he never did. Maybe he would have, but someone began knocking at the now-locked door. "It's Miss Wilson," Terry announced, Clare Colby's *nom de guerre*. I had been reprieved.

Ganner dropped the gun into his jacket pocket and went to the door. The woman slipped into the room, breathless, tense, angry, scared — all of that in her voice as she said, "It's that *friend* of mine, I'm sure of it — that broad I was stupid enough to trust, that bitch with the manners and the nice voice. I don't see her anywhere. She and the guy she came with, they're both gone and didn't even say goodbye. Why else would they go that way and so fast if it wasn't them?" She noticed me. "Who is this?"

"He may be in with them," Ganner answered. Then to Al and Terry, "Get outside and check with the car attendants."

"Let me be the one to answer your question, Mrs. Colby," I said, because I saw the chance to soften things for myself.

"Mrs. Colby?" Ganner said. "Where did you get that name?"

Mrs. Colby's eyes widened and the two bums stopped to listen and Ganner snapped at them, "Come on, for Christ's sake, do as I tell you before those goddamn people are all the way to Acapulco."

The two bums did as bidden and Ganner turned his overly expressive face on me again. "How do you know that name?" he asked.

Mrs. Colby, gazing at me, said, "From my husband, that's how."

"That's right," I said. "I didn't want to talk about it at first. But maybe if you know what's what I won't have to take a bullet or a beating for something I never did. I don't know Joe or Augie or anyone else like that. Mrs. Colby's husband is my client. He hired me to locate Mrs. Colby. It's just a job to me — an ordinary, everyday job."

"To find me?" Mrs. Colby said with a sneer. "Or to get back the jewelry?"

"To find you."

"I don't believe that for a minute."

"I'm glad it's not those shits from Chicago," Ganner said.

"For God's sake, Max, must you use that kind of raw talk while I'm here?"

"Forgive me, baby," he said, and looked at me. "So the old man sent you. But to do the same thing. Oh, sure, for a different reason."

"You've got it wrong . . ."

"Remember what I was going to do to you a couple of minutes ago?" he said. "Well, I'm glad I didn't. It would've been too fast. And I think you're going to get it very slowly, Blaney . . ."

"Oh, God, that kind of thing," Mrs. Colby said. "No thanks, not for me."

"Not while you're here, baby," Ganner assured her.

"I couldn't stand anything like that. But for God's sake, Max, make him talk. I went through five years of hell to accumulate all that stuff for you."

"Mrs. Colby, all your husband wanted to know was your whereabouts," I said. "All that other stuff about the missing jewelry is Greek to me."

"Is it? You must think I'm very stupid."

"See to our guests and don't let on about anything," Ganner told her.

"All right," she said, opening the door to leave. And then she added, "My God, I'm shaking all over."

"I feel sorry for her," I said to Ganner with a certain amount of perversity. "She's a very sensitive woman."

"Feel sorry for yourself," he told me, standing across the width of the pool table from me, the gun leveled steadily at my chest. His suntan was glistening, partly from the pool-table light, partly because he was sweating. "There's no way you can leave here alive unless I get that jewelry back."

I didn't say anything and suddenly Al and Terry were back in the room. "Nobody left the premises, Boss," Al said, and glanced at me. "I talked to everyone of those kids out there and they swear no one has come out of here and asked for their car yet. I phoned the gate and they didn't see no one who might of been a guest drive through and leave yet."

"So that means they're still here," Ganner said, as if it amused him to think so.

"Well, maybe not here," Al said. "But somewhere in the colony and without a car."

Ganner's face lit up. "Why? How come they didn't just drive out?" He looked at me and said to Terry, "Frisk this guy."

Very quickly Terry came up with the car claim-check. "The answer is they don't have a claim-check," Ganner said. "He's got it."

"I told you I drove in," I said. "Naturally I've got a claim-check."

"Yeah, but your friends don't have."

"I have no friends."

"Let's start looking," Al said.

"First get those handcuffs out of the closet," Ganner said.

Al did as he was told, and in mere seconds I was lying face down on the floor alongside the pool table, my hands cuffed behind my back, my ankles handcuffed also. And then I was alone and as helpless as a salmon in a net. It was the middle of a nightmare.

12

I LAY THERE on my belly, my face turned to one side, the metal cuffs cutting into my wrists and my ankles. Time did not pass, it crawled painfully in the dark, and I couldn't really tell how much of it I had lived through since they had left me like this. But I was numb and beyond discomfort when the door opened and they brought Bedelia into the room and switched on the pool-table light-trough from the wall.

She saw me immediately and cried out. "Jim!" The sight of me on the floor like a trussed-up Hefty bag came as a jolt. "Jim, are you hurt? Oh, Jim . . ." And she was kneeling down next to me with her hand on the side of my head, the heel of her palm touching my face.

I could see stress lines in that ordinarily cool marble forehead, and I said, "I'm fine. The worst of it is how stupid I must look lying here like a side of beef."

"Okay," Ganner said. "Nobody is faking. You know each other. And you both came here with one idea — to heist a collection of valuable jewelry. And you've been caught."

"Ganner, let me up," I said. "I can't talk from down here. Come on, you've got the other guy with you. It's just me and a weak woman."

"She doesn't look weak to me."

"Ah, don't be silly. What can happen?"

"What about it, Miss Dean?" Ganner said to Bedelia. "You ready to talk straight?"

"I won't open my mouth until you let him up and take off those handcuffs," she said in cold, almost steady tones.

Ganner snorted breathily. Then he tossed the key to his yegg, the one who had fleetingly entered the room earlier, and the guy unlocked the handcuffs on both my ankles and wrists. I lay there for a few seconds fighting to get back my circulation and unbend my stiffened joints, and Ganner said, "I just hope you're not thinking of playing games with me."

"Ganner, we can all see what the setup is," I said, getting to my feet massaging my wrists. "You've got us, that's obvious."

"I hope it is. Because you've got about half a minute to tell me where the other guy is," he said. "The guy who came with this young lady."

My eyes flicked from his gun to his face, unsmiling and hard and businesslike. He felt close to what he was after now that he had the two of us in tow. "Ganner, I've been here with you," I said.

He took a quick breath and the pitiless mouth distended angrily.

"He's gone," Bedelia jumped in. "And there's nothing you or any of us can do about it."

He turned to her. "Want that face cracked up, huh miss?" he said. "It's bad enough you infiltrated your way in here posing as a friend and double-crossed a goodhearted, decent woman, that you're a liar and a tramp. Don't add a smart fresh mouth to it now. Not while I'm standing here with you like this."

"I'm telling you the truth," Bedelia said in a deliberate, even defiant tone which I think made Ganner uncomfortable, because he had to admire it. "We separated an hour and a half ago, and I haven't seen him since."

"And where are the jewels?"

"He's got them."

"Where?"

"In a belt he's wearing around his waist."

"Where's he gone? Come on. Where's he gone?"

"I don't *know,*" she insisted.

"What do you think I am? A fucking fool?"

"Anyone can see what you are, Mr. Ganner," she said. "It keeps coming out, no matter what you do to hide it. The clothes, the manicures — none of it helps."

It made my blood run cold and it turned out to be more than he could take. His hand snaked out and cracked her across the face, turning her head violently, and he said, "Listen, you stuck-up little cunt, don't you high-hat me if you want to keep all your teeth . . ."

Before he could finish I was making my move, one you didn't have to be a twenty-five-year-old athlete to make. I don't know if it was my own rage that was triggered by the ringing sound of the brutal slap he had given her, or my realization that he was put off guard by his flare-up of temper. But at that very instant I grabbed the pool cue that was leaned against the wall outside the rack and rammed it up into the light-trough above the pool table. I rammed it with such force that the lights exploded like a gunshot and showered the place with glass and plunged the room into what at first seemed like total darkness. But then you could see who was where well enough.

Bedelia got out of the way instinctively, and I was able, almost in the same motion, to ram the stick pointblank into Ganner's face, the heavy end colliding with his teeth and getting a sharp grunt of pain and shock out of him. Then I brought the stick down on his gunhand with a quick, maybe lucky, swing, dislodging the gun from his grip. And as it clattered to the floor, he started to go for it and I brought one down in the general direction of his head. It bounced off his forehead but dazed him and suddenly I had to go for the other guy who had been frozen for just those four or five seconds in the dark and whose gun was now coming up for action.

He was too late, too small, and too thin, and muscle was not his strong point. I grabbed his wrists, bounced the automatic out of his grasp by slamming his hand against the metal edge of the air-conditioning unit in the window behind him and made him cry out on the impact. I then released his other hand and brought a tightly arced, full-shouldered right hand, half hook, half upper-cut, to his jaw with as much snap as I was capable of and I felt my knuckles swell up almost instantly. They say there's no such thing as a right hook. But whatever it was, the little knife-thrower let out a kind of squeal and dropped to the floor like an inanimate object.

Behind me while I was getting rid of him I had heard some kind of scuffling and a thud, and now as I turned I could see vaguely that Ganner seemed to be stirring where he lay crumpled at the base of the wall, not quite unconscious and groaning a little bit. The bracket lights went on and there was Bedelia standing at the wall switch holding Ganner's .38 in her hand and training it on him. "I had to hit him," she said in a slightly choked voice.

I looked at Ganner and the side of his face was swollen and cut and I assumed she had laid the butt of the gun across it, which meant she had to be facing him at least partially.

"He was getting up and going for you."

"Don't apologize, sweetheart," I said. "And hang on to that gun."

I picked up the other guy's gun and now knelt down beside Ganner who was trying to shake off the effects of what both Bedelia and I had done to him. "It's a new game, Max," I said.

"Just a . . . weak woman, huh?" he strained to say.

"I was wrong, Max," I said. And I quickly rolled him face down without any protest from him beyond a groggily muttered string of nasty words.

"Here, Jim," Bedelia said, handing me the handcuffs that had been placed on top of the TV set.

"Smart girl," I said, and locked Ganner's hands behind his back.

"My God, what a mess this has turned into," she said.

"We'll get out of it," I said, trying to be encouraging. And then I dragged the other guy over to handcuff him also and intertwine the connecting links on his cuffs with those on Ganner's. And then they were hooked back-to-back on the floor like a couple of college fraternity pledges.

"Someday I'll kill you for this, Blaney," Ganner said, still with noticeable strain.

"Boys like you always say things like that, Max. But then you get back to the city and you forget."

Bedelia made a breathy sound, halfway between a laugh and a gasp. I got up, tossed the key on the pool table and looked at her. Her legs were slightly parted, her feet planted, the gun in her hand. Her eyes were bright and expectant and both scared and excited, a flush of carmine in the high cheekbones of that beautiful face, the lobes of the nose drawn and a little tense, the expression on her mouth somehow one of satisfaction. She was measuring up to an insane situation none of us had really anticipated or ever been in. "Come on," I said, grabbing her arm.

We were out of there fast, the two guns in my jacket pockets. Voices came on the early night air, a hot desert wind carrying the sounds. The last traces of a reddish sunlight were down to nothing and at any real distance everything was silhouettes and vague outlines of various kinds. We hurried along the periphery of the property in a straight line away from the game room, and we ducked into a gravel passageway formed by the back of the pump house and a ten-feet-high chain-link fence topped with angled barbed wire that bordered the rear of the grounds.

"Where's Don?" I asked.

"I don't know," she answered. "But the diamonds are in the swimming pool."

13

"WE KNEW that you had run into something and that we were in trouble," she said, speaking quickly and in a hushed voice. "So we thought we'd better get out of sight before they came down on us with the jewelry in our possession. Don said it would sink easily to the bottom of the deep end of the pool. So very casually I lowered it in the far corner away from the house, and it sank exactly the way you'd expect ten pounds of diamond jewelry to sink. No one saw me do it because in mobs like this no one pays a damned bit of attention to anyone. And the bag can't even be seen unless you get very close to the surface and make a real effort to see it. It's nine feet at that point. As far as I know, chlorinated water does very little harm to diamonds. The trick is now to get out of here with them."

"Is that when you and Don separated?"

"No. We ducked into the bathhouse shower room because it seemed relatively safe at that moment," she said, a slight tickle of choked laughter in her throat. I could sense a touch of heady excitement seasoning the fear of the moment, and in the quickly deepening darkness of the hour her face was shadowy and almost openly passionate. It would have been hard to be indifferent or remain untouched under the circumstances. I found that I was also breathing a little faster than usual. "We were jammed into the stall together," she said. "And that's something you should never do with anyone but your lover. Anyway we talked and talked and couldn't come up with even a passably intelligent idea about what to do next."

"What happened, for Christ's sake?"

"Don left me there to snoop around and see what he could see and I stayed put until Ganner and that other guy came in to look around." She shook her head ironically. "They almost didn't find me. And then at the last second Ganner said, 'Take a look in the shower.' "

"We're in a mess all right," I said. "There isn't one chance in ten thousand of getting out of here with the jewelry right now. There isn't even a very good chance of getting out of here without it. Unless we call for negotiations and trade it off for safe passage through the front gate."

"Oh, God, I would hate to do that."

"You would hate to do that. But you would also hate to die or get broken into little pieces. So when the time comes we'll make the trade."

"What do we do in the meantime?"

"Stay under cover for a few minutes until I can think of something better. Or try to."

"Do you think Don is out of here?"

"He could be hiding in the chopped liver for all I'd know," I said. "The thing I'm afraid of is Terry and Al. I don't know where they are. Otherwise I'd just walk out to the front with you and have them get our car. Except there's Don. Jesus, that's the worst part of the whole thing right now, being separated."

"Terry and Al," Bedelia said. "Maybe they're looking for Don." Then there was a touch of fright in her voice. "Maybe they've got him somewhere . . ."

"I don't know. I don't think so. But I want to get you out of here, and I think I've got a way to do it. But we've got to move fast before someone comes back to that game room and finds the damage . . ."

"Me?"

"Listen, I made a couple of acquaintances before, not bad skates at all, and if they're still here they'll be glad to give you a lift through the gate."

"I won't go, Jim. I'm no Wonder Woman, but we're in this together," she said. "I'd be afraid to go."

"Like us to be shot together holding hands, huh?"

"I think I would, I swear to heaven. What would I go back to out there without you? — and even Don? Swinging singles?"

"Look, if you're on the outside, Don and I have some kind of security. They won't be as quick to chop us up and put the remains in lime. They'll think twice because you'd be able to tell what you know, and they would know it."

"Jesus, what a mess," she said, and seemed all of a sudden about to cry.

"I know," I said, and then took her arms in my hands and said, "You're a hell of a woman, darling. I was damned lucky the day you read that ad of mine. I only hope you're as lucky."

"I am," she said, and there was enough refracted light to just see the glitter in her eyes and I could hear the emotion in her voice. "I've been lucky to know you, to be with you, to make love with you . . ."

She kissed my lips and her mouth was soft and hot because her blood was racing—partly with fear and anxiety, of course. "We're going to get toward the pool area. We'll stay in the shadows as much as possible, and I'll see if I can spot those people. Mr. and Mrs. Gertz . . ."

But we were trapped.

I reached for the guns in my pockets but it was too late. Someone said, "Let it alone, mister, or we'll blast both of you where you stand."

Both ends of the narrow passage between the chain-link fence and the back of the little building were blocked by a man, each of them holding a Magnum revolver and aiming it from where he stood, catching us from two directions with frightening firepower. Those guns would have torn us apart, each of them a 357 Magnum .38 caliber weapon. "Okay," I managed to say. "You've got us."

"You bet your ass," one of them replied.

14

"JUST WALK this way and keep your hands down at your sides," the other said.

I put myself slightly ahead of Bedelia because the narrow space wouldn't allow us to move side by side, my hand holding hers as if she needed to be guided and protected. And as if I were in any position to guide and protect her. The second one, with the nasty mouth, came into the gap from behind and followed us out at the opposite corner where his friend was waiting in the near darkness, backed up just enough to avoid me, the deadly gun in his hand. "That's it, nice and easy," he drawled. Just two of Ganner's goons patrolling the grounds. And they had to run into us.

The one in back put his gun against my spine and a hand took from my jacket pockets the two guns I had confiscated. He tossed one of them to the main guy who tucked it into his belt and said, "Okay. Let's just move along now."

"Where to?" I said, and looked at the nasty mouth.

"You'll fucking find out, mister," the latter said. "Now do like you're told."

"Has trouble forming his words, does he?" I said, grinning and feeling fear at the same time. I wanted to get him for the language because he was using it the way he would indecently expose himself just because Bedelia was there to hear it. It would have been okay from me but not from him.

"Never mind that," the main guy said. He was about thirty-five, well-built, short-haired, cool, and even-featured. "Just move."

These were locals, non-eastern types, Anglo-Saxons of the highest quality, and I hadn't seen either of them before that very minute. They were both dressed in suntan shirts, light zipper jackets, and half-boots. The nasty mouth, bulky and powerful, tough-jawed and mean-faced, spit on the ground and said, "I hope

I didn't say anything to upset your whore. If I did, well, fuck both of you."

Bedelia squeezed my hand to keep me from getting killed or banged up, and she said, "You're right, Jim. He does have trouble forming his words. Comes of bad early toilet-training."

"He looks that type," I said, and I was almost crazy enough, after all we'd been through to this point, to want to provoke him. But I wasn't that crazy. I knew the other guy's presence would prevent a real blowup.

Then we walked back toward the game room huddled alongside of the date palms. The building was outlined blackly against the early evening sky, and I knew that Ganner and his frail henchman were still where we had left them. I couldn't begin to understand the absence of Terry and Al, not to mention Don.

"Nobody inside?" the main guy said as we reached the door. Bedelia and I had turned off the lights.

"Looks that way, don't it?"

"Maybe we'd better find Ganner."

Ganner's voice came from within. "Who's out there?"

Our two captors were startled. "Gates and Slasser," the main guy answered. "What's wrong?"

"Get in here. We're tied up. Me and Roy."

The door was locked on the snap lock, of course. "Bust it in," Ganner's somewhat remote voice ordered. "Or better. Come around to the back window and jimmy it open."

"You do it, Slasser," said Gates, who was the main guy.

Nasty-mouth went to it quickly and we were left alone with Gates. "Just stand still, trooper," he said like a stranger giving good advice.

Bedelia and I were both looking at him intently. Maybe he would get careless. Her eyes then darted around us as if she were looking for an opening in some high invisible wall. The smell of the day's heat lingered and the sounds of people a hundred yards away were as remote as a foreign country you will never visit. Slasser's efforts in back of the building could also be heard.

"What did you do in there?" Gates asked, looking right into my eyes. "Something dumb, huh? Don't you know it don't pay to be a hero, trooper?"

"How would ten grand sit with you, pal?" I said, as if it were a deal no one could turn down.

"You trying to corrupt me, fella?" he teased.

"I'm not playing games, pal. Ten grand. I've got it and you can come with me to the bank while I draw it in cash tomorrow morning in L.A."

"By God, you *are* trying to corrupt me," he said, because he didn't believe a word of it, wisely enough. "Hey, trooper, can't you think of something better than that? Shit, man. Excuse me, ma'am."

"Okay, pal," I said, excitement welling up in my chest. "Don't ever say you weren't given a golden opportunity."

And the tough but good-looking wide-skulled face with its dumbly superior grin lost all expression as a sickening crack sounded. It was the sound of a gun butt colliding with cranial bone. The face went slack and the unseeing eyes disappeared. Don had come up in back of him, let him have it, and caught him under the arms so that he wouldn't be heard falling down or cracking his head on the flagstone.

Bedelia and I stood rooted in our tracks. Don lowered Gates and then quickly stood up, his .38 revolver in hand, his face tense. He looked disheveled, his jacket torn in the shoulder-seam, his collar open, his white shirt soaked with perspiration, his face red and flushed in the evening light refracting from other parts of the grounds.

We all stood still, Don off to one side of the door, Bedelia and I where Slasser could see us when he finally would open it. It took another couple of minutes and we could all hear him getting into the room from outside the building, and also the impatient sound of Ganner's seething voice. "The key is on the pool table. Come on, get us unlocked."

"Where's the fucking lights?" Slasser said.

"There's a wall switch."

The light went on inside and through a garble of talk Slasser apparently unlocked Ganner and the other guy. Then the game-room door opened and Slasser stood there, Ganner visible inside rubbing his wrists, his hair carefully coiffed and styled earlier in the day to cover his baldness, no longer even pretending to be altogether real. His anger could be smelled like the heat itself all around us.

Slasser's eyes flickered and the question in them had only two seconds to travel to his brain. It never got answered. Don stepped into the doorway and separated Slasser from Bedelia and me, and laid the gun butt across the bridge of Slasser's nose with fearful power and precision and the bone shattered. You could hear it collapse under the blow. Blood gushed and Slasser cried out as his gun clattered to the stone walk just in front of the door but fortunately did not discharge.

As Slasser fell back into the room and thudded to the carpeted part of the floor, Ganner shouted, "What the fuck — ?"

The man who was called Roy sprang at Don with a show of real daring and a lack of sense. I said to Ganner, "Don't move," and was pointing the two fallen 357 Magnums at him while Don racked up the hapless Roy with a punishing left hook on the chin, his right hand still holding his own gun. Roy went down for the second time that evening like a shot. He would have been smart to have an electroencephalogram made as soon as possible. Don could hit like Rocky Marciano or Joe Frazier even with the left hand, and he had used more than the minimum force necessary. Roy lay on his back, blood spilling over his lips, Don's blow one backed up with bad temper. He had evidently been through something on his own all this time and was a big and quietly ferocious enemy no one would choose to have. "Just stand there, Ganner, as if you were riveted to the floor," he commanded in a tight-lipped drawl, his eyes narrowed and blazing.

Ganner's face was drained of its blood and his own anger was dead-white, his dark eyes sparkling with hate and, for the first time, with fear. He didn't know what to do. "Let's get away from here," Bedelia said. We were knocking over the opposition ruthlessly and there was something about it that seemed to be a little shocking to her.

"Where's Mrs. Colby?" I said.

"How do I know?" Ganner snarled in a choked voice, his face twisted with rage and disbelief. This had all turned into a nightmare for him beyond any he could have anticipated. His eyes sprang with angry anxiety to a point beyond us through the open door which Don then quickly slammed shut.

"Don't look for them, Ganner," Don said. "They're not coming."

We all knew he meant Terry and Al, and I said, "Where are they?"

"They took me for a little ride out into the desert," he said, his eyes staying on Ganner's face. "I guess they thought it would be a romantic setting for my murder. But I slipped through them like water through a sieve. You should send them back to crime school, Ganner. They could stand a refresher course."

I looked at Don, six feet four, a lean, hard two hundred and fifteen pounds, the broad shoulders smoothly muscled under the white shirt, the waist narrowing down like a bat handle. "Get Mrs. Colby in here, Don," I said. "Just tell her the spot Max is in. She'll come without a fuss."

"You won't get away with it," Ganner said, his voice unwavering and oozing with hints of vengeance.

"For today we will," I said. "Your army is gone."

Don went outside and dragged Gates across the threshold and dropped him next to Slasser. They were both out of it, and I wondered vaguely, as I looked at them and also at Roy all splayed out on the floor, if any of them would ever be the same again. "I'll find her," Don said and went out again.

"You're pretty quick with calling names and holding your noses," Ganner said emotionally, the welt and the cut on his face a purple and scarlet mess. "But what are you except two-bit stickup artists?"

"We're just recovering stolen goods, Max," I said. "The cops could have been brought into it if Mr. Colby wanted to take that course. But he did you a favor and got it back the hard way. Why complain?"

Don came back with a grim-faced Clare Colby who looked at Bedelia and said in quiet but bitter tones, "You two-faced, hypocritical, phony little bitch."

Bedelia didn't answer and it was hard to tell what she was thinking. Maybe she agreed. Clare walked over to stand next to Ganner with an air of superiority, clear contempt in her face for all of us. "What's my husband paying you for this?" she said. "Whatever it is, it won't be worth it to him in the long run; you can tell him I said so. He won't get away with it. And neither will you."

I said, "One of us is going to stay behind while the two others get safely out of the compound. Try to take it calmly and quietly."

"Fuck yourself," Ganner said.

Clare winced slightly and he glanced apologetically in her direction but said nothing.

"I'll hold things down, Jim," Don said. "And I'll see you back in L.A."

Bedelia and I walked across the grounds to the swimming pool, where not more than half a dozen people were still congregated. In plain view of all of them, I poled Bedelia's bag from its resting place at the bottom of the pool, using the long-poled leaf-strainer to do it. One man said, "Fall in, did it?" and no one else was sufficiently interested to give us more than a perfunctory glance.

At the top of the broad stone staircase leading to the street Sylvia and Irving Gertz appeared. "Leaving?" she said.

"All good things come to an end," I said.

"Do they?" she said in that elusively tart way she had, pointedly not looking at Bedelia but acutely aware of her. "Well, sooner or later anyway."

Irving nodded pleasantly at us and Bedelia smiled vaguely at them. Then I gave the claim-check to the kid who within thirty seconds delivered the rented Dodge to us. I gave him a dollar and we got into the car, Bedelia holding her wet drawstring canvas bag no differently than any woman holds such an item when it contains little more than her lipstick and credit cards. And an hour and a half later we touched down in Burbank. Carrying one thousand thousand dollars' worth of diamond jewelry with us.

15

WE DIDN'T TALK during the forty-five-minute flight, and as tired as we were we didn't doze even once. It was nearly eleven when we reached the airport parking area. Bedelia carried the bag slung on her shoulder, and we looked as if we were returning from a weekend that had tired us out and left us no more satisfied than before we had gone away. We had had a dream together and weren't quite awake from it yet. Except that it had not been a dream. As we got to the car Bedelia said, "I'll breathe easier when we know that Don's out of there."

"He's fine. He's out of there a long time by now. With Mrs. Colby for company all the way to the airport. It can't have gone wrong."

"I was a little sorry for her," she said.

"She's a tough cookie. Save your sympathy. There are worthier causes all over the place."

We reached my Galaxie standing in a slot in the almost empty rectangle. A two-engine jet came in over us, the landing lights flashing, the wheezing screech of its retarded speed filling the air for a few moments. I went to the hood of the car and lifted it. I leaned in and couldn't see too much detail in the dark but I carefully groped for the starter rod. Bedelia was standing a few feet away and she said, "What are you doing?"

"Nothing much, just checking a loose wire."

There was nothing under the hood to alarm me and I slammed it down tight and then unlocked the driver's door and looked inside, though the likelihood of someone having broken in and then relocked the door was remote. Bedelia noticed the fractional hesitation. I slammed the door and walked around to the passenger side and unlocked it and held the door open for her. She came around, gave me a faintly questioning look, and then got inside. In a minute or two we were driving back along Hollywood Way, a typically wide street in the Valley, toward Burbank Boulevard. The streetlights were like markers on a strange planet, because we were still back at that house, still in the game room facing Ganner's hot scowl, men settling things with guns, the hot desert air still baked into us in spite of an air-conditioned airplane ride.

She said, "I guess it's a little late to start worrying now, isn't it?"

"You can always worry a little. It never goes to waste, if that's what you like to do. But it never does much good. Are you worried?"

"No. Just thinking."

"About Ganner?"

"Yes. We completely and utterly humiliated him. He'll find that harder to take than anything. I suppose we should be ready for him to show up, unless we can get away — I mean, out of L.A."

"He'll never show up," I said. "Sure, he was humiliated. And he'll want to keep it quiet. Especially since he knows the jewelry is out of his reach. That's why I let him know where it was going. Once it's in Colby's hands his stake is gone. There's no percentage in tangling with us after that, because he can lose more than he can gain. No, I think we're sitting pretty as far as Ganner is concerned."

"I didn't think we had it in us to do things like that, did you?"

"Not unless we were going to get a hundred and fifty thousand dollars for doing them."

"And do you realize that if that movie had been sixty seconds longer that night," she said recollecting, "there might not even have been a Colby case. And if there had been anyway, we'd have walked out of Ganner's house the way all the other guests did, because no one would have recognized you."

"It was all or nothing. Colby never would have come to us otherwise."

"I can never get over how thin the threads are."

"Thin and plenty of them. There's something in my jacket pocket. Take it out and read it. Use the map light, it won't bother me."

She did as I told her to, and her reaction was a sharp intake of breath. "Oh, God."

"I should probably have waited; you've had enough for one day," I said. "But you'll have to know about it sooner or later if it's on the level."

She refolded the note and said, "That explains what you were doing under the hood of the car. You were looking for a bomb."

"Maybe I was overreacting."

"That one insane moment *did* follow us," she said in a pensive voice that seemed to have overtaken everything she now talked about. "Do you remember? I said, I wonder if you ever got away from something like that . . ."

"Yes."

"What are you going to do about this?"

"Just keep as cool as I can and watch my step as much as possible for a while. But don't worry about it. Most threatening notes are never followed up. They'll tail off."

"Darling, we'll never be sure as long as we're in the Yellow Pages," she said.

"It's okay. We're going on a trip. Or did you forget?"

"But how soon?"

"As soon as we wind this up. I may even retire from the detective business. I've been thinking about it a long time."

I didn't say anything more as we drove along the freeway, and neither did Bedelia until we had reached Coldwater Canyon, got off, and parked in front of her apartment building on the dark, hilly little street.

"Ready to drop, baby?" I said.

"My juices are all dried up," she said. "I've never felt so squeezed out."

"Sleep late, sweetheart. There's nothing to do in the office anyway."

"What are you going to do with that?"

"Put it in a safe place."

There was a pause and she said, "Keep your gun under your pillow, Jim. That note scares me." Then she kissed my cheek. "Good night, darling. Don't get out."

She went in by herself and I drove away.

I drove directly back to the Burbank-Hollywood Airport, because I wanted to use a public locker for securing the bag and its contents. I didn't want even Bedelia to know where it would be reposited until the moment I could deliver it to Colby and get my big payoff. It was useless and dangerous information and it would have been unfair to make her carry it around with her even overnight. That was why I didn't place the bag when we arrived. As soon as it was done, I called Colby's house and woke up the housekeeper, who knew nothing of Colby's whereabouts and suggested I call in the morning. I then returned to my apartment and tried to sleep. I was dog-tired, but it took some doing. By then it was about one in the morning.

16

I AWOKE FEELING different than I had felt on other mornings, the shutters on my bedroom windows tightly closed against seven a.m. light. I was on my stomach and my head was at the edge of the bed.

I could see my .38 on the carpet not two feet from my face within quick and easy reach. This in spite of the fact I didn't think there was anything to be afraid of.

I sat up and put my feet on the floor and reached for the bed-table phone and dialed the Colby residence. No hour would have been too ungodly for this call. The butler answered and sounded as if he had been awake for hours. "Mr. Colby is out of the city," he informed me.

I wasn't happy about that at all. "For how long?" I said.

"That I couldn't say, sir. You might try calling his office. Perhaps they can tell you more."

It was too early for that because Brooks was not apt to be available before nine o'clock, if by then. I picked up the phone again and dialed Don's number. Halfway through the second ring his voice came on. "Hullo . . ."

"This is Jim. You okay?"

"Sure thing . . . How about you?"

"Everything's perfect. Go back to sleep. Talk to you later."

I hung up and sat there staring into space in the vague and shadowy room. The idea of more sleep was out of the question, so I shaved and showered, knowing full well that I would need to shave again by seven o'clock that evening if I wanted to be fastidious. It didn't matter. I was dressed and ready to leave the apartment by seven-thirty and that's just what I did. For the second day running my .38 was in a holster under my left arm. This even though I knew how low the danger level probably was. It was an uncustomary sensation.

I walked across the enormous recreation area opposite my two-story building, four baseball diamonds marking the extreme corners. The place was like lonely prairie-lands under gray morning skies, children's swings and seesaws deserted and silent for the moment. I spent about twenty minutes configuring the grassy surfaces and the cemented playground and finally had had enough. Maybe I was really testing the danger level anyhow, I don't know.

I came back to my apartment and fixed myself coffee and toast. I drank the coffee, ate the toast, and read the L.A. *Times* slowly and carefully, half-expecting to find out all about what had happened at Ganner's house in Vegas the day before. Then I slammed the door on an empty apartment and began to drive over to the office. By then it was exactly nine o'clock and the KFWB news was coming over my car radio. And very shortly the well-lubricated tones of one of the announcers confirmed something I had suspected since the night before.

"The bodies of two known underworld figures were discovered early this morning by Nevada State Highway Patrolmen. Terry Mannino, aged thirty, and Al Big Dago Scalzi, twenty-eight, were evidently shot to death sometime last night and left in the desert fifteen miles from Las Vegas, about a hundred yards off a minor road, seven miles away from the main highway. Both men had been shot twice, and from all indications the gun used for the purpose may have been one belonging to Mannino and now missing. A gun found at the scene had been fired once and was registered in Scalzi's name. Police and Highway Patrol officials have not ruled out the possibility of a gangland murder attempt by Scalzi and Mannino that backfired and left them dead at the hands of their intended victim. The influx into the area of certain eastern mob personalities has been of recent concern to Nevada authorities . . ."

The story droned on for a few moments longer but I didn't pay close attention to it. When I reached the office none of the shops were open yet and only the two insurance guys were at their desks a few doors down from me. A few pieces of old mail, not today's, lay on the carpet just inside the door. An envelope with Rita's familiar hand was among them, and inside was the key to Jan's personal vault-box, something apparent to the touch even before the envelope was opened. I stuck it in my pocket and shuffled through the other pieces as I walked to my desk through the morning light. A bill from Pacific Telephone, a bill from Union Oil, a car insurance premium notice, an announcement from Brooks Brothers, tickets to a new show at the Ahmanson Theatre that I had promised to attend with Bedelia, a few other inconsequential items. But there was one significant piece of mail. The Colby contract, bearing his signature. I sat right down and dialed Colby's office and asked to speak with Simon Brooks.

"Yes, Mr. Blaney," he said, as if I were looking for a job. He had a little of that in him. "What can I do for you?"

"You can tell me where Colby is," I said. "Because he is paying for the very breath I draw."

"I'm sure he won't object to that. But he happens not to be in the city."

"I knew that before we started."

"Oh?"

"I called the residence."

"I see."

"What's the story, Brooks?"

"Well, it's as I say, and I've no real gauge of when he'll be back. Though I imagine soon enough."

I had had enough. Yesterday had finally caught up with me. "Listen, Brooks. I've knocked my ass off and did a lot of mean, hard work for that son of a bitch — put my life and the lives of my associates in danger and I'm not going to sit here quietly while he cools his ass somewhere, got that?"

"It's perfectly clear, Mr. Blaney. But it will change nothing, unfortunately, because I have no more idea of where to contact him than you have."

"That bastard knew I might be back in L.A. at any time with dogs nipping at my heels and he didn't even bother to leave a message?" I was immediately sorry I had said that much.

"It's typical of him," Brooks said. "He's a secretive man, sometimes needlessly, I needn't tell you. It's part of his — ."

"Style, yes, we've gone into that already."

"Is it anything that won't keep another day or two?"

"That's a good question. The answer is, you never can tell."

"I promise you, Blaney, the first thing I bring to his attention will be this conversation."

"It had better be or it's liable to cost him," I said, trying to keep from raising my voice too much but steaming mad. "And I don't mean expenses and normal fees. So you better let him know that I said that and fast."

I hung up and was a little sorry I had poured it all over him as much as I had. But he was there to take some of what people wanted to give directly to Colby and couldn't. That's what he was being paid for. Not that I was someone who enjoyed anything like that, I didn't for one minute. But this setup suddenly unnerved me because I hadn't expected any delays. A delay in a situation like this could have been fatal. I didn't know exactly how but the thought wasn't farfetched. It got to my nervous system and so I let Brooks have it. But at a certain point you stop feeling sorry for everyone. Especially those who are earning a hundred thousand dollars or more a year.

The front door opened and Don came in. He looked tired, fatigue on the chiseled features under the suntan. As he crossed my threshold I turned my eyes downward to the surface of my desk on which rested pictures of Jan and Loretta, and I said, "What did you do with Mannino's gun?"

Then I looked right into his eyes. He was frowning and looking like a big running back who had overrun his interference and knew it and was embarrassed by it. "You figured it out right away, didn't you?" he said.

"Only part of it. But even if I hadn't, it's on the news this morning," I said.

He spread his hands in a philosophical gesture. "If they had come back," he said, "I *wouldn't* have."

"It was them or *you*?"

"I was dead from the word go," he said.

"Why should they have gone that far with you? They weren't that *nuts*, were they?"

"That's right, but they wanted the rocks for themselves," he said, sitting down on the desk and leaning toward me. He picked up Jan's picture in its leather frame almost without knowing he had, glanced at it, and put it back without pausing in his story. "You see, they had no idea that the jewelry even existed up till yesterday . . ."

"Yeah, I caught that myself," I said.

He shrugged. "Greed before loyalty. And I don't think that they had much faith in Ganner's future anyway. So they were going to do a number on him and the only way was to get rid of me," he said. "Get me to talk, that is, and tell them where the stuff was hidden, and then not tell Ganner about it. That kind of a dodge means you can't have someone around who knows about it — namely me, in this case."

"How did they get to you?"

"Mrs. Colby pointed me out. After I had separated from Bedelia. Did she tell you about how we were hiding in the shower stall?"

"Yes."

He shrugged faintly, his eyes slightly clouded and pink from lack of sleep and misted over with the memory. "So I took my shot," he went on. "And I was faster than either one of them. Thank God. They were big and strong but not that quick."

"Yeah," I said and watched him relive it.

He looked at me with deep concern. "Listen, Jim, don't ever tell my mother about any of this," he said.

"I was going to send her a written report. You must think I'm pretty dumb," I said casually. "Anyway, what happened?"

"I took a swing at Scalzi, I guess it was, and I caught him right on the nerve. He went down and I got locked into a wrestle with Mannino and ripped hs gun away and shoved him off. Scalzi pulls his gun and starts shooting from the ground and I had everything with me because he missed me and I got him twice with my shots. I was on the ground myself at that point because I was ducking away from Scalzi's fire. Mannino by then was coming back at me and I hit him twice in midair and he went down." He paused, shrugged, and said, "If you can follow that."

"I can follow it," I said. "How did you get back into the compound?"

"Over the back fence," he said. "Couldn't you guess? Ganner's grounds go all the way to the edge of the area. I nearly ripped the Jesus out of myself . . ."

He looked at his hands and I could see some of the scuffs and cuts he had sustained, which I hadn't noticed at first.

"Anyhow, I didn't aim to kill them, Christ knows," he said.

"But we're on the spot for a story," I said.

"You mean for the police."

"The self-defense angle is easy enough, especially since the police have it figured that way already. But it complicates things for us," I said, swiveling in the chair. We should have been on the phone to the Nevada cops without hesitation right that minute. But here we were trying to figure it out first. "The fact is, it becomes inconvenient for us to come out in the open with it right now — while those rocks are still in our hands."

He nodded and said nothing.

"Part of the problem is the agreement I have with John Colby," I went on. "No publicity, no police, nor anything else that would reveal his personal circumstances in connection with Mrs. Colby and the jewels. That was the specific and paramount condition." I shook my head. "He might just hold me to it. And we might wind up with payment for services plus expenses and nothing else."

Don shook his head slowly and with a pained thin smile. "*That'd* be tough shit in the extreme, wouldn't it?" he said.

"That's where the problem is," I said. And then I added in a philosophical tone, "Of course, we're talking about a pair of sewer rats."

"You mean, who would cry over them?" he said.

I stared out of the window, and Don was looking at the pictures of Jan and Loretta as if he wanted to discuss it with them also. I turned to discover him studying them. Bedelia was just entering the office. She looked none the worse for wear, her eyes wide, the cornea absolutely clear and white, her blondness bright and creamy, and I marveled at what a night's sleep could do for her, glad I hadn't ruined it. Not because I was king of the studs. God knows, but I was almost always at her beck and call. And she had fortunately not beckoned or called the night before.

Everyone said good morning or hi in appropriately subdued tones and then said nothing. Bedelia glanced idly out of the window. "And what shall we do today?" she said.

"Close this place up to begin with," I said, getting up from my desk.

They looked at me and I went on. "Colby's out of town. Yeah, nothing ever goes from A to B to C. So that leaves us to tread water — I don't know honestly for how long. Probably not more than a day or two. A very long time. I'll stick it on the bill with penalties. But I don't want any business or activity of any kind in the office in the meantime."

"I've got files to clean up, Jim," Bedelia said.

"Well, just pretend you don't," I said. "I wasn't worried yesterday and I'm not worried today," I said, looking at Bedelia as I said as much. "But just in case Ganner *should* somehow get wind of this little bottleneck and figure it gives him a fighting chance. It might tempt him to try to catch up with us. It's a thousand to one, but we're going to be chicken about it.'

"I'll go down to La Jolla and see my mother," Don said.

"That's all it takes," I said. "In fact, as far as *they* know, you're Miss Dean and Mr. Peabody. They can't even look you up."

"But they can look *you* up, Jim," Bedelia said. "You're James Blaney to them, and you're not only in the Yellow Pages, you're in the *white* pages too."

"I'll check into a hotel or something just until Colby gets back. After that we'll see what happens."

Don said, "Is there no way we can get a line on him? Jesus, if he knew we were back, that old son of a bitch'd come a-running. I mean, just to gloat."

"He probably thinks we've been murdered," Bedelia said.

"Give him a day or two," I said. "And let's not grind about it."

"Did you show Don the little love-note you received?" she said, an urgent sound creeping into her voice.

"No."

"That's as good a reason to get out of sight for a while as any," she said.

Don looked at me questioningly and I gave him the thing. He read it and handed it back. "The pushers' friends," he said flatly, a faint and mirthless smile on his lips. "When did you get this?"

"Last week when I came in from Vegas for a few hours."

"Show it to the cops?"

"What are *they* going to do about it?"

"You ought to tell them you received it anyhow."

"I think you should, Jim," Bedelia said.

I shrugged, put it back in my pocket, and said, "Let's go on our furlough."

"Is your mother well, Don?" Bedelia said. "I mean since she's out of the hospital."

"Well, not too bad. Getting back into things. I'll give her a surprise. Just grab a couple of changes of socks and one or two unmentionables and tool on down there. You've got the number, don't you Jim?"

"Yeah. Send my best."

"Will do."

He moved out of the office substantially ahead of Bedelia and me. "Why the hell would you even dream of going to a hotel, for God's sake?" she said with a mildly exasperated smile.

"I didn't. It just sounded better."

"Jim, darling, Don's a good friend and he knows we sleep together."

"Yeah, but I don't want to announce it officially."

"Do you think that makes sense?"

"No more sense than tipping your hat to a lady," I said, and then remembered something. "Wait a second — one quick call before we check out."

I dialed the number Jan had given me and let the phone ring eight times before giving up. I would try again later. "Come on, you liberated young thing, you," I said.

"Okay, Life With Father."

We locked the door behind us. It was ten a.m.

17

I WENT BACK to my apartment to pack a suitcase and I parked in back of the building in my assigned stall, reached by a cut-through. I came and went without being seen on the street from any one of a number of possible vantage points, moved to and from the apartment by the inside staircase. I wasn't sure which of the threats I was protecting against, which was the more significant or if either of them was really worth the caution. Sometimes you play games with yourself and you don't even know that you're doing it. I moved like a shadow anyway. At least I hoped I was moving like a shadow. I drove to Bedelia's apartment and she opened the door to me like the lookout in an illegal horse-room. "Didn't bargain for this when you came to answer that ad, did you, kid?" I said.

I followed her to the kitchen, where she had a pot of coffee ready to pour as she said, "Nobody can say it's been humdrum. But you could have been in the plastic key-ring business and I'd have taken the job." And as I sat down at the Formica tabletop and she began to pour the two cups, she added; "Except that there would have been no excuse for you to move in with me like this now. And that's what I like about the detective business."

"And that's what I like about the south. Let's go to the races and have lunch at the track."

"Feeling that expansive and *joie de vivre,* darling?"

"Whatever that word means, yeah. Why not?"

We left the apartment shortly, and as we drove down on the San

Diego Freeway, she said, "Don killed those two men, didn't he?" And her tone was somewhat solemn.

"You heard about them on the news?"

"Yes. The conclusion is obvious."

"Yes, he did it. They were going to do it to him and he did it to them instead. A much better outcome that way."

"God in heaven, yes. But we're sitting on it, aren't we? We're not telling the police."

"That's right."

"It's the cold and logical thing to do undoubtedly," she said acceptantly. "And it's all right except for the two dead and God knows how many with blood in their eyes."

"Neither of them was a model citizen."

"I know. But I guess I wish none of it had ever happened — even for all that money. Or maybe I don't feel that way at all. Maybe it's just that I know I *should* feel that way." She looked at me and I glanced away from the freeway at her. "Do you know what I mean, Jim?"

"Sure. You think it's wrong to enjoy the dough because of everything around it, the dead hoodlums and so forth."

"Do you feel a little like that about it?"

"No, sweetheart. But you're sweet and young and moral underneath everything and you know we've done a few things that aren't exactly among the highest of traditions."

"I go back and forth about it."

"Yeah, I know. But this is the arithmetic for me. The dough gets my daughter Loretta into first-year med school, the way she's always hoped; Don gets a nice chunk of it for himself; and you and I go off on a quiet spree. Courtesy of Cole Porter. For this we were very nearly murdered, and some hoodlums got killed instead. I don't anticipate sleepless nights over that, sweetheart, and neither should you."

By the time we got to the track, had lunch, and were making a few small bets, the pleasure and the excitement of the warm and golden day had taken over. The hoofs thundered, the crowd roared, and we even came up with a winner in the fourth race that paid five-sixty. On the day's tally I had dropped a couple of hundred but didn't let it affect me because I am not a habitual horseplayer anyhow and it was the outing itself that was important. And it had been altogether enjoyable and I didn't fret about the money. But it did drive me for some reason to silently curse John Colby and his highhanded ways, and just before we left the track after the eighth race I put in a call to the Colby office. But not even Brooks was around by that time. Another try on Colby's home phone also produced a zero.

Bedelia and I did some shopping at Ralph's in the Valley and then went back to the apartment for dinner at home because we were both sick of restaurants, even good ones, and we were keen on a change of pace. She decided on meat loaf and baked potatoes and got things going in the kitchen. I fixed a couple of martinis in the living room and turned on a side of Glenn Miller. I still went for that kind of thing. Bedelia joined me. We had a drink and didn't say much. As the side ended and the arm clicked back into place, we began to make love.

We were on the sofa, the shutters closed, the room unlit. She flattered my ego lavishly and made me younger, and even dynamic in a way I could not have been with anyone else. "You're terrific," she murmured sweetly.

"For an old cock," I said.

"Ha. You're better than all the young studs all rolled into one," she said, and sighed.

"How would you know?" I teased.

"I read books."

But a pang of envy and the thought of eventual loss were just under the skin. You can't fight off a gap of twenty-five years indefinitely. "Rita is right about us," I said. "She always points out that I've got a daughter only a couple of years younger than you are, sweetheart."

"The hell with Rita," she came back at me.

She kissed me with erotic intent and she was not pert or cute but a grown woman in every way, and again I reacted to her in the most gratifying and desirable manner. For a second time. At my age that says something. "Abelard was thirty-seven and Eloise seventeen, darling," she said after some time had gone by.

"We've got *them* licked," I said brilliantly.

"We've got everybody licked," she said, confident and sultry. "Oh, my God — the meat loaf."

She leaped up, her breasts dancing, and ran naked to the kitchen. The meat loaf was saved and we got dressed and had dinner. And then I remembered Jan and the key in my pocket, and I went to the phone in the living room while Bedelia put on the coffee. I wanted to let Jan know I had done her errand and could simply put her key in the mail, or, if she liked, give it to her in person. I thought I might like to see her again anyway. This gave me the excuse. A man answered, someone thirtyish or less, I thought. "Is Jan there?" I asked.

"Jan?" he replied vaguely.

"Jan Blaney."

"Oh, Jan Blaney."

There was silence. "Have I got the right number?" I said.

"Oh, you've got the right number," he said.

I had reached the limit of my tolerance and I distinctly didn't like whoever was doing the routine on the other end. "Who are *you*?" I asked.

"Jan will be around in a little while," he said. "Why don't you come by if you want to see her?"

He hung up and the hackles on my neck rose. I got off the sofa fast and went into the kitchen and said, "Sweetheart, the coffee will have to keep."

"What's wrong, Jim?"

I don't know," I said. "Something with Jan." I started to put on my jacket and move toward the door. "I'm going to look in on her."

In about fifteen minutes I was driving up in front of the ratty apartment building where I had picked her up on the other occasion. I had a feeling I had left something out of my arithmetic when I was doing all the toting-up for Bedelia earlier in the day. It was a sinking feeling. And I had every right to it. Inside I found Jan, wearing only a brassiere and tight-fitting jeans, lying across an unmade bed, her arms flung out, her legs splayed and grotesquely arranged, one foot touching the floor, her eyes closed, her mouth pitiably agape. And she was dead-to-the-world on smack. Heroin. I knew the signs. The sight made me weak in the knees. I had never had as hard a jolt.

18

FORTY-FIVE MINUTES LATER Rita and I were sitting in the waiting room of the UCLA narcotics section while Dr. Feldman did whatever had to be done on the ward with the resident people. And I was saying, "Who is this guy Strelli? Where the hell did he come from? I mean, I would like some answers."

"For God's sake, Jim, this comes as much of a shock to me as to you," Rita said.

"Well I mean, didn't you see something like this coming?"

"Oh, what a naïve question."

"Is it? I don't think so. It's you, not me, that she's been living with."

"And may I remind you that it was you who saw her last. And at that time, if memory serves me, you refused to divulge her whereabouts. To me. Her mother. And now, all of a sudden you're acting as if everybody is accountable except you." She added, "And lower your voice, please . . ."

"I'm not shouting," I replied, and in fact we weren't talking loud. But the tensions were there, and even people who were looking the other way couldn't help being aware of those they were sharing this deadly room with, this common agony. It was always parents sitting outside with a kid inside.

Rita stood up and paced slowly to the louvered window. Dark-haired, tall and trim still, her slightly triangular face with its faintly scoffing mouth and sea-green eyes hadn't lost too much of its particular kind of beauty in the press of time. Except there was moisture in the sea-green eyes, the remains of quiet tears, and the mouth was chastened by distress and anxiety. I hadn't seen much of her in the past few years, but she was still someone on whom a tiara would go just right. And that particular capability wasn't commonplace among women born in Long Beach. Not that Rita was some kind of an imperious snob, just that she had certain needs that a helter-skelter private eye could never have taken care of, much as he might have loved her at one time.

I got up and walked over to where she stood. "Rita, just answer me as directly as possible and maybe we'll come up with something," I said, facing her, trying to get back on some kind of a footing. "Does it make sense to you that Jan would go in for this? She's twenty-two and she's never had a drug experience, has she? Or has she?"

"How do I know for a certainty?" she said resentfully, vexed not only by the situation but by me. "To my knowledge, no."

"That's the point. That's what's nagging the hell out of me. Why *now?*" She shook her head and I went on quickly. "There's a big piece missing somewhere. And I'd like to find it."

Several more people entered the room, one a pitiably overweight woman with unkempt hair, the other a thin, gaunt, curly-haired boy of seventeen, probably her son. As they passed by I continued. "All right, we won't talk about what made her leave the house and take up with this guy Strelli. We'll just accept the fact she did."

"Jim, there's a natural conflict today between people like Jan and people like Steve and me — and you. There's nothing that can be done about it really. The funny part of it is, I'm sympathetic toward it, I understand it . . ."

"Sympathetic toward what? She said you raised hell about Strelli," I said.

"You're missing the point," she said. "Of course, I raised hell about it. First of all, I couldn't understand the choice . . ."

"Oh?"

"Or maybe I could and didn't want to."

"I can see how being fair-minded can land you in a lot of trouble, Rita," I said. "I can see what you were doing — the kind of thing liberals always do: giving away more in principle than you can live with when somebody takes you up on it and comes to collect."

Her eyes flashed and were very dry now. "Oh, what are you talking about?" She wanted to eat me for that one.

"Only that you tolerated and sympathized instead of drawing lines a kid can understand. And when all the tolerance and sympathy turned into a seal of approval for all the new ideas and your daughter decided to try some of it out, you suddenly wanted your money back. But it was too late."

"Jim, you're so smug and so damned wrong," she said, and I could hear the tightness in her throat.

"That could be. If I'm wrong I'm sorry. But what did you mean when you said first that you *couldn't* understand the choice and then that you *could*?"

"That I didn't approve and I pulled back at the sight of someone as — well, someone who lets it all hang out to the extent he did. Which I suppose is about the most accurate way of saying it . . ."

"Lets it all hang out?"

"He oozed with whatever it is that lets you know he wants to seduce you and can do it better than it's been done before."

"*You?*"

"Don't be clever — anyone! I have eyes and an I.Q. over eighty-five. I could see what was going on and what it was about him that got to Jan. Tall, dark, one of those Zapata mustaches, eyes to turn a young girl's will into bread crumbs, which he then eats up like a fat blue jay . . ."

"Where did all this note-taking go on, Rita? Did he come to the house?"

"He drove her home from a date one night and I ran into them accidentally," she said. "It was very brief, but I guess I could see the handwriting on the wall. They had only met a couple of nights before."

"When was this?"

"A few days before you called me."

I wasn't sure I had heard right. "A few days before I called you?" I repeated. "You mean she's only known this guy a little over two weeks at this point?"

She said nothing and I said, "That's incredible."

Suddenly Steve Pembroke was coming into the room, flushed, grim, a little big for his lightweight suit, the lantern jaw set and reconciled. He was about forty-five, Rita's age, not overly bright but steady, good for about twenty-five thousand a year. I was sure Rita both liked and respected him, but no more than that. He talked with a twang and a rasp along the edges of his voice, a not unpleasant but somewhat boring sound. "Can someone tell me in a way I can understand what is happening," he said. "I don't get it. You try your level best and you think you're doing the right thing, and then something like this hits you in the face."

"Well, we're all asking the same question," I said, as if nothing could change that fact. "And yet Jan said — or at least she strongly implied when I talked to her that you and Rita and she had a blowup. What about that?"

"That's a fair enough description," Steve said. "She just came in and announced that she had to leave home, and that she was going to." He shrugged and looked regretful. "It was honest. But we all got a little agitated about it."

"That was the mistake," Rita said. "That was why she went off in a cloud of dust and wouldn't contact me when she wanted her safe-deposit key. I should never have said the things I did and I'm ready to admit it."

"Why didn't you tell me that on the phone when I called you instead of telling me I was being duped?"

"Because you *were* being duped — you with your tough nose and reactionary outlook on things. You're more hidebound than any of us. You're the last one to go along with the various trends of the day, and here you were being her confederate. You were in league with her . . ."

"In league," I scoffed. "I was trying to be a friend to my daughter because she needed someone to help her, for Christ's sake. She wasn't going to contact you whether I turned her down or not."

"We're all beginning to misunderstand each other and it's getting us nowhere," Steve said. "And we're attracting attention."

At that instant Feldman stuck his head into the room and beckoned to the three of us. We followed him into an empty examination room. He was a gray and sallow man of fifty, successful and smart and unavoidably complaisant. He let us have it cold. "Not good," were the first words he uttered.

"Is she . . . ?" Rita started and stopped, her eyes full of remembered mistakes, pain and fright in them.

"She's crashing," Feldman said. "That means sleeping it off."

"What's the prognosis?" Steve said urgently.

"Psychoanalytically, I can't speak with authority," Feldman answered. "It's not my field. But I do know that anyone who has had as many injections as she seems to have had in the past week has a serious addiction problem. If it's not physiological yet, it's certainly mental. It's a habit and there are going to be problems breaking it. You're going to have to find the key before it's too far gone."

All of our mouths were tightened by the news and Rita seemed to be fighting tears. "What can be done, Doctor?" she said.

"See what her reactions are in the morning," Feldman said. "Cold turkey is one way. Sometimes the best. Maybe this par*tic*ular time because the use doesn't seem to be prolonged."

"Then what?" Rita asked anxiously.

"She has to be watched carefully, perhaps given some sort of psychiatric attention." He pressed his hands together and worked the knuckles. "I've seen so damned much of this." He shook his head.

"Can I talk with her tomorrow?" I said.

"If she'll talk with you, why not?" Feldman said. "Do you know anything about this, any of you?"

All of us made hopeless little gestures or just shook our heads and said nothing.

"No previous experiences?" Feldman said with tired disbelief.

"She left home a little over two weeks ago," Steve said. "We were just talking about it and trying to get a clue, but . . ."

I had stopped listening. I couldn't share anything with Rita because she was not someone I shared things with any longer. I knew Steve felt like hell in his own way, though it wasn't his natural daughter, and I wanted to leave them to themselves and get off by myself. "I'm going to say goodbye now," I said quietly.

"I guess we've got a problem," Steve said.

"Jan is the one with the problem," I said. "No matter what we do about it, it's her problem now."

"Any girl might want to live with a man," he said, with perplexed eyes trained off in space. "She's young and normal. But why the drugs?"

"That's what I've been asking you," I said.

"As if we have the magic answer," Rita said.

"Maybe there isn't any," Feldman said.

Our words were all embarrassing and empty. Something didn't stack up and all of us were about as wise as penguins figuring out what it was. Especially me. It nagged me like an untreated wound as I walked along the hospital parterre away from the red-brick building, its lights burning in windows of grief and discomfort in back of me. I reached the parking area and actually found the answer attached to the windshield of my car, and there was nothing magical about it. It was a flawlessly typed note which I read by the map light on the dash. The words were put together carefully and their intent was very clear.

> You've had your day of glory and being a hero. Now you've got a hooked daughter. How does that feel to you? Not so good, huh? Too bad. You'll just have to live with it. If you want to know who hooked

her, the answer is you did. The day you stuck your nose where it didn't belong and killed someone you didn't even know. This is your punishment for that stupid action. Sleep tight, hero. But your daughter won't do the same ever again.

Friends of the deceased

I must have sat there about two full minutes without moving before I snapped out of it and began to drive away. I felt as if someone had hit me with a sandbag.

19

I SAT HUNCHED over with my elbows on my kness and my hands loosely folded, staring at the carpet on the living-room floor and seeing very little. Bedelia was seated on the sofa wearing the sexy black peignoir I had bought her, but only because it was too warm to wear anything else. One leg was curled up under her; her face was pensive, her expression solemn and composed.

I shook my head. "They got to me through her. And I'd like to get them for that. Killing me is one thing. They're scum and you can expect nothing better of them. But this? I'd like their blood for it."

"Jim, you can't help Jan that way," Bedelia said. "You can only spend yourself."

I didn't say anything. It was one in the morning and we had been talking for hours. The phone rang. We looked at each other. Bedelia picked it up without moving. "It's for you," she told me, and I got up and took the receiver from her.

It was my answering service. "A Mr. Brooks just called and said it was very urgent that he speak with you immediately," the operator said. "I hope it was all right to call you this late."

"Yes, it's all right. Did he leave a number?"

She gave it to me and I dialed it instantly. Brooks picked it up on one ring. "I thought you'd want to know he'll be back tomorrow," he told me without preliminary. "You were so overwrought about it this morning I was quite sure you would have no objection to my calling at this hour."

I won't say it took my mind off Jan. But the news did improve my outlook somewhat. A hundred and fifty thousand dollars was no less attractive now than it had been before. I stayed awake and watched a very bad movie on a local channel while Bedelia slept beside me, covered only by a sheet on what had turned out to be a muggy night. Even if I had been bursting with unspent passion I would have had little desire for her right then. I was glad we had made love earlier. I loved her, but I couldn't get Jan out of my mind and all kinds of old recollections came back to torture me, memories of her at earlier ages, various mixed impressions of a sweet face with a ready and brilliant little smile, all the good moments long ago. And finally I felt myself dropping off and I clicked off the set by the remote control with my last speck of consciousness. It was a bad night and Bedelia and I were both awake at about seven o'clock with very little to do.

"You can't blame yourself, Jim," Bedelia said to me, as we lay there sharing that overalert nervous quality that masks fatigue. "There's got to be some responsibility on Jan herself."

"They went after her because of me," I said in a hoarse croaking voice.

"She fell for it," Bedelia said, quietly uncompromising.

I said nothing and then we were silent. I finally said, "So she fell for it. What does that make her? A Nazi spy?"

"No. But some girls wouldn't have. She was evidently made to order for the kind of thing that happened to her. It's heartbreaking, darling, and it's tragic. But where does the responsibility lie?" She stopped and seemed to think it over and then said, "I don't know. But it can't be with you. Not after all this time."

"Let's get some breakfast," I said.

"Okay."

She cooked bacon and eggs for both of us and we were both ravenously hungry and ate them appreciatively. "I want to stop by the hospital this morning," I said. "Maybe she'll tell me something about it we don't know."

"You know already, don't you? They found out about her and cultivated her with this evidently crack seducer and then deliberately turned her on. Is there more than that?"

I didn't answer.

"You know there isn't," she said. "But you want information so you can go after them. You want vengeance. Don't do it, Jim."

"Just ignore it, huh?"

"No. See her. But cut yourself off as far as anything beyond that is concerned," she said with earnest eyes. "She is not your responsibility."

"I think you're being very tough about it," I said.

She looked at me for a moment then lowered her eyes and said, "I'll shut up." Her voice sounded choked and she got up from the table and took our empty plates with her to the sink. She began to wash them. I felt lousy from about three different directions. "She's my daughter, sweetheart," I said.

She didn't answer and I came up behind her. "Don't you think I owe her something?" I said, putting my arms around her waist, pressing upward and lifting her breasts.

"Not any more, Jim," she said. "It's me you owe something to. Staying alive and keeping out of trouble. If you don't owe me that much . . ."

"You don't know how bad I feel about the fact it was me they wanted to hurt," I said.

She turned around in my arms and faced me to say, "She let this Strelli deceive her. He's no good. But he attracted her. If he hadn't it never would have happened. And if you go out and kill somebody or get killed because of it, you're crazy. Because you'll change nothing for her. But you'll change everything for me. And I'll just love her for that, Jim."

I didn't answer. I knew she was basically right. I called Rita and discovered that she and Steve had taken Jan home and were going to try to do whatever they could for her, that she seemed lethargic and withdrawn but not in need of a fix upon awakening. So there may have been hope. Her habit was apparently not yet a ravenous one. Maybe I felt a little better about it. But I knew she had been injured very badly and there was no telling whether or not she could remain off the stuff and how the experience with Strelli's brutal emotional swindle would leave her.

But I had some fence-mending to do elsewhere. I got off the phone and went into the bedroom where Bedelia was getting dressed, and I could see that a sense of injury if not outright defeat lingered in her manner. "Let me take you down to La Jolla for lunch," I said, coming up to her and trying to make things right. "You've never met Don's mother and you'd like the house. A real stinkin' pink palazzo."

"Are you going to the hospital?" she said.

"No. It'll be okay. They're taking care of her at home."

She didn't say anything and I said, "And listen. You take a back seat to no one, sweetheart. I'm crazy about you and I can't tell you how glad I am that you're crazy about me. And I guess we're both pretty crazy when you come right down to it."

"I take it back, Jim. You don't owe me anything. I don't know why I said such a thing before."

"I owe you plenty, sweetheart, and I'll never be able to pay it. Not all of it."

"You don't. I'm the one who owes *you*."

"Let's stop trying to out-owe each other before we go bankrupt or something. I'll give Don a call as a matter of common decency while you make yourself decent."

"Don't get yourself killed or thrown in jail, darling. That's all I ask of you."

"Okay, it's a deal," I said slapping her behind, and walking out of the room. "All I want to do beforehand is drive by my apartment and pick up the mail."

In about half an hour we were on our way and the atmosphere was very much improved. Driving into that cut-through in back of my apartment building to visit my mailbox and spending two and a half minutes in the process didn't really take a lot of guts. We were just going through the motions of precaution at this point. All the dangers had run downhill somehow. You could feel it.

Bedelia remained in the car which I had parked in my stall while I went inside. There were two or three junk items. And one envelope whose contents I never expected to receive at this stage of the game. Another neat typing job.

> The days grow shorter and soon you will be a corpse. Dead for dead. That's what you get for being a friend of the heat and killing one of us. You're as good as laid out, fink.
>
> Slow Death

A few minutes later as we drove along Bedelia examined it. "They're crazy, aren't they?" she said, quiet and astonished. "Absolutely crazy."

"You could say so."

I continued to drive toward the freeway. It was a very sunny morning and sudden moderate winds had blown away the smog of the day before.

As soon as we got down there I told Don what had happened to Jan. I waited until Bedelia had gone out in the garden with Mrs. Price for a preliminary look around the place, because I didn't want to reintroduce the subject in her presence. Don and I stood on the front terrace overlooking an oval of grass circumscribed by gravel driveway. He was upset by the information, and when I gave him the note I had found on my windshield his eyes burned with the quiet anger I had seen in them before. I then gave him the second death-threat I had found in the mailbox and said, "What do you make of that? On top of the other thing?"

His eyes still burning, he said through tight lips, "I don't." He was outraged in my behalf.

I took them back from him and replaced them in my pocket and he continued to stare with that same look toward something that wasn't present. I said, "They don't go together, do they? They did their job on me with Jan." I shrugged. "Or maybe they see it as a two-part thing. First I suffer. Then I die."

"They were typed on two different machines," Don pointed out. "That might mean something, but I wouldn't know what offhand." Then he looked at me with the eyes of someone who never gave a promise lightly. "You know you can count on me, Jim," he said, "if you want to track those bastards down. But don't tell my mother about Jan. It would upset her too much."

Jean Price was a tall, broad-shouldered, regal-looking lady of sixty-two, her silver-gray hair coiffed like a small, neat crown, her nerves like the flutter of birds' wings under a pie crust, her eyes faded from a former sparkle, a touch of Parkinson's plaguing her physical stability. Recent illness had left its signs, but she was a gracious lady and a good hostess. Her Spanish house dominated the top of a sloping street in an exclusive configuration of such streets overlooking the littoral. It sat on an acre of land with inner gateways, a port-cochere, fancy grilleworks, a big terrace in front, baked-tile walkways, a stunning patio overhung with eucalyptus and wisteria, the inside floors of expensive red quarry tile, the swimming pool like a turquoise off to one side — in short, the works. What I am saying is that Don's paycheck had never been a big factor in our relationship.

Our conversation was ended when the ladies joined us, and pretty soon we were having lunch in the lee of a lovely shade tree, from whose birds we were protected by a striped umbrella. Mrs. Price, even in a state of diminished strength, was not one to mince words, honed and well-enunciated as they might have been. And how it came up, I don't quite know, but while I was digging out a divot of avocado vinaigrette, I heard her saying, "I like you, Jim. Like you a lot. But you never grew up entirely. I hope you don't mind my saying that. It's meant without malice. And I suppose it's a part of your charm. Women never really love men who become fully mature."

I smiled my suavest smile and said, "Coming from you, Jean, there's no sting in it."

"I mean, that's true of all of you," she went on in that nervous, compulsive way some people might have when they are not feeling well or completely calm about life. Her smile was there but tight and wan. "You lives are will-o'-the-wisp things, all of you," she said. "Children's dreams being carried out in the guise of adult activity."

"You might not think so if you ever needed a private detective, Jean," I said.

"I can't think of why I might. But there could be a reason, I suppose. But that doesn't in the least alter what I'm saying. It can be so grimy, can't it, and not that lucrative."

"Mom, it's not always money that counts," Don said, with a respectful smile to mask his criticism. "Jim would be bored in almost any other business."

"Your father avoided boredom and died of bullets pumped into him," Jean Price said to her son. "I suppose that's preferable to boredom."

"Mother, my father was a small-town D.A. in a town full of gangsters and a wide-open field of political corruption. He bucked all of that because that was the way he was. He never had a chance. They were bound to get him."

"I never knew that about your father, Don," Bedelia said.

"He was gunned down in the streets of Newton City, Montana," Don answered. "He was in the midst of building a case against the mayor and his whole city council at the time. It never got done. I was about twelve."

Jean Price looked into the past with faraway eyes and I got the feeling she lived a good deal of the time there these days. But she made a quick return-trip and said for Bedelia's benefit, "Don's father was my first husband; George Taintor, my second. My name is actually Taintor now. He made us well-to-do beyond the wildest of my dreams and he was a good man. But not like Don's father."

Don looked at his mother in obvious accord and then said, "I swore I'd get every one of the people who had anything to do with it. I was going to grow up and become a special prosecutor. And if I couldn't, I was going to get them one by one on my own."

"Something you never would have done," his mother said. "It was a child's thoughts and reactions."

He shook his head with a covert little smile. "It didn't matter anyhow. There were eight men with little black crosses next to their names in a little book I kept for years. But not one of them was still alive by the time I got out of Stanford."

"You mean you were still thinking about it even then?" Bedelia said, her eyes widening, her smile slightly horrified.

He shrugged. "Why not?"

The butler wheeled the main course out of the house right then and began to serve us. We talked about a lot of other things after that, and finally finished eating and began to drink coffee. A little while later Jean showed Bedelia around the big house and exposed her to all the thing I had already seen long ago, and Don and I walked around the grounds and stopped at the swimming pool, where we sat down in rattan chairs and looked at the lapping chlorinated water in front of us. Neither of us were cigar-smokers, but we lit up a couple from the supply his mother kept for male guests.

"I've disappointed her," he said reflectively, and took a puff on the cigar.

"You've got to live your own life, Don, with all due respect to Jean," I said with great wisdom.

"When George died he left Mom all of this and also the business to run. She deserves it. And I've always been glad about it. But I guess she's reached the age where she's lonely and keeps thinking about her one and only son who didn't turn out to be a big corporation lawyer or governor, or even a district attorney somewhere, but a private eye." He made a little ironic hand gesture. "And, of course, now she's not well . . ."

"Yes, that's tough."

He shook his head again, his eyes again reflective. "You know what she told me?" he said, and looked at me. "She had a dream that I was shot down, just like my father. She's had it a number of times. What do you think of that?"

"I think she has strong anxieties."

"Listen, Jim . . ."

"Yes, Don?"

"I got to come right out and say this, because I can't beat around the bush with you or hem and haw about it."

"Okay, Don. Go ahead."

"You see, because of all I just said, I have a strong responsibility here. And so . . . well, I'm going to have to quit the business and take over down here. She just can't go it alone."

He looked me right in the eye, because he was that kind, and I could see that it had been a tough decision for him. I cut his discomfort short. "Now, I'm going to tell you one, Don," I said. "I've been seriously thinking about getting out of it myself for some time now. So all you've done is swing my vote, kid. Don't let it bother you."

He was visibly relieved. "Jesus, you took the curse off that for me," he said. "I didn't know *how* in the hell I was going to tell you."

"Just the way you did. Right out. You did fine."

"I guess that's the only way. But I didn't look forward to it."

"What the hell."

"The thing is, I knew it as soon as I got down here last night and got a look at things, if you know what I mean."

"It was your only move. Don't let it bother you."

"What are you going to do?"

"I haven't given it much thought."

He hesitated before saying, "Is there a chance you'll get married, Jim? Or is that none of my goddamn business?" He added, "I wouldn't ask if you and Bedelia weren't my two best friends in the world."

"That's okay, Don," I said, and put the cigar in the standing ashtray next to my chair. Maybe it was the peaceful and lush surroundings and the feeling of letdown setting in after a fine luncheon. But I had no hesitation in telling him what I had in mind. "Someday I'm going to do the decent thing and get out of her way," I said. "I'm too old for her."

"But you're in love with her, aren't you?"

"I'm in love with her but I'm too old for her."

"She might not feel that way, Jim. I never think of you as old anyway, that's the truth. You're more of a man than any guy half your age that I know. Hell, you don't even have gray hair."

"Look a little closer," I said, and then patted his shoulder. "Let's find the ladies, okay?"

We got up and began to walk away from the pool enclosure toward the house. We walked several moments in silence. Then I said, "Can I ask *you* something?"

"Go ahead."

"When you shot Mannino and Scalzi . . . were you in a way getting even for your father?"

He didn't answer right away, and then said, "It crossed my mind."

When Bedelia and I were driving away from the house at about four o'clock I told her about Don and she was obviously glad. "It's the best thing for him and the best thing for you and me," she said. "There should be something else we can do with our lives."

"That's a switch. I thought you always liked it."

"Don's mother put her finger on certain things in her vague way. At least for me she did. We've all had enough for a lifetime."

"Anyway, that's the way it stands," I said. "He feels a strong devotion to her and she needs him."

"She's nearly broke, you know."

"No, I didn't," I said. "Did she tell you that?"

"She only said that she was going to sell the house because she couldn't keep it up."

"The recession. I imagine the business has been hit."

"I guess that's why Don feels he has to take over. And she has faith in his magical powers. I just hope that they're magical enough. What was she in the hospital for, by the way?"

"Mastectomy," I said.

She shuddered just a little in sympathy. "Oh, that's awful . . . At any age."

We drove along and were silent for a good deal of the time until we got back to L.A. When we walked into Bedelia's apartment I called the service and was given a message to call Brooks. I did so, as Bedelia stood by with an intent expression on her face, waiting for results. "It's the same time and the same place," Brooks said.

"As last time?" I asked.

"Yes, of course."

"And not the time before?"

"The same time and the same place as last time," he said again, this time in the careful way you repeat something for an idiot.

"I like to be absolutely sure of these things," I told him. "Okay. I've got it."

I hung up and said to Bedelia, "Another midnight meeting. There are easier ways and safer ways. But this is Colby's idea of how to do things."

"He's like all paranoids," she said. "He has to be sly. Nothing is ever in a straight line."

I began to take off my jacket as I said, "He may be emotionally retarded, sweetheart, but his checks don't bounce."

"Money," she said with an ironic little mouth. "It makes people into what they are. I had to laugh when Don said to his mother that it's not always the money that counts. Well, okay. If you're talking about a baby's life. Or making love." She moved into the kitchen and began to fix me a martini and herself a sangria, and she said, "But otherwise it counts in all ways, in every way, and forever."

I nodded. "Amen," I said, and took a drink.

"I'm glad you're getting rid of those damned diamonds tonight," she said.

"So am I, sweetheart," I said. "It will be like graduation day."

21

THE FIRST THING I did was go to the airport at Burbank and take the stuff from the wall locker and transfer it to the pouches of a money belt I had for the occasion. I did it in a booth in the men's room, all of it going fairly easily, if bulkily, into the ten sections. Only the small tiara wouldn't fit and I locked it in the glove compartment of my car. I put Bedelia's canvas bag into the trunk and was finally headed north on the Ventura Freeway to where John Colby was going to meet me. My left rear tire blew out and altered my schedule a little bit.

It was just past Sepulveda. I barely heard the explosion but the car jerked and thudded fiercely because I was doing sixty. I kept my foot clear of the brake pedal and I held on to the buffeting wheel as I steered toward the shoulder of the freeway. I then had the great pleasure of changing a tire on the bad side while sixty-mile-an-hour cars tore by me in the dark and rocked me in their windy wake. My blinkers were going but I didn't feel that safe while I worked with feverish speed, trying to take it in stride and sweating like hell. Getting off the lug-nuts with the small wrench I had really put me to a hard test and took plenty out of me. They were rusted in and each one was a fight to the death. But the other steps in the process weren't too tough and the whole operation took about fifteen minutes. Twenty minutes later I drove into the isolation and mystery of undeveloped Mariposa Canyon, my headlights cutting into the faint mist rolling in from the ocean a few miles ahead. I was, according to my watch, twenty minutes late for the appointment.

The vague but unmistakable shape of that old Ford appeared about a hundred yards away and parked on the shoulder to my left. I slowed down from my twenty-five-mile speed and then stopped the car. I cut the engine and kept the heads on momentarily. I didn't move out from behind the wheel right away. And then I saw him approaching. A hundred-and-fifty grand was about to fall into my hands.

I got out of the car and moved very slowly toward Colby's hulking-old-man figure and deliberately let him cover most of the ground between us. The darkness made it impossible for me to see his face, but when he got to within fifty feet of me he began to slow down, and then stopped moving altogether. I couldn't make it out and I moved more quickly toward him now than I had been moving. Before I got anywhere near him I knew what was what. He was struggling to stay on his feet. He was lurching suddenly. He was reaching out in front of him with one hand like a drowning man. "Blaney," he cried out hoarsely and with terror in his throat.

The hackles went up and I froze as he kept staggering toward me and finally pitched forward on his face in the middle of the road. And then he lay there very still, not moving at all as far as I could tell from where I was standing in the vague grayish mists.

I raced to him and knelt down and turned him over and could see nothing clearly in the dark, only the washed-away look of a face illuminated by a smattering of stars poking through the misty night. My first thought was that he had had a stroke or a coronary; he was that type. But then my fingers touched the sticky substance that runs out of people who have been stabbed or shot or whose flesh has otherwise been rent. I said out loud, "Jesus Christ," down on one knee next to him, my hand near a wound under his heart. He had been shot at least twice, I thought, and it had happened within the past few minutes. And he was now dead.

I yanked my gun from my holster with desperate haste and felt my flesh crawling, every muscle in my body tensing. I got to my feet and ran back to my car and I unlocked the panel compartment and took from it a flashlight and then relocked it. There was a killer who was still very close by who undoubtedly knew exactly where I was but whose own hiding place I couldn't begin to guess.

I crouched for a moment or two next to the far side of the car, away from the road, and I turned on the light and sprayed it around and could see meaningless samples of the terrain — the brush-covered slopes running up from the road and certain indistinguishable and vague shapes at the edges of the beam. It all meant nothing. I shone the light toward Colby's body and he was still dead. That's not meant to be funny, but merely to say that what had happened hadn't altogether sunk in and gained my acceptance yet. And I remained crouched there waiting to see if Colby's murderer would make a move of some kind before I walked out in the open where he might be able to see me and shoot me down. Nothing had moved in or out of that area after Colby had been shot and the killer was positively still close by.

A minute went by. Then something moved straight ahead of me and very close to Colby's car. I flashed the light toward the vague sounds just as the engine turned over. And then someone depressed the accelerator with a roar almost like a warning to stay clear. Like something gone crazy the car came screaming past me and drove away in the night. I couldn't have done anything about it because there was no way I could have maneuvered a turnaround in that narrow defile to chase him without a crucial loss of time. I didn't get a look at the driver but I knew he had just made what the next day was going to be a big noise in the world of international finance.

I got into my car and negotiated the turnaround and drove out of that canyon in about five minutes and hit the now-darkened shopping center of the adjacent town. There was no sign of Colby's car and I wondered where it would show up if it ever did.

A gas station, locked up tight, appeared across the highway to my right, and I swung into it and went to one of the phone booths and called the local cops and told them who I was and as quickly and as simply as possible what had happened. I was put onto a Lieutenant Carrodas, who seemed to talk through his teeth and was not happy with what I was telling him. "I don't understand why you're not available for questioning right now," he said, after I had taken nearly a full minute to go through it with him.

"Look, Lieutenant, if I wasn't on the level I wouldn't be taking precious time to explain things to you. Right now I have to attend to something that won't wait. I'll come back here from L.A. voluntarily tomorrow. So be a good guy, okay?"

"I've got no choice at the moment," he said grudgingly, and hung up.

I got back in the car and began a long, tiresome drive down 101 and was above the speed limit most of the time, the traffic very light at one-thirty in the morning. In half an hour I picked up the San Diego State Freeway and whipped along its smooth wide surface to Los Angeles International Airport. I wanted to get there while the getting was good. I was tired and jittery and sick of the whole thing. But someone was going to honor that contract I had with Colby. That was all I was interested in at that moment.

It was two a.m. when I drove into the vast complex of airline satellites that surrounds the huge parking-ellipse, everything brightly lighted and like another world, depopulated and half-dead. The passenger traffic, arriving or departing, was reduced to sporadic trickles, and as I walked toward the public wall-lockers in the TWA building my footfalls clacked and echoed like warnings that ghosts hovered everywhere. Maybe it was just the hour.

I had already slipped off the belt before getting out of the car and dropped it *and* the tiara into a leather attache case I had in the trunk. The information desk was unattended and a couple of nightworkers went at things in silence and indifference. I took a box at random, stuck in my coin, left four dollars inside to cover eight additional days in case they were needed, and locked the jewels away once again in disgust. I pocketed the key and then went to the front of the terminal where a weigh-in steward was for some reason on duty. "Do you have a small envelope you can give me?" I asked him.

He had, and gave it to me. I thanked him and went to the information desk where I took out my ball-point pen and addressed the envelope to my Hollywood post office box. I slipped the key inside and bought a stamp from the vending machine in front of a semidarkened locked-up boutique. I mailed the envelope just outside the electronic doors and then walked to where I had parked the car across the street. The place was all but deserted. The whole experience was like coitus interruptus.

BEDELIA was awake when I let myself into the apartment and she knew something was wrong before I even said a word, her eyes both disappointed and inquisitive. "Still an open file," I told her immediately as I took off my jacket and laid it acorss the back of a chair. "And the peaceful little colony of Mariposa Beach has a very big murder in its lap."

Her lips parted and her eyes grew perplexed and she obviously hadn't expected anything like that. "What?" she gasped. "Murder? Oh, my God, no."

"Colby," I said. "Somebody killed him. Shot him maybe less than a minute before I arrived to meet him. He died right in front of me."

"Did you see who it was?"

"I wish I had for purely selfish reasons. No, he got away in the dark. But he didn't get what he came for because I still have it."

"The diamonds?"

"What else, sweetheart?" I said, sitting down wearily on the sofa.

"Jesus. Even after what happened in Vegas and that night in the parking lot I can still be shocked. I guess that's a good sign."

"Maybe, darling. But I'm sitting with those rocks which I don't want and a bill that may go unpaid for a very long time. And that's what shocks me the most."

"For the first time I'm a little scared," she said.

"I know. But you'll feel better in the morning. Come over here and sit down," I said, patting the cushion next to me.

She came over and said. "What happened?"

I told her all there was to tell, leaving out no detail from the moment I got the blowout on the freeway until I called The Law in Mariposa Beach. I told her that the stuff was back in hiding again and that a big can of worms had been opened up and that there was no telling how it would work out for us personally or in what length of time. "There's only one thing that's clear as day for me," I said, my arm around her shoulder all the while. "Anybody could have done the murder. But not without the help of Mr. Simon Brooks."

"Brooks?"

"Brooks was the only one in the world, as far as I know, who had any idea of where John Colby was going to be at the moment he was murdered. That is, besides me. And I know *I* didn't tell anybody else."

"You mean deliberately?"

"It was either carelessness or collusion. And Brooks isn't careless. You can bet that John Colby didn't say anything about where he was going to *any*one. Only Brooks knew it, because even a John Colby can slip up about who to trust."

She was silent and thoughtful and I went on. "Every loner needs a wall to bounce his ball off if he can afford it. And Brooks was Colby's wall. No one else."

"But did Brooks know about the jewelry? I thought that was hush-hush."

"A million dollars' worth of jewelry is a tough thing to keep hush-hush forever. Brooks could easily have found out about it."

"Unless the murder was one of those insane accidents," she said. "They do happen all the time. Could it be just that crazy a coincidence in this case?"

"No. There were five such last month alone," I said. "But this wasn't that kind. A kid with a detective-kit from cereal box-tops could tell you why in about sixty seconds."

"Then I guess I should be able to."

"Nobody who is looking for trouble wanders through a completely unpopulated canyon ten miles long, because he won't find it and he'll spend a couple of hours going from end to end. No loose nut or psychopathic killer is going to do anything like that on the chance that John Colby or someone like him is going to come by, park his car in the dark at that very spot and get out and wait to be murdered. Uh-uh. Someone was waiting there — someone who knew plenty about the whole thing because Brooks told him."

"But isn't it just a guess anyway, darling?"

"Yes. But a good one. And I'm going to come down on it very hard with the cops as a matter of self-defense. We've got our flanks to protect."

"You don't think he committed the murder."

"Not the type."

It was by then ten to four in the morning and my mind had stopped functioning. There was a whole bunch of angles on the thing and I couldn't keep track of them any longer and I let them crawl back into the woodwork. Bedelia's eyes were drooping by then. It made her pretty in a strangely sullen way. We staggered to bed.

Bedelia was still asleep when I woke up at nine o'clock after four solid hours of slumber. I forced myself to sit up on the edge of the bed and come to. I then walked the twenty-five-foot telephone cord into the living room, the phone in my hands, and in a minute I was talking to Don in La Jolla. "Are you awake?" I said.

"We're just having breakfast," he said, and he knew it was more than just hello. "What's the matter?"

I told him. I gave him the story as I had given it to Bedelia but in a fraction of the time. I stuck to bare facts, and when Don said, "What does that do to us? Where does it leave us?" I replied, "We'll analyze it later. I've got to check in with the police up there and look as cooperative as I goddamn well can and I don't know how long that will take. Maybe a couple of hours with everything thrown in."

"What are you going to tell them about Vegas when they ask what Colby hired us for?"

"Nothing. Not a goddamn thing. I'm not even going to mention the word. I'll *have* to tell them about the jewelry, but that's all. I'll just say the jewelry was recovered. Not when, where, or how."

"Boy, I'll bet they'll want to talk to *me*," he said.

"Not if I can help it, they won't," I said. "Anyway, get up here and I'll meet you at the office as soon as I'm done. There's no point in keeping locked up anymore, I don't think."

"Okay," he said. "Hell of a turn, isn't it?"

"Beautiful," I said brilliantly.

I showered, shaved, got dressed, and was ready to leave. Bedelia woke up and caught me at the door. "Going to talk to the fuzz?" she said, still mostly asleep, a faint and somewhat fetching puffiness to her face. "Give me a kiss first."

I kissed her with sweetness but no passion and said, "I'll meet you and Don at the office as soon as I get through with them."

"The office? Good. I'm glad. I don't like ducking around corners." And then with a kind of childish mischievousness that seldom came out in her she said, "I like *fuck*ing. But not *duck*ing."

I tousled her hair. "You're nuts," I said and walked out.

23

I GOT UP TO MARIPOSA BEACH about forty minutes later. The murder had already made the second editions and was all over the dial. The town was pretty and affluent and there wasn't any smog at the moment, just nice, made-to-order sunlight. The police station was off the main highway on a quiet street along with City Hall, the public library, the local mortuary, and a playground. The station itself was a red-brick one-story building fronted by a few palm trees and a wide yellow sidewalk, a parking area off to one side.

As I drove in, a gray Mercedes SL 300 was driving out. Behind the wheel, impeccably dressed, a look of deadly concentration on his face, sat none other than Brooks. We slid by each other in close quarters. There was a nervous glisten in his eyes. If he saw me he pretended not to have, and I had a sinking feeling that he had already undercut me with the people inside because he was as smart as hell and certainly as quick to anticipate things as I was. My feeling proved more than warranted when I told my story to plainclothes Sergeant Praxy a few minutes later.

He was about forty-five and his face was that of a bored marriage-license clerk. We sat in an office with two other desks, a uniformed sergeant busy at one, the other one vacant, the nameplate of Lieutenant Carrodas placed on it. Praxy was polite enough while I laid out the buildup to the murder, carefully leaving out anything that could lead to Don's killing of Mannino and Scalzi and all the rest of what had happened in the process of getting back Colby's diamond jewelry. I wanted to get to Brooks as fast as I could and make myself look as good as possible. And then he gave me, "Well, you know, of course, we've talked to Mr. Brooks."

"Oh, yes, I thought I caught a glimpse of him leaving," I said noncommittally, waiting to hear it from him.

"Yes, he came up here to look at the body and we did a little talking."

"Anybody send for him?" I said.

"He came up here voluntarily to see if he could be of any assistance," Praxy said, looking at me and telegraphing his thoughts.

"Fast, wasn't he? Get in and look good before they come after you," I said with a skeptical grin. "Let me ask you, Sergeant, so we can stop the little minuet we're going through here, did Brooks say anything that contradicts what I'm telling you?"

A smile cracked his saturnine face and then disappeared. "Everything," he said. "It's got its humorous side. Sergeant Baring over there and I talked to him together, and one thing I can tell you, and Sergeant Baring will tell you the same, is that Mr. Brooks made it pretty clear that he didn't have the slightest idea where your meeting with Colby was going to take place. He says he never heard of Mariposa Canyon."

"He does, eh?"

"Well, you know, in an indirect way. That is, he didn't come in here and say straight out that he never heard of Mariposa Canyon or anything like that. This came out in back and forth conversation over twenty minutes." He glanced at the other sergeant. "Would you say that, Charley?"

"That's close," the other replied and went on writing.

"That's what emerged, in an indirect way," Praxy said. "I mean, what comes out is that he *did* do certain things in connection with engaging your services to begin with. To track down Colby's wife — the one you're refusing to discuss with me."

I ignored the remark and said, "But?"

"But that he had no part in the actual details of how you and Colby met or where and exactly when your meetings took place. He says you arranged that yourself — you and Colby — as far as he knows."

"He's lying," I said without emotion. "His calls came through my service on both occasions pertaining to the meeting in

Mariposa Canyon. He even left his name because I wasn't in, so there's a record that speaks for itself."

"Oh, I don't think he would deny calling you on the phone. But what emerged, you see what I mean, is that he didn't give you any details concerning when and where you were to meet Colby. According to him he never knew anything about it. He says that he called you and put you in touch with Colby directly, nothing else."

"As you say, he came in voluntarily to see if he could be of any assistance," I said.

"I'm not drawing any conclusions, Blaney. But as far as last night is concerned, I can tell you his alibi is airtight. His whereabouts is accounted for and he was nowhere near here at the time of the murder."

I shrugged. "I don't think he was either. But he *knows* who was."

"You'll get a chance to tell him that before it's over, you can bet on it," Praxy said.

Two Los Angeles detectives, Birney and Saunders, neither of whom I knew, walked in at that moment, both young and good-looking, wearing open collars and cardigan sweaters, their .38s barely noticeable in shoulder holsters. They introduced themselves and we began to talk about the same things all over again and within ten minutes were at the point Praxy and I had reached just as they walked it. "Would you face him and say that and see where the chips fall?" Saunders said to me.

"My story stands up because I've got roughly a million dollars' worth of jewelry I'm looking to get off my hands so I can collect my fee. That cancels any motive for either my murdering Colby — "

"Which nobody has even breathed to you, Blaney," Praxy said.

"That's right," I said. "Or anything per*tain*ing to the murder. Like lying about Brooks being the only other person who knew about that meeting — time and place."

"Right," Praxy said. "Unless there's a motive we don't know about. Maybe someone hired you for a lot of dough — for so much dough that the jewels are chopped liver by comparison."

I looked at him solemnly. "What are you doing stuck away in a place like this, Sergeant?" I said.

"You think what I'm saying is impossible? You don't read the papers or watch TV then."

"Sergeant, you're writing a script. Get a literary agent."

"Maybe I will. But there's untold wealth in the dead man's estate and a lot of people who might benefit from the death. A relative; a business partner. Even a business rival. Any one of them could have hired someone to do the job. Even you."

"And you may be the head of the Mafia in Mariposa Beach," I said.

"Oh, what a witticism," Praxy said. "You got any more like that?"

Right then one of the visiting cops, Saunders, I think it was, piped up, "You might be right on the button about this man, Brooks. But what gets me is all the wide-open spaces in your story, Blaney."

"I haven't left out information that's vital to this investigation, gentlemen," I said walking to the window and looking out to the sunshine and the cluster of reporters and the TV camera outside the building. "You can take my word on that."

"You won't be hurt if we don't," the other one, Birney, said.

"What else can I say?" I said with complete sincerity.

"Tell us exactly what Colby hired you to do," Birney said. "I mean *exactly*. Not a lot of shuffle about confidential matters and all of that. Where are the jewels you're talking about and how did you get them back and who from?"

"That's right," Saunders said. "Who's the thief in the first place?"

"All I can tell you is it was a family matter without the slightest bearing on this case," I said.

"I don't get you, Blaney," Saunders said, his even-featured young face filled with disgust. "What are you holding out on us for? Are you hiding something? That's what it sounds like."

"Look, I'm not supposed to go around embarrassing people

who pay me to keep their law-abiding skeletons under wraps," I said.

"But that client is dead now," Birney said, openly exasperated. "He's not going to be embarrassed by *any*thing."

"Sure, but his family might be," I lied.

"Blaney," Sergeant Praxy began. "I've heard about you and I'm sure these men have too. Saw you on TV when that shooting took place."

"Everybody did," I said. "And my life hasn't been the same since, gentlemen."

Praxy didn't bat an eyelash. "You didn't say much at the time, and I remember thinking you must have been the real thing. After that we heard all about you . . ." He scratched the back of his neck and looked away, I guess to show how cool and blase he could be. ". . . you know, about your outlook on crime and the police and so forth. It turned out you were a big law-and-order man. Quiet maybe, but that was what emerged. And I guess it's true, huh? Except when it gets personally inconvenient."

"Not nice, Sergeant," I said, but I was a little embarrassed because it wasn't altogether untrue. "I came in voluntarily and I'm trying to give you the best lead this case has right now or probably will have. I have no reason to hold out on you and *every* reason to want to see this murder cleared up, if that's possible. Only because the murder is bad for *me*, not because I'm that civic-minded. I wouldn't protect the Pope if I thought he knew anything. And I certainly wouldn't protect Mrs. Colby or anyone else if I didn't know they were clean. Not at my own expense. That's why I'm giving you Brooks. He makes sense right off the bat because he was Colby's confidant and prat-boy, number one through ten. There was no other. All this business about how and where I got the jewelry back from Mrs. Colby is sawdust, gentlemen. Brooks is lying and you *will* eventually find it out and see for yourselves that I had every legal and moral right not to talk about Mrs. Colby or her present whereabouts, which I don't know, or where I've got the jewelry hidden right now, which is really none of your business without a court order. Think about it logically for a minute. You'll come up with it."

"Okay. So you're saying Brooks tipped someone off," Birney said.

"More than that — drove him to the spot. I can't prove it but, gentlemen, I *know* it. Because the killer drove out of the canyon in Colby's car and there wasn't any other in sight. So it needed that kind of a move. And if Brooks was the murderer's accomplice, he also provided the transportation." I looked at Praxy. "Have you found Colby's car yet?"

"Yes," he said. "We located it hours ago. Abandoned about five miles down one-oh-one."

I turned my palms up. "Five will get you ten the killer switched to his own car which he had parked previously at that very spot. For whatever reasons — and there could be a couple of good ones — they wanted it that way. So that the killer was scheduled right from the start to get out of Mariposa Canyon in Colby's car."

"What's the motive for the murder then?" Saunders said challengingly. "Or can't you dream that part up?"

"That's simple," I said. "I say as much because I was there. To start with, the murder was an accident. At least, it was unplanned. I've got another ten for a five that says Brooks never, but never, started out to be part of a killing."

I happened to glance out of the window again, and I saw Colby's own daughter, Merrilee, narrow, flat, tall, wearing a beige pantsuit on the occasion of her father's death, her husband Craig with her, arm-in-arm, as they walked toward the building. Craig's hair was merely over the ears, and he was dressed in an open shirt and a puka-shell necklace, a pale-blue jacket, and flared check pants. The reporters converged on them. I said to Praxy, "Two of John Colby's heirs are on their way in right now."

Sergeant Baring looked up for the first time and lit a cigarette. Praxy got up from his desk and said, "Which ones?"

"The daughter and her husband," I said.

"That's right. We've been expecting them. They're here to

make a next-of-kin identification. We haven't had that yet."

They both entered the office at that moment, and Merrilee introduced herself and Craig, her face composed, her voice steady and haughty, not the slightest trace of tears in her eyes. She and Craig recognized me immediately but didn't bother to say hello.

"Right this way," Praxy said, and began to lead everyone out of the office and down the corridor toward the rear of the station. "We'll go out the back way to the mortuary. That's where we put our occasional corpses. But we haven't used it for a murder case until now."

The building was about a hundred feet away and we walked to it in utter silence, eluding the reporters on the other side of the station house. Colby was in one of the four refrigerated drawers, and the mortician pulled it out by the handle and uncovered the face. Merrilee looked down at her father, commanding even in death, and she showed no signs of emotion. "That's him," she said, and Craig merely nodded and turned away. His stomach wasn't as good as hers.

The cops looked and I looked and then Praxy said, "The M.E.'s report just hit my desk, as a matter of fact, so you can claim the body any time, Miss Colby."

"Mrs. Smith," Merrilee said. "It will be picked up. That's been arranged."

"I'd like a look at that report," Saunders said.

We all walked out. "Shot with a thirty-eight caliber weapon three times," Praxy said, then stopped as if suddenly overtaken by a sense of delicacy. He needn't have bothered.

"Can we ask a few questions, Mrs. Smith?" Detective Birney said. "I know this must hit you pretty hard, but I'm sure you'd like to help the police find out who killed your father."

"Of course," she said. "But can you make it some other time? We've a terribly important engagement in Los Angeles and we're dreadfully late already."

"If that's the way you feel," Birney said with no small touch of disdain. "When *can* we call on you and Mr. Smith for a little talk?"

"Here's my card," Craig said.

Birney looked at it, read it out loud. "Twenty-first Century Enterprises," he said and passed it to Detective Saunders. By that time we were at the back door of the station house and walking in.

"You know how it is," Craig said with a nervous laugh.

"Sure," Birney said with hard eyes and a faint sneer.

And when Craig and Merrilee flounced down the corridor and right out the front door into a pincer movement of press corps members, visible from where we were standing, Birney added, "What a pair of shits."

"They're just not bothering to put on an act for anyone," I said. "No one who knows them would believe it and they know it. They may be shits but they're smart ones."

"You know that much about them, do you?" Saunders said.

"I picked up enough here and there while I worked for Daddy," I said. Then I turned to Praxy and said, "You were starting to tell us about the bullet wounds."

His hand was on the doorknob to his office and he said, "Three bullets penetrated the body from a thirty-eight-caliber weapon. Two in front — one under the heart, the other through the left shoulder. A third bullet went through his aorta from behind. Two in front, one in back."

"So that he was facing the killer to begin with," I said in a speculative voice, "got shot twice and started to run away, and was shot a third time. A few seconds later he was coming toward me." I shook my head as if it all might mean something eventually. "Anything in the car? Fingerprints? I guess all over, huh?"

"That won't mean too much because a lot of people might have been in the car."

"Not in Colby's car," I said.

"They're going over it for latent prints anyway, naturally. Oh yeah, and there was blood on the front seat. But it's the L.A. boys who'll be doing all that crime-lab stuff."

"Who's out at the scene right now?" Birney asked.

"Everybody," Praxy said. "There must be fifty people out there. "They've closed the area off."

Birney looked at me and said, "How about coming out there with us? You can tell everybody your theories."

I looked at my watch and wanted to get away. "I've been up here over an hour," I said. "I've got to leave now and find out who pays my fee and when. And that might take a little doing."

"What are you? Money-mad?" Saunders said.

"A day's pay for a day's work, boys. What's wrong with that? It's called free enterprise." I tossed them a lazy and flippant two-finger salute and walked out. It was the right time. They were still just a little off balance. Footwork and bluff were what it was all about.

24

I HAD TO RUN the reporters' gauntlet before I could get away. I kept it as polite as possible and finally wound up saying, "Most of what I know about murder I learned from the six o'clock news." Then I caught up to the Smiths in the parking lot because they wanted me to. We all stood next to their red Stingray parked a few slots down from my Galaxie, and I said, "Sorry about your father, Mrs. Smith."

She looked at me with her father's cold eye, the same facial cragginess of the man somehow managing not to be unattractive in the girl. "Did you ever locate that two-timing tramp my father was married to?" she asked without raising her voice or showing great emotion.

"Now do you think that's very nice? Particularly on an occasion like this?"

Craig stirred uncomfortably and said, "Merrilee thought Clare wasn't what her father needed in a wife, that's all."

"Don't spoil your image now with phony solicitude, kids," I said. "I was glad to see there were no fake tears before."

"What a suspicious person you are, Mr. Blaney," she said with arrogant indifference and a brittle smile. "Are you suggesting I didn't love my Daddy-poo?"

I looked at her and shook my head with a certain amount of awe. "You're a real number, Mrs. Smith," I said, and then looked at Craig.

I was ready to walk away when she said, "If you went to meet Daddykins last night on that dark old deserted road, Mr. Blaney, it must have been for more than just a conversation about Clare. He didn't give that much of a damn about her."

I looked at her with renewed interest. "Oh? Then tell me, Mrs. Smith, why you think I was meeting him. I know you're just dying to."

"And aren't you just dying to hear it?"

I fluttered my hand like a bored Italian waiter being asked how the minestrone was. "Dying is an overstatement," I said. I looked at my watch. "But I'll listen. If it's short."

"It's short," she said. "Short but expensive. She stole the diamond jewelry he bought for her."

"Oh?"

"I happened to be there the day he found it out. I was on a peace mission. That's code for down on my knees. Anyhow it was the wrong day for it. My timing has never been exactly golden. He was so dear though. I remember he looked at me and with all the love that was in him he said, 'Shut your mouth about this.' "

I said nothing, just kept glancing down at the ground every so often when looking at her became too tough for some reason. I think it was because she and Craig were so damned desperate to be rich and famous and it stuck out all over and was embarrassing. Because they didn't know how to do it. Not yet.

"Well, I did shut my mouth," she went on. "But that was then and this is now, *n'est-ce pas?*"

I looked at her and then at her husband and said nothing. Then they looked at each other, and Merrilee, who was her father's daughter in so many ways except winning, said, "He hired you to get it all back, didn't he, Mr. Blaney?"

"It's a fact, Mrs. Smith. It will be in all the papers by tomorrow and on TV tonight."

The admission was a source of satisfaction to her. "What was your arrangement with my father, Mr. Blaney?" she said.

"Why? Want to take care of my fee?"

"Is it much?"

"Plenty."

Her eyes flashed and her breath grew a bit short as she said, "You know there's really no law against handing the jewelry over to me instead of the estate. I *am* the legal heir."

"What's coming, Mrs. Smith?" I said, tilting my head.

"I won't play games with you, Mr. Blaney. And I'll show you I'm no piker. Forget your agreement with my father. He's not going to care, I think we can all agree. If they honor your claim, you've got x-number of dollars. And it might take weeks, maybe months, before it's all worked out. You know the red tape an estate like this might make you go through."

"Yeah?"

"Fifty-fifty. Take half of what's there and give me the rest."

"Just like that."

She looked at me with hard, wise eyes. "Why not? Can you give me a reason that stands up?" Then, "Look, let's drive somewhere for coffee and sit and talk."

"Mrs. Smith, the best thing for you to do is sit down and think quietly and calmly and let your head clear."

"I knew he wouldn't go for it," Craig muttered to himself.

"May I say the same to you, Mr. Blaney," she said. "But don't just think. Do some lateral thinking. Your client is dead and I'm his daughter and legal heir . . ."

"Mrs. Smith . . ."

"Let me finish. There's no risk whatever to you, only a completely legal profit." She edged closer to me, and I could smell her eau de cologne, her jaw just faintly the jutted affair her father's was. "You have to think of it in a new way, not the way you did before my father's death. And you have a perfect right to."

"That's jail talk, Mrs. Smith."

"Why? Who presses charges and what the hell are they?"

"I'm not a lawyer. But I know that contractual arrangements with a deceased person are not nullified by the death."

"Oh, that's just technical."

"Let it alone," Craig advised.

"Be smart," I said. "Wait for the will."

She gave me a look of withering contempt and with a slow incredulous voice said, "You dumb flatfoot. No wonder you're a private detective peeking in keyholes and following tramp wives, and you'll never be anything else . . . What makes you think I'm in the will?"

I let out a breath and said nothing.

"I'm not *in* the will," she said, some of the hate she had felt for the old man all of her life now showing. "Couldn't you figure that out for yourself?"

I shrugged and was uncomfortable in the face of her vehemence.

"Because I married Craig and wanted to do something with my life he didn't approve of," she spewed out at me. "It was perfectly all right for him to marry someone who wouldn't have made a third-rate whore in a second-class cathouse, but not for me to marry someone like Craig, with all the brains and talent in the world . . ."

"Take it easy," I said.

"And here's a chance to right the wrong. . . ." She was almost ready to choke on it, now groping for words as we stood there off from the reporters and others but starting to draw some attention. "No one would be hurt and Craig and I could get our company on its feet and make something of ourselves and of others at the same time. And someone like you without the brains to reason things out and see the benefit to himself even just stands there and ruins it all. And for what? . . ."

"Take it easy," I said just to calm her.

"Go fuck yourself," she answered.

"Come on, Merri," Craig said and took a strong hand in guiding her into the car.

"I'm not trying to hurt you, Merrilee," I said.

"Who gave you the right to use my first name?"

"The same person who gave you the right to vilify and abuse me. For whatever it's worth, your father's wife never uses that kind of language and I've seen her under fire."

"What does that prove?"

"I don't know. I'm just mentioning it."

They drove away and I watched them go. Birney and Saunders came out of the police station and brushed by some of the reporters. I wondered what the hell they were all waiting for, who they were hoping to see. I got into my car and drove out of the parking lot before Birney and Saunders had a chance to spot me.

It was only eleven o'clock and I didn't want to go back to the office until I took a shot at tracking down the location of the pay window. I got off the freeway at Sepulveda and pulled into a gas station and telephoned Brooks's office, not even sure that he would be there the morning after the boss had been murdered. He was not and I called him at home. A lady answered the phone, asked who I was, and I said, "Tell him it's Arthur Baldwin of the Boston branch of Valley Forge Steel."

"Arthur Baldwin? . . ."

"Of Valley Forge Steel. It's quite urgent."

Brooks got on and his voice revealed his uncertainty and caution. "Yes? . . ."

"Brooks?"

"Yes. I'm sorry, I don't . . ." He broke off the apology because he suddenly realized who was calling him. "Who is this?" he asked snappily even though he knew.

"Blaney. I tried your office first. I need some information and I didn't want to wait."

"What convoluted concept motivated the little charade,

Blaney?" he said, his voice both jittery and resentful. "Do you often assume fictitious identities for no apparent reason?"

"I've lost faith in you, Brooks, and I wanted to be sure you came to the phone."

"I suppose that has some sort of meaning in your mind but I'm sure I wouldn't know what," he said, trying not to lose his composure. "What is it that couldn't wait a respectful interval following the death of Mr. Colby?"

"My money, Brooks. I'm owed a good deal of it for services rendered. Who is it that runs the estate?"

"I wouldn't know," he replied. "You'll have to bring your problem to Arnold Ackerman, not me. My work is not in any way connected to administering the estate."

"Who's Ackerman?"

"Colby's attorney."

I recalled the name suddenly. "Ackerman, Styles, and what's the other guy's name?"

"Lewis. Ackerman can answer your question."

"Thanks, Brooks," I said. "It's too bad you made the move you did. Who's the other guy? The one who squeezed the trigger?"

"A nice, crude frontal attack, Blaney. It's almost amusing."

"Be smart, Brooks. Tell them about it. Tell them you may be greedy but that you're no murderer, that you never bargained for that. The faster you do it, the less rap you'll take."

That was when he hung up.

25

IT TOOK A PHONE CALL and a little gentle talk with a secretary to learn that Lawyer Ackerman was both out for the day and on the tennis court of one of the big hotels. And that was where I caught up with him. He was about forty, tall, dark-haired, suntanned, and looked like someone who had gotten rich because he didn't trust anyone. He was handsome in an uneven, slightly coarse featured way, and he played his game against the hotel pro as if he thought he had a chance to win. When I approached him during a break at the baseline, staying on the outside of the chain-link fence, he looked at me coolly because he knew immediately I wanted something of him and was going to impose on him and break his concentration to get it. He was right.

"Maybe you didn't notice, he said, toweling himself off, his body lean and stringy, his gray-green eyes sharp and avid. "But this isn't my office. I happen to be playing tennis."

"It's not my office either. But this won't take more than a few moments if you just give me the answers to a legitimate question or two."

He didn't lose that surly and contemptuous look that was a part of him but he told the pro he would be with him in a minute, and then said to me, "Go ahead in as few words as possible."

"I was working for Colby on contract. I did a tough job for him and I want to collect on it pronto. How do I do that now? Through you? Or a bank? Or what?"

"What kind of a contract? I don't remember drawing one between Colby and you."

"Well, someone drew it for him," I said. "And I have my copy with his signature right in my inside pocket."

"What's it for?"

"I recovered a collection of diamond jewelry that had been — removed from the premises."

"Stolen?"

"Removed but not stolen. The contract calls for my discretion concerning the circumstances of my employment. You want to read it, as his lawyer?"

"No. The original copy has to be in Colby's effects. And as I say, I never drew such a contract for him."

"Maybe he used another attorney."

"Go find him, in that case, and tell him your troubles," he said, obviously taking satisfaction in thwarting me. Sometimes that kind of thing happens between total strangers. Hate at first sight. "For all anyone knows you might have stolen the collection from Colby yourself in the first place, and now are trying to palm it off for a payment you say he promised you."

"I've got the contract."

"Which could be a forgery."

"Can't that be ascertained?"

"Listen, my friend, nothing is going to be that simple, because the decedent is a murder victim and nobody knows the identity of the murderer yet."

"What about his tailor? Or you, Ackerman? And if bills come in from Brooks Brothers or the tree nursery or the maintenance company, what happens? Does everyone sit and wait for Perry Mason to work the whole thing out before they get paid for goods and services?"

"This is not in that category and you know it," he said, with a little flash of anger now. "You have an unusual claim on an arrangement no one else knows anything about. That's going to take some testing, and you'd better get used to that right now."

"Are you the executor?"

"No, I am not." He was getting ready to walk away.

"Then I'd appreciate your telling me who is," I said. "And you had better if you want to go on enjoying the rest of your game."

He glared at me and said, "Call Steven Elson at Coastal Manufacturers Trust and Savings," and then walked back to resume his game. He served a hard shot with an angry snap as I was leaving, and I assumed he was playing over his head. His belligerence and irritability seemed wasted and petty. I was nothing in his life. But some people are like that. Maybe I reminded him of a kid who had beaten him up when he was little or a teacher who had flunked him in geometry.

Steven Elson was another breed altogether. He was a tall,

handsome, cool, and easygoing man trained to do a job and to be pleasant doing it, even when it entailed telling you that you were financially ruined. About forty-five, with silvery-blond temples, ruddy cheeks, candid blue eyes, a leonine head, he sat across from me in the expensively paneled office, racehorse prints all over the walls, somewhat inappropriately, I thought, and he told me the contract would need to be filed with the court and there might well be a delay, particularly since Ackerman had no knowledge of it.

"What are you telling me in terms of time? Forty-eight hours? Six months? Or what?"

"Or what," he said dryly. "Let's see. This is Thursday. Tomorrow is dead. Which runs us into the weekend. Leave the contract with me and by late Monday I should be able to have some idea of where we stand with the court, what demands they may or may not make on you."

I tossed the document on his desk and said, "How does that work? What do they do?"

He separated his palms about eighteen inches and brought them back together with a faint clap. "The court's position is simply one of making certain that executors and attorneys don't squander a deceased person's estate, either through carelessness or design. Everything — especially something of this kind — has to be carefully accounted for. It's a good system because it protects not only the estate but the people administering it. If they're honest, that is. It keeps mistakes at a minimum."

I got up and put my card on his desk and shook his hand. It was faintly clammy. "I'd appreciate as quick a rundown on this as possible. Colby was — let's say, a little eccentric. And he might not have wanted Ackerman to know the details of the job he hired me for. That could account for it."

"Not unlikely." He got up and walked me to the door and said, "I'll do my best. But regardless of the immediate outcome, you're going to have to turn over the jewelry."

"I can't imagine I'd be breaking a law if I didn't."

"That's right. But you'd be liable to a lawsuit. And that could make your claim a dead duck for a very long time."

I didn't answer and he said, "Very candidly, how's your reputation?"

"My reputation?"

"Anything about you that's shady?"

"Nothing that can be proved."

"That's not unimportant in a situation like this. And I'm playing devil's advocate now, you understand."

"Any time, Mr. Elson."

He smiled a warm and friendly smile. "I'll contact you as soon as I've anything to tell you."

We left it at that. It was the best I could get.

26

IT WAS ONE O'CLOCK when I got to the office. Bedelia and Don and I were pretty hungry and we drove toward Hollywood to have lunch at Musso's. Don said, "What about the hundred and fifty thousand? How do you collect that?"

"That's what I was looking into before I came back to the office," I said, hitting the freeway on-ramp at Van Nuys Boulevard. "Talking to the people you're supposed to talk to."

"Who say what?" Bedelia asked.

"Who don't say much. The point is, whenever someone like Colby dies there's a lot of stuff to hack through. It's not just a couple of bonds in a cigar box or some cash stuffed into a mattress. And when he dies because someone has *killed* him — God knows what complications that can set in motion. If the executor thinks something is fishy, he can put everything in probate. A claim like ours would be the first victim. That's why I was ducking the cops on Clare Colby this morning. Because if they ever tie her to Ganner the killing of Scalzi and Mannino is sure to come up and this thing could go on until nineteen-ninety."

"Did the cops buy your story about Brooks?" Bedelia said.

"Enough of it. They're not exactly thrilled with me but they know I'm not too far off with them because they have nothing else that's as solid."

"Well, Brooks sure had the opportunity and the knowledge," Don said.

"It almost couldn't work any other way," I said. "Unless there's something or someone in left field we know nothing about. But this is the kind of case that looks closed-in and will probably turn out to be just that. Just so many possibilities and only a single motive — the jewelry."

"If it was the jewelry," Don said.

"Right. But what else do we have? Nothing. So if the motive is the jewelry, you're narrowed down to less than half a dozen people. Two brothers, a sister, a daughter and a son-in-law — the last two really only a single suspect. Good candidates. But they couldn't have pulled it off without Brooks. Because none of them knew where to go or when. He supplied that. But as far as the question of who approached whom goes — it could have come from either direction. Or both directions at the same time."

"Without Brooks, in other words, you can't even have a real theory about the murder, can you?" Don said. "Unless someone just played a hunch and followed Colby to where he was going."

"Too vague," I said. "Besides, there was no other car. Only Colby's, and the murderer drove away in it and abandoned it five miles from the scene. Which means someone had to have driven him in with the intention that he would drive himself out or be driven out in Colby's car. He then was either picked up at the point he abandoned the Colby car or he got into his own car which was waiting there for him."

"Maybe somebody saw him."

"Maybe. But that will take some doing, digging up a witness," I said. "No, I'd say the killer is off the hook. Brooks is the one that's on it. If he can convince the cops that I'm lying, he'll wriggle off and the heat'll be on me."

"Do you think he can do that?" Bedelia said.

"Well, if he keeps his head and doesn't crack he can make an open question out of it. Which might not be too good for our claim. It's the claim I'm concerned with. Because they'll never stick me with the murder. It's just that as long as there's doubt about it — well, the jewels could be impounded by the State and the court could nullify the contract." I shook my head. "Just hope it doesn't drag on too long."

"You've already put in the claim then," Bedelia said.

"I didn't see any point in waiting," I said.

By the time we were sitting in a booth in the restaurant waiting for three orders of filet of sole, I was saying, "Brooks delivered his man to the spot well ahead of time . . ."

"Man and or woman," Bedelia corrected.

"Slim chance of it's being a woman, even if Merrilee *is* in on it," I said. "But okay. Whoever it was. Let *he* cover both genders. So he's in the brush waiting. But something went wrong and Colby discovered him. And when that happened, whoever it was had to kill him. He couldn't face being unmasked. So he let Colby have it. But that's not the whole thing. The whole thing hinges on the fact that I had a blowout on the freeway and was twenty minutes late to the meeting with Colby. And that was what tripped the guy up. It might have worked otherwise."

Don and Bedelia were both looking at me intently and I said, "This is just guesswork. But that's the way us detectives do it."

"I can see what you're driving at," Don said. "There was too much time left over for mistakes."

"There had to be. No murder was planned. We know that. There was Colby, on time and waiting. But no me. I can just imagine how gracefully he took my tardiness. He must have gotten out of the car and started to do a little pacing. He keeps looking toward the direction I'm supposed to come from, ready to explode because I'm not there, looking at his watch in the dark and maybe muttering a few choice terms of endearment about me. And then somehow, for a reason you can easily make up for yourself, he stumbles on the killer, who is waiting in hiding — not to commit a murder but to heist a million dollars' worth of diamonds. And let's assume that the would-be thief planned to get himself into the back seat of Colby's car — not an impossible task by any means — while Colby was distracted with me. The purpose of that would have been to get himself driven away in Colby's car after the transaction. Then, if all had gone well, he'd have sprung himself on Colby, stopped the car, and taken what Colby had. The final step would have been either to unload Colby in the dark and let him fend for himself — that's if he was the good-natured type — or shoot him. His own touch, not Brooks's. Either way he drives off with what he came for and everyone can go whistle." I shrugged. "Guesswork, but I'll bet it's close."

"Could he do that?" Bedelia said, enrapt at my speculations but skeptical. "Sneak into the back of the car? Without a sound? Without attracting attention?"

"In fact, that's almost surely what happened because there was blood on the front seat of the car when it was found," I said. "Maybe Colby came pacing back to the car because I still hadn't shown up. He either opens the door and happens to see the guy crouching in the back seat, *or* — if you like this better — he caught the man making the attempt. The murderer made a dumb move because he was also thrown off schedule by my blowout on the freeway. That is, it gave both Colby and whoever killed him too much time alone together in that small area near the car, too much room for a nervous mistake. Just as you said, Don."

"And if he didn't get himself into the back seat of the car?" Bedelia said. "If you had come along exactly on time and he couldn't get quietly into the back seat because you were both too close to Colby's car? What then?"

I shrugged. "We might have caught him," I said.

There was a faint smile on her lips, but there was a kind of latent fear in her eyes. "Is that your honest appraisal of the situation?" she said.

I said, "No. He'd have had the drop on us and he'd have shot us full of holes as soon as we batted an eyelash — if we turned at his sound or even just looked startled. Or he could have taken what he wanted and left us in one piece. Maybe wearing a stocking mask over his face or whatever."

"That's not my guess," she said. "My guess is he'd have done away with you both like houseflies."

I grinned. "Gives you a better shudder that way, huh, sweetheart?"

"I just think he's that type," she said. "He wouldn't have killed Colby otherwise."

"If you're right, then Brooks, if he's the accomplice for sure, could be in trouble," Don said. "He'd be damned well advised to go to the police and spill the whole thing, not even wait for them. Maybe we ought to point that out to him."

"I already did," I said. "I talked to him on the phone. He wasn't ready to crumble. But I could hear the shortness of breath."

"I think he *will* talk," Bedelia said. "If all this is true."

"He's in with a very unsentimental type," I said. "This guy's got the stomach for whatever comes along. And I think Brooks knows it. And that's what I'm counting on."

"Then again, it may not matter to us," Don said. "Brooks might hold out forever, and whatever consequence that might have might not necessarily mean a damned thing to us, and wouldn't affect the claim at all."

"That's true," I said.

"I guess we wouldn't give much of a damn about who killed Colby then," Don said.

"Funny thing," I said. "I would still want to see him caught."

"Yeah, I guess." He was suddenly a little sheepish.

Bedelia just gazed thoughtfully off to one side. "Thank God you got a flat tire," she said softly.

The waiter was coming toward us with the filet of sole just about then.

27

THAT NIGHT Bedelia and I went to the theater at Civic Center. The evening was very nearly ruined when we ran into her mother in the lobby during intermission. She was with a man of about fifty-five, thin, balding, maybe her escort for the evening, maybe her steady boyfriend. Her looks were a distortion of Bedelia's, the nose a bit more pointed, the mouth just slightly soured, the skin no longer lustrous and a little raw from the sun, the same blue eyes, but full of old schemes and envy, her body shorter, the figure fuller and verging on topheaviness. She said, "This is Sam Orkin. Sam, my daughter, Bedelia, and Mr. Blaney, her boss. They're in the private-eye business, just in case you want someone followed sometime."

"Christ, mother, you're a doll," Bedelia said through a clenched white smile.

"I've been calling you but you haven't been in," Mrs. Perry went on. "I wanted to let you know that your father's brother, your uncle Kyle, passed on. I thought that might be of some interest to you."

"Oh, I'm sorry to hear that."

"I came by your apartment. But I didn't go in. I could tell it might not be an appropriate time to visit."

She looked at me with an unformed expression I couldn't fathom. "You have a Ford Galaxie, don't you?" she said.

"Yes, I happen to have a Ford Galaxie."

"Yes, I was sure you did."

Later on Bedelia said, "She's such a — " She stopped in frustration and then said, "I'd love to say the word but I guess I shouldn't. I suppose she can't help it anyway."

"Now you're being a big girl," I said.

We went home after an after-theater ice-cream soda, and the next morning I announced my departure. "I'm going to move back into my place, sweetheart," I said. "Nobody's after me at this point. And if they are, they can find me here anyway."

We were having a cup of coffee and some toast, and she was not happy with the idea. "It's because of my mother's little needle, isn't it, Jim?" she said.

"No, no."

"It's a matter of ritual with you. You'll visit. You'll make love, you'll stay half the night. But you're not comfortable unless you go home."

"It's not that."

"Then it's something else. Too domestic maybe. Is that it, Jim? Don't let that bother you. Because you can walk out on me anytime, Jim, whether you're here or not."

"Look, sweetheart, living together is a very significant thing to do," I said weakly, groping for the right words and knowing there weren't any.

"Bullshit, Jim darling. That's the only way to say it. Maybe you *should* go and maybe that should be an end of us."

"You're getting a terribly wrong slant, darling. And I know I'm not helping it any. I just want to say that if I didn't have you I'd go into a nose dive and never pull out until I hit the ground and splattered. And maybe that's all I can look forward to at the end."

"What a pretty speech."

"I love you, Bedelia," I said, taking her hand as we sat at the table at right angles. "But it's got to be under separate roofs." I shook my head. "I can't stay here and be your common-law husband. Do you understand?" I looked right into her eyes. "If I had seen you twenty years ago, I'd have fallen all over myself trying to get you to take that plunge with me."

"I was not even five years old, you imbecile."

"Yes, I know. Don't remind me."

Then we stopped talking and sipped the coffee and chewed on the toast and stared into space for a moment or two. "When we get on the ship to go cruising, will we have separate cabins?" she said.

"No. That's different."

"A time out of reality, you mean. The ship sails from one place and arrives somewhere else. It doesn't stand still. And then it's all over."

"Listen," I said. "I'm just hoping we can even *get* on that ship, sweetheart. Without the Colby fee we won't. We're not out of *that* reality yet."

We didn't say much about anything after that, and shortly we both showered and got dressed. I said, "I'm going to get my hair cut, sweetheart."

"All right," she said.

"I should be back inside of an hour."

She was standing in front of the bathroom mirror brushing that lambent blond hair, and she said, "All right," again, and I walked out.

The trip to the barbershop and the haircut itself came to about forty-five minutes. And when I got back to Bedelia's apartment she wasn't there. I thought she might have gone to the office because the files she wanted to work on were still waiting. I packed my suitcase and went downstairs and put it in the trunk of my car. Then I drove to the office directly and found that it was locked up tight and that she wasn't there either. I didn't know what to make of it. But I had an idea I was being punished just a little bit. It was okay with me as long as it didn't go on too long.

28

I TURNED ON THE AIR CONDITIONING because it was the beginning of a hot day, and then sat down at my desk and went over a couple of folders on cases I wanted to get out of the way before closing down the business. I was about ready to hand over that unpaid thousand-dollar fee to a collection agency when the phone rang and Lieutenant Carrodas of Mariposa Beach announced himself. "We missed each other yesterday," he said. "I'd like to come in and have a talk. It won't take long."

"Sure. I'll be here." Always look cooperative. At least until you had collected a hundred and fifty thousand dollars that may have hinged on it. "Come on up."

I hung up on him and immediately I dialed Rita's number. As soon as she heard my voice she said, "You don't seem to be able to stay out of the headlines lately. Murder and diamonds and God knows what. You're going to get yourself killed one of these days, Jim."

"Would you shed a tear, Rita?" I said.

"That's a bastardly thing to say."

"I didn't mean it that way. But you sound as if I'm some kind of publicity hound trying to attract attention. Somebody murdered my client. Nobody's as sorry as I am, not even his family. Or I should say, especially not them. And I may have a hell of a time collecting my fee. A big part of which would see Loretta through a couple of years of college. I know you and Steve can't swing it any other way."

"It's out of the question, I'm afraid. Med school is wildly expensive."

"Well, I know that."

"That would be marvelous of you, Jim."

"No, it wouldn't."

"That's not exactly a customary fee, is it?"

"Tell me about Jan."

"Why not the story of my life? Or yours?"

"What's that supposed to mean?"

"Jan may be beyond all of us now. There is only so much you can give as a parent or a friend. And then it's beyond you. And she is. At least beyond me." I heard a slight break in her voice. "She left the house yesterday."

I took it in and said, "Why did you let her?"

"What were we to do? Chain her to her bed?"

"What was it? The heroin?" I said, frustrated.

"No. Strelli. Like it or not, he was suddenly all that mattered. And when he gave her the heroin, she took it and liked it and associated it with him. He could have broken her of it too, according to Helder . . ."

"Who's that?"

"He's the psychiatrist we've been talking to. According to him Strelli became the focus of everything, bad, worse, and rotten. And when he threw her on her face and walked away from her, he was telling her she was less than nothing and that's the way she sees herself."

"Jesus Christ, these headshrinkers and their theories," I said, irked and upset at the same time. "That guy is probably nothing more at this point than her fix. Her connection." I shook my head with disgust and anxiety. "Ah, nuts."

"I suppose the courageous thing to do is to look at ourselves," she said. She laughed without a trace of joy. "Where did we go wrong, you and I and Steve?"

I took a deep and woeful breath and couldn't think of an answer at the moment. I said, "Rita, I've got to hang up now. I'll call you tomorrow. Maybe we can get together."

"Goodbye, Jim."

I didn't move for a moment or two and then I opened my desk drawer and took out the different sets of threatening notes I had received in connection with the shooting in the parking lot. As if it could bring back my little lost girl.

I sat there staring at the three messages with their venom and hate, and then came out of the trance at the sound of the front door opening. Lieutenant Carrodas came toward me through Bedelia's little section, now empty. I knew him immediately because he had the right look and I was expecting no one else. He was thirty-eight to forty, a humorless man with a trim black mustache on his longish upper lip, his smooth black hair combed flat and cut short. He sat down across the desk from me at the crest of my bad mood. "I've done a lot of talking to a lot of policemen about this thing, Lieutenant, or at least it seems that way, and I'm getting awfully bored," I said. "So I hope you're not going to drag me over the same damned ground again."

"Oh, you're bored, are you? Isn't that too bad?"

I made a conciliatory gesture. "Sorry. I happen to be having some personal problems. The bums I shot a couple of months ago had some friends or relatives or something and they decided to take revenge. You know the type. Anyway they got to me through my daughter." I tossed the notes on the desk and he leaned forward to pick them up. "Two of them signed Slow Death don't make much sense, but the other one does. You just caught me at a bad moment."

He examined them carefully and shook his head. He said, "They hooked your daughter?" I could see he was sympathetic as he put the notes back on my desk and said, "That's the kind of animal we're dealing with. Have you shown these to the L.A. department?"

"No."

"You should."

"I've been intending to."

He nodded and wanted to get off the subject suddenly because he remembered what he had come for. "Look, this won't take too much time and could be of great benefit to both of us," he said. "This thing happened on our doorstep, not L.A.'s. That's why I'm here."

"Okay."

"You see, I believe your story about Simon Brooks. At least it's not too farfetched. And I'm ready to take you up on it. Why don't we have a talk with him?"

"When would you suggest?"

"What's the matter with right now?"

"Not a thing," I said. "Have you talked to him?"

"Briefly. Late yesterday. And I think he'll tell all once he breaks. He's that close." He held up his thumb and index finger to demonstrate the distance. "As soon as I saw him I could tell."

"I'll take a chance on it with you," I said, getting up and taking my jacket from a hanger hooked to the filing-cabinet handle. "On the other hand, I don't want to see a murder pinned on him that he didn't do." I slipped into the jacket. "He was just the towel boy. He never squeezed the trigger, the way I see it."

"If you're right, I want a look at him with you right in the room."

A few minutes later I was following Carrodas's car in my own to the Colby Building on Wilshire Boulevard. Brooks's secretary said that he had not come in that day and was probably at home. He lived in a high-rise cooperative also along Wilshire Boulevard about two miles from the office, very expensive and towering above everything.

We took an elevator to the ninth floor and got out and walked along a thickly carpeted and silent corridor of closed doors behind which very rich people lived their very rich lives. The door to Brooks's apartment opened after Carrodas had set off the chimes, and there stood a small, harried-looking woman of forty, her face almost fleshless, her dark eyes bright and troubled, her mouth thin and suspicious. "Yes?" she said, looking at both of us.

"I'm Lieutenant Carrodas. This is Mr. Blaney."

She looked at me with a flash of open resentment. She knew the name. "My husband is not here."

"You're Mrs. Brooks?"

"Yes, I am." She made no move to invite us in. "My husband left a little while ago. I don't know when he'll return." Her voice had a fractional quaver and she was anxious to close the door. "I'll tell him you were here."

"We don't want to disturb you, Mrs. Brooks," Carrodas said. "But I wonder if you've any idea where Mr. Brooks could be found."

"I've no idea, I'm sorry," she said, and began to close the door, but then stopped suddenly, everything about her withering with tension. "Is there something that urgent?"

And it was while he was giving his answer that I caught sight of the child in the living room because my angle happened to allow it, a boy of about ten. "Nothing to worry about," Carrodas was saying. "There are some questions that have to be asked, that's all. Just part of investigative routine. Okay, Mrs. Brooks. Thank you. I'll call back."

Downstairs, as we prepared to go in separate directions, I said to Carrodas, "Thanks for the buggy ride."

"That woman knows something," he said, the thought fixed in his eyes.

"Oh, that woman knows quite a lot," I said.

"It was worth the trip just to see how unnerved she is."

"You might be pretty unnerved yourself if you were the mother of a kid with multiple sclerosis," I said.

"What?"

"Sure. Didn't you get a look at him?"

"No. Jesus."

"You must have been standing in the wrong spot. I saw him. That would be enough to set her off by itself."

We were silent as we walked along toward the cars. "Well, we'll get to him later," Carrodas said quietly.

I nodded. "Call me."

29

I SPENT THE AFTERNOON hiring a collection agency, for the first time in my experience, consulting with my tax accountant, and fixing myself a five-o'clock drink which I drank in solitary regret at my apartment. When I got downtown to Parker Center it was six o'clock and there were two detective sergeants on duty in Narcotics, both of them doing the paperwork of a backbreaking case load. One was John Keely, a flaming red-haired man in his late twenties, and the other, Elwood Poulter, square-jawed, pleasant, about thirty. Both of them knew me immediately and were only too willing to stop what they were doing when I told them what was on my mind and showed them the three messages I had received, the two from Slow Death threatening me with extinction, and the one from Friends of the Deceased which referred to what they had already done to Jan.

Red-haired John Keely's boyish face belonged to a very mature and seasoned policeman. "The two death threats get to mean less with every day that goes by," he said, pushing them to the center of his desk where Poulter picked them up. "I think somebody read about it or saw it on TV and decided to throw a scare into you if they could."

"Crank notes, you mean?" I said as Sergeant Poulter, who was standing next to Keely's desk examined all three messages very carefully.

"Maybe," Keeley answered. "I don't think they should be ignored. But they don't look connected to that gang."

"We'll run these through the lab for whatever might still be on them," Poulter said, sticking a pipe in his teeth and slipping the three notes in the breast pocket of his Hathaway. "Let's look at some names."

"And the mugs that go with them," Keely said, getting up.

"You don't go out looking like that, do you?" I said, referring to their close-cropped hair, their clean shirts, Keely's open at the neck, Poulter sporting a blue-and-maroon-striped tie.

"We both got tired of the long hair," Poulter said. "We use wigs. You can't tell them from the real thing. Tight jeans, T-shirt, denim jacket. Instant hipster, dealer, junkie, or whatever it takes."

"We'll be going out tonight," Keely said. "But not from here. We keep rooms downtown. It's the only way. If you want to be safe."

"If we could get your daughter to look at mug shots we would probably make the guy," Poulter said as we entered the large file room. "Just in the event that Strelli is not the name that goes with the face."

"I suspect she won't. But maybe her mother can. She's seen him."

"Then that's the answer," Poulter said.

"Let's check the name out first," Keely said.

And after using the computerized index finder, we got right to the section where Richard Strelli would have to be. But no such name was on file.

Outside in the corridor Poulter said, "The best thing is to have the girl's mother go through all the jackets."

"The guy in jail — Kramer," I said, referring to the survivor of the two guys I had shot that night. "*He* can tell you just who and where Strelli is."

"We could ask him if he knows Strelli and he'd say no and that would be the end of it because we have nothing more to go on than that," Keely said. "The best thing in this situation is to identify the man and then lodge a complaint against him. Or actually your daughter would have to."

"I know most of the technicalities and I can guess at the rest," I said. "The point is, all I want to do is find out who Strelli is and what he looks like."

"We wouldn't mind that either," Poulter said. "We might

recognize him ourselves. Get the girl's mother to go through our files and there's a damned good chance we'll come up with it."

"After that, Mr. Blaney," Keely said as we stopped at the door to their office, "you'd be wise to let us handle it."

"What makes you say that, Sergeant?"

"Because I read minds as a sideline," the young cop said. "If we find this guy and there's a reason to put a tail on him — let *us* do it. The slow, safe way." He looked at me wisely. "Okay?"

"Of course, Sergeant," I said. "You must be reading someone else's mind, not mine."

He nodded and Poulter just sucked at the unlit pipe in his mouth. "Get in touch," Keely said. "If we're not on, someone else will be — probably Myers and Dodd — and they'll know all about it."

The uniformed black female officer at the check-in point took back my ID plate from my lapel, and I went to the nearest phone kiosk and called Bedelia. There was no answer so I called the service. The operator came on and I announced myself. "No messages, Mr. Blaney," she told me. I thanked her and hung up.

I WALKED into my apartment and there she was, perched in my overstuffed armchair like something ready to spring, her legs bent under her, her hands tensed on the wings of the chair, her bare arms firm with her kind of youthful strength, and looking as if the sound of my key in the lock had alerted her whole body. She had the look on her face of someone who wasn't sure whether she was waiting to strike or be struck. And it made her particularly beautiful and alluring and maybe more than I was finally going to be able to handle. Her mouth questioned me, her eyes defied me. Or maybe it was the other way around. But I don't think any of it was calculated as much as it was exploratory, or like some sort of probing action. She didn't know how she stood with me at the moment. She couldn't have known how high it was, how much I longed for her in a way I could never fully express. "Have you had enough of me?" she said. "Demands, tantrums, sucking at your throat like Dracula's great-granddaughter. Have you had all you want?"

"Do you think I'm crazy?" I said. "Of course not."

"Oh, Jim."

"What, sweetheart?"

"I don't want to fail you. I don't want to be less than what it takes to be the woman you need. Does that sound overblown and full of pounding drums? I guess it does."

"I like it. I don't deserve it but I like it."

She got up and we came toward each other and embraced and sat down on the sofa together, she holding my hands and sitting at the edge and turned toward me. "I did a disappearing act," she said. "I wanted you to miss me. Definitely kid stuff, huh?"

"Maybe. But it worked. Where did you go and what did you have in mind when you went there?"

She smiled as if the joke was on her. "I drove out to my friend Gay Siegel's house in Westwood. We spent the day. I wanted to see how long I could stay away from you."

"And then you felt sorry for me and you came back," I said.

"You're toying with me, you bastard," she said.

I took both of her hands firmly in mine and, looking right into her eyes, I said, "Look, I want to tell you something and I want you to understand it and file it away. You see, I don't want it all to sneak up on us, sweetheart — me with busted veins in my nose and white hair and stiff in the joints, and you still just a bloomer. I don't want that to sneak up on us and I know it could. It would embarrass me and it would ruin you."

"It wouldn't. You're too obsessed with age."

"Maybe. But that's the way I am. And you'd never walk out and maybe you'd wind up hating me and not even knowing why you were doing it. That's why I am back here in my own apartment now and not yours. We'd have settled in and I'd never have left. All it might have taken was another twenty-four hours. And then some day I'd be too old and scared to leave. And if you showed good sense and tried to leave *me* I might break down and blubber and grab you around the waist on my knees and cry, Don't go, don't go. And wouldn't that be a sight?"

"I somehow can't get that picture in my mind," she said.

"I might even die in your arms," I said with a little grotesque humor. "Picture that."

It stung her and she punched me on the arm and it was no love-pat. "You stink," she said with more than mock anger.

I laughed.

"I mean you're a terrible man sometimes."

"Am I?"

"A pain in the ass."

"But lovable."

"Like hell. My God, why do I have anything to do with you at all? What strange malady of the moon draws me to you?"

"Let's get out of town for the weekend, sweetheart, and find out," I said.

"And what do I do if you die before Monday morning?"

"Just leave my corpse where it is. Somebody will find it."

We drove down to Laguna and checked into a place we had liked in the past, big but nice, and right on the beach. For two days we lay in the sun, took walks, watched the stars and the whitetops on the water at night, and listened to the sounds of the surf and the faint humming breezes that carried the tingling smell of sand and sea to our nostrils. We made love once or twice when it was nowhere near bedtime. The sun and the sea air worked wonders. It was lovely. By Monday morning I hadn't died and we came back to L.A. with terrific suntans and memories of muted cries and arching backs and of moments when I made love to her as if I were,

I won't say sixteen, but substantially younger than I actually was.

Don joined us at the office and we did not compare weekend notes except in very general terms. He had been in La Jolla part of the time and in San Francisco the rest. We didn't ask him with whom. Our minds were hardly off the gentler matters in our lives when Bedelia went forward to her desk to get a phone call and buzzed me for a pickup. I could hear her voice both from the desk up front and through the receiver. "Mr. Steven Elson of Coastal Manufacturers Trust and Savings."

I felt a little thump in my gut and I said, "Put him on."

31

"Mr. Blaney," came the smooth voice.

"Yes, Mr. Elson."

Bedelia had moved away from her desk and Don had hung up his phone and both of them had their eyes riveted on me. I put my hand out vaguely to signal for patience. But suddenly Don picked up the earphone on his desk that was tied to all three lines in the office and Bedelia went swiftly to share it with him, her face close to his. And then all of us heard Elson say, "I'll have a decision for you by tomorrow at noon."

Faces fell and I said, "Uh-huh," feeling as if I had been hyped by someone just for the fun of it, which wasn't at all true.

"But you'll be interested to know that the contract between you and Mr. Colby has been located — the original, that is. So that's a good sign from your point of view."

"I'm glad to hear that."

"It was drawn by another attorney — a man named Billings in Pasadena. That aside, the approval will come — assuming there are no unforeseen encumbrances — from a court functionary," he said. "Normally it would be a superior-court judge to whom we would present the claim, you understand, and you could find yourself waiting for God knows how long. I'm cutting through all of that for you, you understand."

"Thank you."

"And your reputation isn't too bad at all, by the way. We've been checking, which comes as no surprise to you, I'm sure. And it turns out you're something of a hero. I had no idea."

I laughed feebly. "Neither did I."

"I must have been out of town at the time. But it certainly didn't hurt your claim any. But just one thing, and that's the jewelry itself. You'll need to turn it all over to Coastal for examination at least forty-eight hours before a check can be issued."

"All right."

"The reason is the need for enough clearance to be absolutely certain there's nothing wrong with the jewelry itself, that it's all genuine and that there are no conflicting claims concerning any of the pieces. Just a formality."

"Don't explain."

"I'll call you, as I say, tomorrow. If the claim has been honored by the court, we'll make arrangements to receive the jewelry sometime in the afternoon."

"I won't bring it to you, it's too risky. The best thing is to have a couple of specials accompany me to the place I've got it all secured. Even a Brinks truck wouldn't be a bad idea; you use them normally anyhow. So I won't need to transport it by myself. The way I did last time."

"That makes sense. In fact, I was going to suggest it, but I don't think it can be tomorrow in that case. Let's talk about it when I call you."

I got off the phone with him and looked at Don and Bedelia. "Think we're home-free?" Don said.

"You can't buy a box of Wheaties on it yet," I said with restraint. "But maybe."

"Let's all just not say anything about it," Bedelia wisely suggested. "This is the morning I get to those files. Better me than the IRS."

Don and I both gave her some help for a while until she said she didn't need us and was better off on her own. Don then went to his desk and began to thumb through a copy of *Sports Illustrated* and I went to mine and put in a call to Rita.

"I was just stepping out of the door," she told me.

"I won't keep you long. Have you heard from Jan?"

"She called over the weekend, I don't know from where and she refused to tell me . . ."

"Yes? And?"

"Just to say she was all right and not to worry. She said she was with her *man,* as she put it, and that everything was okay. So what does one say to that? Not much — just *bon voyage.*"

"Her *man?* Do you mean Strelli?" I said, keeping my voice low.

"I didn't ask, but I would assume as much, wouldn't you? She wanted me to know that he hadn't deserted her, I suppose."

"Listen, Rita, that's what I'm calling you about," I said, letting my chair come forward and swiveling it to one side for no good reason. "I'd like you to take some time off and come down to police headquarters with me, say tomorrow or the next day, so that you can look through the files and perhaps pick out Strelli . . ."

"Pick out Strelli?"

"You won't be able to go through all of them in one visit, and maybe it will take a second or third . . ."

"But why?"

"Why? Well, for God's sake, isn't that obvious?" Then I realized it wasn't obvious to Rita because I had never told her the whole story. "This guy Strelli deliberately hooked Jan on heroin, and there's every reason to believe he did it to get back at me for killing that dealer in the parking lot that night."

"What?"

"That's the long and the short of it. We don't want him to go scot-free, do we?"

"Then why is he still with her, if that's the case?" she said in a suddenly demanding voice.

"What's the difference? Maybe he has more damage to inflict. In fact, if it's him she's with, that's what I suspect. I think he's the brother of the guy who was killed — that's my personal guess."

"Oh, Christ, you had to be there and be so ready to get into the middle of things. . . ."

"It wasn't like that at all, but I'll take the blame for everything up till that point. And even for *that,* if that's what you want to hear . . ." I caught sight of Don and Bedelia both being very absorbed by what they were doing, never letting their attention wander toward me. "She was ripe for it when it happened, Rita, we have to face that. A happy girl could never be that easy a target. She was a pushover, our little Jan. And I'll take the blame for that too. Only come with me and look over those mug shots."

There was a moment of silence and then Rita said, "I'll go with you tomorrow morning. Make it as early as you like."

"I'll pick you up at eight o'clock," I said.

I hung up, came forward to Bedelia's section. She looked at me with eyes that were a little too neutral, and I assured her, "Strictly a police matter, sweetheart."

The door opened and in walked a man who was immediately familiar to me, fifty, gray, conservative in manner and dress, and I was on the brink of recognition when he announced himself. "Lieutenant Wagner," he said. "Remember me?"

"Yes. That night."

"That's right. How are you?"

"Okay. Yourself?"

"No complaints." He nodded to Bedelia with a faint smile, took off his hat and said, "And how are you?"

"Fine, thank you."

"What's up, Lieutenant?" I asked.

Don had looked up from the *Sports Illustrated* by now and Wagner said, "I'm on the Colby case — one of the fifty detectives who are."

"Yes, I know, I've run into a few of them."

He smiled a little. "But that's not what brings me here. We've got a related matter and I'm in charge of it. I thought it would be of interest to you and that you might even be able to shed a little light."

"Always willing to shed light, Lieutenant. What's it all about?"

"Simon Brooks has been found dead. Someone stabbed him through the heart and left him at the bottom of an elevator shaft in the building where he lived."

"Jesus Christ," Don said softly in disbelief, and Bedelia just stood there looking shocked.

32

"A BUILDING CUSTODIAN found him at seven o'clock this morning," Wagner said. "The official M.E.'s report isn't complete yet but a ballpark guess is that Brooks was killed about three days ago."

"Meaning Friday," I said.

"Can you tell us anything about it?"

"Have you spoken to his wife?" I said.

"Yes. She was a pretty big help, in fact. Before she went into shock. Gave us the key factor as far as the murder itself is concerned. I'll get to it with you, if you're interested."

"Sure."

"You were up there, weren't you, and saw the woman on Friday?"

"That's right. With Lieutenant Carrodas of the Mariposa Beach Police Department. We tried to see Brooks to settle the little differences in the stories he and I were telling about the Colby thing. Brooks wasn't there and Mrs. Brooks wasn't inclined to talk about anything and we left. From what you say, the chances are he was dead at that very minute. He never even left the building that morning."

"Is that all? Nothing funny that you can remember."

"There's a young boy with multiple sclerosis, and there's nothing funny about that. That was what stayed with me. There was nothing else."

"How sad," Bedelia said. "You didn't mention it."

"We've seen the boy," Wagner said. "Damned shame."

"How was Brooks killed and then dumped in an elevator shaft?" Don said, frowning. "How does someone open an elevator shaft without being seen to begin with?"

"Someone takes a chance," Wagner said dryly. "It happened at the swimming pool."

"Swimming pool?" I said. "Sounds like Philo Vance in *The Dragon Murder Case*."

"I remember that," Wagner said. "It's not that kind of thing." And then he laughed. "You've got a good memory. I must have been ten when I saw that movie."

"Is there a swimming pool in the building?" Don said.

"My God, there's everything in that building," Wagner said. "There's a restaurant, a sauna — everything." He dropped his hat on Bedelia's desk. "Now this is how the murder gets pinned down in regard to opportunity, if you want to hear it."

"Go ahead," I said with a touch of impatience.

"According to Mrs. Brooks, her husband went to the pool every single morning like clockwork before leaving for his office. He would do the same thing on Saturdays and Sundays. He was a swimming enthusiast, you could say. But he wasn't killed in the pool obviously. The chances are he was killed in the locker-room area. They have lockers. It's a convenience for people who want to leave certain things at the pool instead of lugging them back and forth to their apartments. On Friday morning he went through the same ritual. Whether he had his dip or not, the M.E. may be able to determine through chlorine traces, if there are any. But, either way, that was when he was murdered. Stabbed by someone who was waiting for him, we're pretty sure — who knew he'd be there, just the way he was every morning for the past five years."

"Why didn't Mrs. Brooks call the police or tell someone in the building when he didn't come back from his swim?" Bedelia said. "May I ask?"

"You may ask anything you like. Mrs. Brooks says her husband would always shave before leaving the apartment. And after his swim, he would shower right there and just put his street clothes back on and leave for wherever he was going. So she didn't think anything was wrong until a couple of days had gone by anyhow."

"A couple of days?" I said.

"Mrs. Brooks was very candid with us. She said that Brooks planned on getting out of town for the weekend. He didn't want to be around in case the police decided to move in on him. He wanted to lay low and think things out, from what she tells us." Wagner shrugged slightly. "It doesn't matter any more, so she's not holding anything back. She admits she knew he had some explaining to do to the police."

"And his murderer knew the same thing," I said.

"Maybe," Wagner said. "Anyhow, we can pinpoint the murder almost to the quarter of the hour. What time did you and Carrodas call on Mrs. Brooks?"

"Come to think of it, it was after twelve," I said. "He was dead a long time by then."

"That's right," Wagner said, and took a brief pause before going on. "And whoever did it knew Brooks's habits, his routine. At least as far as this swimming ritual every morning. And he moved fast. Not many people use the pool that early on weekday mornings from what we can gather. So not many people were moving around and the murderer had a very fair chance of not being seen."

"But what about the elevator shaft?" Don said. "How did he get the body into it?"

"The locker area is maybe fifty feet from the nearest elevator,"

Wagner said. "And we are dead certain that the body was transported from the lockers to the elevator. How? An absolutely perfect way. In one of the laundry wagons. They are very big and deep, if you can visualize the kind I mean, and a body of any size could easily go into one and be covered over with dirty towels and never be seen. And in fact, we are sure that that factor alone was the major reason why the murderer hit on doing it there. And we actually have *the* wagon, bloodstains and all. We're waiting for the pathology report, but we're sure we're on the right track."

"It sounds like it," I said.

"There are workmen and delivery people in and out of that building all the time. The murderer had that advantage. It looks as if he carried the body to the basement level where he got off the elevator with the cart, got back in, and stopped the cage a few feet above floor level. There's a door release on the panel for emergencies. He uses it, climbs out of the cage, dumps the body in the shaft, climbs back in the cage, closes the doors, and goes on his merry way. Getting out of the building after that is the easy part. Who's watching?"

"He took chances, didn't he?" Bedelia said.

"That's what I said before," Wagner said. "But it worked because as far as we know no one saw him." He shrugged. "He took a few chances and he might have had a few close shaves. But then we have to assume his motive was a strong one."

"And I've told all the cops in Los Angeles and Mariposa Beach what that motive was," I said. "The guy killed Colby, and Brooks knew it because they were partners in the attempted heist of the jewelry. Brooks might not have seen him do it, but he knew about it."

"And who is it?" Wagner said.

"Start checking all of Brooks's contacts," I said. "What people knew him that long and that well that his habits and routine were that familiar to them? Check on their whereabouts between nine and ten o'clock on Friday morning for a starter."

"Just out of curiosity, where were you?" Wagner said with a thin smile.

"I happened to be getting a haircut from John Tomiari on Ventura Boulebard at about ten o'clock," I said. "After that I was with Carrodas. Could I have been in better company?"

"Where were you before the haircut?" he said. "Just curious."

"With me, Lieutenant," Bedelia said.

"Oh?"

"From sundown to sunup," she said. "You can have a sworn statement, if you like."

"That won't be necessary. At least not for the moment."

"Don't hesitate," she said.

I shrugged slightly when Wagner looked at me, and for no reason I could fathom I said, "We were discussing the possibilities of a concerto built around the kazoo. Between seven-thirty and nine-thirty a.m."

Wagner said in his sometimes dry way, "You won't need to go into the details."

He was picking up his hat and I said, "I'll get in touch with you if anything comes up that would interest you or is related to the killings. I guess I don't have to tell you that."

He walked to the door and said with a smile, "And that goes the other way around." He looked at us all briefly, said, "Goodbye," and walked out.

"What's he fishing for?" Don said.

"What else has he got to do?" I said. "He'll poke around like this with everyone who knew either Brooks or Colby until he either gets a break or gives up on the whole thing. They all will."

"I feel sorry about Brooks," Bedelia said.

"If there wasn't a kid there with MS you wouldn't say that," I said.

"I know," she admitted.

"He wanted a big score. What he had wasn't enough," I said.

"But he must have made close to a hundred grand a year," Don said.

"Sure. But the cut on the jewelry would have come to two or three times that in a lump sum, nontaxable," I said. "A nest egg. Security for his wife and the boy." I walked back to my desk and added, "Or maybe it had nothing to do with his wife and the boy. Maybe Brooks was just greedy. Like so many people."

"And reckless," Bedelia said.

"He didn't have anything to fall back on," Don said. "Someone like him has to be insane to take those kinds of chances." He shook his head. "What the hell. Tough all around. But I guess his insurance is pretty good."

The rest of the morning slipped by slowly, and when Don had finally gone off on some errand or other and Bedelia and I were alone for lunch at the Farmer's Market, she said, "You didn't mind my telling Wagner about us, did you Jim?"

"Why not? It was part of my alibi. There's nothing like having a dame who will stand by you."

"What's a dame for, you sexist bastard?" she said, and took a bite of her cornbeef on rye.

33

IT WAS NINE O'CLOCK when Rita and I reached Parker Center and went to the mug-shot room where we sat for about two hours in the dark while a thousand faces flashed on the screen in front of us. Not one of them was familiar to her, even though once or twice she hesitated before making her decision. "You know how it is when you've seen someone on only one occasion," she said. "You're not that sure a second time."

"But you're sure you haven't seen Strelli so far?" I said. There were a couple of those faces that stared out sullenly that I had cast in the role and I was frustrated and disappointed when Rita either shook her head and muttered, "No," or "Uh-uh," or just shook her head and said nothing.

"Yes," she said, answering my question. "I'm sure none of the ones we've seen so far is Strelli."

The uniformed police officer who worked the projector for us finally said, "We're out of jackets. Do you want to pull some others now or come back?"

"How many roughly are there?" Rita said.

"More than twenty-five thousand in this section."

"Oh, my God. No, I can't take any more for the moment."

"Okay," I said, weary and resigned.

We left Parker Center just before eleven-thirty and as I drove along, Rita sitting beside me, I said, "By noon I'll have the word on the Colby fee. And unless something goes wrong I'm going to be able to put ten grand into Loretta's college fund."

"You weren't kidding about that, were you?" she said with mild astonishment that irritated me somewhat.

"The girl has the grades and wants to be a doctor," I said. "She's my daughter and if I've got that kind of dough it's hers if she needs it. Why should that bowl you over?"

"Don't be so thin-skinned."

"Look who's talking," I said as we drove onto the freeway at Los Angeles Street.

"You mean you're actually collecting that much from this Colby thing?" she said.

"Hundred and fifty grand with a quarter split for Don Price," I said. "Of course, something could blow it at the last minute. The court could get cranky and table the claim, especially now with the murder of Simon Brooks."

"Yes. Murder isn't cute like in Agatha Christie. It's not just a nice neat puzzle that's going to be solved in the last chapter, is it? And you're right in the middle of it, aren't you?"

"Well, not the dead center exactly. I'm somewhat connected."

"You've always kind of longed for an adventure like this, haven't you, Jim? I mean the mystery and the attention and all of that."

"Do you believe that?"

"I don't know."

"Forget it. I just want my money, darling, nothing else."

"Yes. And I suppose you're looking forward to a little flyer with your mistress on all that money."

"Now, now. You're too big a girl for that kind of thing."

"Am I?" she said with a laugh. "You mean I should be."

"I think you are."

"How sweet of you."

Then we drove along in silence for a few moments before she said in a deep and thoughtful way, "What if she never gets over Strelli?"

I glanced at her, a little surprised by the thought. I said, "That's why I'd like to catch up with him."

"You? You mean the police, don't you?"

"Either I or them."

She sounded a little bit alarmed. "You don't intend to take things into your own hands, do you?" she said.

"No, no, of course not."

"Let me ask you something. What if Strelli has actually fallen in love with Jan? What then?"

"Oh, come on."

"It's not impossible," she said. "What if without wanting to he simply found himself that way about her? What then?"

"That's about as likely as snow in July." I said as much and then realized that there are all sorts of places in the world where there is snow in July. So I added, "In the middle of Los Angeles."

I took her home and said I would call her about going downtown again and she wasn't disagreeable about it. She said goodbye in that wistful-queen way she sometimes had and I left her. I called Steven Elson at Coastal etcetera from a phone kiosk in a gas station on Sunset Boulevard. "Come to my office tomorrow at eleven, Mr. Blaney," he said. "A guard truck will accompany you to your depository and by Thursday afternoon, if all goes well, you'll have your check for a hundred and fifty thousand dollars."

"Swell," I said. And I took a deep breath as I hung up. It's not that I'm that mercenary. But it was the sweetest deep breath I had ever taken. I'd have bet on it.

34

THE NEWSPAPERS and the television news had played Brooks's murder up big the day before because it was like something in a detective novel or a movie. First the super-powerful industrialist of gigantic wealth is murdered on a lonely road where he went for a mysterious midnight meeting. And a week later his right-hand man and confidant is also murdered and dropped into an elevator shaft. How could they pass up that kind of juice? The connection had to be there, all part of a diabolical and ruthless plot, a tough, clever, and maybe desperate murderer behind it. It was sheer dynamite for the five o'clock news. I was glad it didn't get in our way and was even a little surprised it hadn't. Though in fact a couple of reporters from two of the big networks' local outlets had moved their portable equipment and crews into the patio, and as I was coming back from my morning with Rita, they moved in on me. But I didn't lose the slight spring in my step. "Are you working with the police on Simon Brooks's murder?" one asked, sticking his hand mike as close to my face as he dared.

I kept walking but I didn't want to make waves so I said politely, "The police don't need my help. I'm like any other citizen and whatever they might ask of me I'll comply with to the best of my ability."

"Do you have any theories about what kind of person the murderer might be?"

"The kind who can kill," I said, reaching the bottom of the staircase.

"Is it true that you and Simon Brooks each told contradictory stories about the facts surrounding the murder of John Colby?"

"Why don't you ask the police about that?" I said, uneasy, wondering fleetingly if the order to pay the claim could be rescinded between now and the time I was scheduled to have that check put in my hand. "I told the police what I knew about the situation from the point of view of having worked on a private matter for Mr. Colby. They seem satisfied."

"What's the story on the jewelry you're supposed to have recovered?"

"That's all for now, gentlemen," I said, and started up the steps.

"Do you have any idea of the whereabouts of Mrs. Colby at the moment, Jim?" one of them said, a pushy snoop with a head of massive blond hair, straight as sticks and sprayed stiff.

"Ask your police-department leak about it," I said, and kept going. There were no more questions fired at me, but the strapped-on cameras kept grinding until I had disappeared inside the office.

Bedelia had been standing at the window overlooking the patio and she said, "You might be able to go on some of the local talk shows if this keeps up. If only you were a publicity hound."

"It will all be behind us in a couple of days, sweetheart," I said, coming toward her. "And you and I are going to be drifting and dreaming and smelling purple passion flowers on a nice long cruise somewhere in the South Seas. And there's plenty of it left that still looks like the travel folders."

She knew what I meant. "It came through," she said. She was almost solemn at first and then quickly the joy spread in those timeless blue eyes.

"That's right, sweetheart," I said, enjoying watching her face and then hugging her very hard.

She hugged me back and said over my shoulder, "Oh, boy, I could walk on air. What an effect money has, darling."

"I know the feeling," I said. "We'll be left with close to ninety grand after taxes and the money I'm giving to my daughter."

"That's a lot of money, darling. Even today it's a lot of money.

Gosh. When you said drifting and dreaming and smelling purple passionflowers . . ."

"Is there such a thing?"

"Only when you need them," she said. "They'll be all over the place when we get there."

I kissed her and she kissed me back with a lot of energy for an office kiss in the middle of the day. Our mouths drew apart and she said, "I don't know what to hope for, as far as the rest of your morning is concerned." There was a somewhat cautious, probing closed-mouth smile on her lips.

We stepped apart and I picked my hat off her desk and tossed it on top of the filing cabinet. "We didn't locate Strelli, if that's what you mean," I said.

"Is Jan off with him somewhere?" she said.

"It's possible."

"Did you ever stop to think that possibly he's in love with her?"

I looked at her and said, "If I didn't know better I'd say you've been talking to my ex-wife."

"Is that what she thinks?"

"She just poses the possibility. It would never cross *my* mind. It's so strictly a woman's idea."

"Does that make it superior or inferior?"

"Superior, definitely. But nasty."

"Not necessarily."

"How can you say that? What a twist. It makes me sick to think of it."

"But maybe it would be the best thing that could happen . . ."

"What? My daughter hooked up with a thug?"

"She already is. But if he returns the feeling, Jim, maybe he could reform. He might be that one in a hundred."

"You're groping for a happy and convenient ending, sweetheart. And I know why. But there aren't a lot of them around anymore."

"There's nothing on him, is there?"

"Only what I have on him myself," I said.

She didn't answer and I said, "Let's go to lunch. And after lunch we'll get hold of a stack of travel folders and go off somewhere and look them over. Sound good?"

"Intoxicating."

That was what we did and it was a nice relaxed afternoon. We sat at the kitchen table in her apartment and lost ourselves in the dozen or more possibilities, the trade winds already playing on our senses, the swaying palms beckoning from sandy white beaches in the distance. "This is the best thing people can do, isn't it? Dream," she said. "You do it when you're a child and you keep doing it until you die, I guess."

"Maybe not quite that long," I said.

By five o'clock we had charted a couple of tentative courses and the whole thing was starting to be more real to us than it had ever actually been. Finally I telephoned Don and found him just in from his golf game. I told him we were in the winner's circle, and you could say he whooped with delight. We made a date to meet at Tail O' The Cock in the Valley, where we could listen to the piano while having dinner.

Bedelia looked as beautiful and fresh as new flower petals, and Don was tanned and he looked like somebody who could still play a lot of football, as we all sat at our table waiting for cocktails. Everyone felt good. The big apple was at hand. Success was in the air. The drinks arrived and we all drank. A Rodgers and Hart tune came from the piano not far away from us. *Wait till you see her, See how she looks, Wait till you hear her laugh.* Bedelia hummed a little bit of it, and I thought that the song suited her from my point of view because that was the kind of soft, boozy mood I was already in. Don said, "I guess we could, if we wanted to, call this a celebration. Except it's a damned funny kind of celebration, isn't it? Busting up and going off in separate directions. And, in a way, I'm the one who triggered the whole thing, I guess."

"It had to go, Don," Bedelia said. "Nobody murdered it. It just died of old age."

I laughed and Don said, "I always thought you enjoyed the

business, Bedelia. The laughs, the chills, the spills and thrills."

"The rocks and rills. Oh, I did. It was always better than a ribbon counter or paper boxes."

"Oh, honey, you could have done a lot better than ribbon counters and paper boxes if you had wanted to," Don said. "I mean there were a lot of reasons for — well, for your not doing anything else. I mean, that's true of all of us. None of it's right down the line and simple."

"Sure. And wherever Jim is I'd be anyway." She took a little sip of her sherry and said, "No, it's just that it was cool and terrific all the way, and the three of us were keen together. But the psychopaths were starting to get to me with the guns and the knives and the notes and all of it. I'm just glad we're getting out while we can still tell ourselves apart from them."

Don laughed. "Hell, I'd never have any trouble with that. We were the good-looking ones."

Bedelia and I both laughed, and Don snapped his fingers, suddenly recalling a neglected obligation. "Damn, I forgot to call La Jolla. I'm going down tomorrow, not tonight. Will you excuse me?" And he left the table to make his phone call.

Bedelia drank a little of her drink and said, "Have you noticed I've taken to dry sherry? Do you think it does something for me?"

She was a little giddy, relief from all kinds of tension and pressure untying some of the knots. I felt pretty good myself, of course. "You don't need a *thing* done for you," I said. "It was all done long ago."

"Listen to the sweet man."

The piano played and dinner arrived and we ate and talked about a lot of different things, some of it forgettable, some of it nonsensical, some of it not so forgettable. Like what had happened in Las Vegas. That was still hanging over us in a way and probably always would. We got to the topic because I was saying it was a boffo finish to everything, the Colby case and all that went with it. "We're quitting while we're ahead and way up high," I said. "That's the best way to do it. Just ask anyone who hangs on too long. I had fifteen years of it. How much better could it get?"

"Twenty years from now I'll wake up in the middle of the night and get the shivers thinking about it," Bedelia said. "They'd have buried us out in the desert and nobody would ever have known. I can see it all through a pale red filter like in a dream."

"Not bad, sweetheart," I said. "I can see it with you." And I went on eating my steak and drinking the Burgundy I had ordered for the occasion.

"We were just damned lucky that Ganner dropped the whole thing," Bedelia said.

"He had to. There was no way he could gain anything by trying to track us down," I said.

"Not at first," she said. "But he can read. He knows what happened."

"Yeah, but there's a funny machismo thing working here in a head like Ganner's," Don said. "Even now he knows he couldn't get the rocks back back without a hell of a big try and a fight. He's not strong enough. And it's not worth it to him to take a chance with what's left of his image. He doesn't want people to know how he got taken by the likes of us and lost two soldiers into the bargain. Very bad for that image. He'd rather write it off than take the chance on that coming out."

"And he would just as soon not take a chance on getting tied into any murders either," I said. "All of which could be dead wrong."

We went on eating and drinking and listening to the music, and suddenly I could see that something was on Don's mind and he was getting ready to talk about it. "Listen, Jim," he said, his fork lowered, his eyes serious. "Bedelia knows about this so I can talk freely. There's still that thing back there."

"Yes?"

"With those two guys," he said. "I've been giving it a lot of thought and I'd hate to have it catch up with me." He put the fork down altogether. "You see, if you pick up that money in a couple of days and the check clears the bank, that's it. Nothing could compromise the claim any more. I could probably get off with self-defense because of the known character of the two guys I . . ." He lowered his voice though it wasn't necessary, there was so much noise in the place. ". . . left out there."

"There's no way they can connect you," I said. "Ganner isn't going to open his mouth, as we just said, and he'll be damned glad if *we* never do. So my advice would be, don't open *your* mouth about it either and it will all go away because no one is too interested in seeing it solved."

His eyes widened, half in relief, half in surprise.

"See, I've had time to think about it myself," I told him. "And I have no doubt about what I'm telling you."

There were several moments of silence again among the three of us, the piano very noticeable, the melody very arresting. Bedelia said, "What is that?"

Because I can probably recognize a couple of thousand songs I was able to tell her. "That's one of the few things Oscar Levant ever wrote," I said. "It's called 'Don't Mention Love to Me.' "

"Yes, I can hear where it goes," she said. "I can just see him with a drink and a cigarette, sitting and staring into space. All those old songs with the no-more-love-for-me theme. I never believe them. They sound good but I don't believe them."

"You're not supposed to. You're supposed to see through the whole thing."

"I mean, who says no more love for me if he really means it? Why bother?"

"Are you sure of what you're saying, Jim?" Don began, not really hearing a word of the prattle between Bedelia and me. "Or are you just trying to make it easy on me?" Then deliberately and with a world of serious purpose in those vivid blue eyes, almost the exact shade as Bedelia's, he said, "It involves you as an accessory after the fact, Jim. I don't want you to carry that around for me all your life."

"Don't overstate it, Don. I'll go along with anything. But it's *your* conscience. I'm just telling you what I myself would do in your position. The rigmarole isn't worth it. Scalzi and Mannino weren't exactly innocent children shot down in a school yard."

There wasn't anything more said about it and we finished our dinners and went on talking and getting just a little bit high on the Burgundy and the Chablis that had followed cocktails, and we couldn't have asked for mellower feelings. Finally Don said, "Listen, you two. You're the best friends I have and I — well, hell, I love both of you . . ." The wine and whiskey had loosened up some of the lurking sentimentality in Don. ". . . But between the twenty-seven holes I played today and the booze I've soaked up, I'm ready to go on my face."

"You're no Cossack, kid, but okay," I said.

"I'm going to miss the two of you," he said.

"Hey save it, we may have to see each other eleven more times before it's all real," Bedelia said.

He got up, leaned over and kissed her on the cheek, gave us both a jaunty salute and a faint goodbye-smile and was gone. And Bedelia looked at me, her eyes shining, and she said, "I love you. And *do* mention love to me any time the mood moves you."

I took her hand below the table level, and she said, "You *do* love me, don't you, Jim?"

"We're about to go on a vacation for six months together," I said. "I had damned well better love you. Or both of us are liable to go nuts."

In a little while we drove back to her apartment, and as soon as we got inside she leaned against me and said, "Give me a little loving before you go, sweetheart."

The wine had gotten to me too but had done nothing to stir me, and in fact had had an opposite effect. It had been a long, hard day in many respects and I had no sexual urge left in me, glistening and beautiful and open as she was, as she looked into my eyes inviting me to take her. "I know I'm being aggressive and unladylike but that's nothing new, is it?"

So I tried and did badly. I was spent in just a few minutes.

"Sorry, sweetheart," I said. "You're on an old horse. Steady but not flashy anymore."

"Shut up. Who cares? It's the wine and the whiskey and all the emotional stress of the day. I was an ass to press you. It doesn't matter to me that we didn't go screaming out among the stars one time."

"I like your choice of words," I said and kissed her. "But what do you really see in me?"

"I'm a degenerate, darling."

I got up, got dressed, and left her about five minutes later. It was about eleven-thirty and it was dark.

I walked across the little street toward my car which was parked under a tree. I didn't feel too bad about it, though I knew it had something to do with my encroaching limitations and was not altogether a matter of too much wine and whiskey. I was thinking about it as I was opening the car door. And then I heard something stirring. Not leaves in the breeze or an animal, but feet. Feet with shoes on. But it was all too fast. I remember that I intended to turn around. But I never did.

And only after I woke up did I know that I had been hit behind the ear with a sap by someone rotten to the core and not afraid to kill or maim. He gave it to me good but not enough to murder me. I was knocked unconscious for the first time in my life. Swallowed up by a blackout, feeling nothing and knowing nothing.

35

I STARTED to come to life slowly with no idea of how much time had gone by. My head throbbed and my muscles ached and I felt as if I might throw up. I was lying on a coarse material you might find on the floor of a bathhouse, my jacket gone, and my feet bare, and I could smell salt air and hear faint sounds of the surf in the distance. I forced my eyes open. It was a very bad thing to do.

I was looking up at two men who were a blur to me except for their general outlines and their leather jackets. A dullish red glow coming from behind them mixed in with the light of a lamp on a table just a few feet away. I was in some kind of a small house or a shack along the water. Where, I couldn't guess. I took in that much quickly and before I could move or entertain another thought, one of them said, "Now just lay there and take it nice and easy for a minute and don't try to get too lively and I'll tell you what's what, mister."

I didn't say anything but lay there peering up at them, straining to see what they looked like. The one who was the talker was about six two or three, heavily muscled, thick-necked, not graceful, just solid and strong. The other one was well under six feet but thickset and tough also. Their faces were smeared behind the press of nylon stockings which they had pulled down over their heads. They didn't want me to see more than that. It meant I wasn't going to be killed — at least, not deliberately. I lay there in a daze. I couldn't have gotten lively, the way the talker said, even if I had wanted to.

He waited for it to sink in, saw I was making no moves, and said, "That's a nice fella. Okay." He knelt down on one knee next to me and I caught a quaff of Budweiser or something coming through that nylon stocking. He said, "Here's the pitch. My name is Jeff and my friend is Babe. That's not our real names, but in case you want to say anything to either of us it makes it easier." He spoke in a flat, midwestern voice without too much education in the sound. "Now the two of us have a specialty. We beat shit out of people for a living. We both got a Ph.D. in it and that's why we get paid so well for doing it. We will beat it out of you in ways you never dreamed unless you tell us what we want to know. And believe me it won't be worth it to you in the end. So be sensible and maybe we can all go home early — even you."

I knew what they wanted before they said another word. Someone had committed two murders — one because an original plan had gone wrong, the other to cover up the first. It had all begun with the jewelry. It was back to that right now, I knew that. What I didn't know was who had set these two guys on me.

"I always like to start off with the subject so that he understands what's what and has a chance to adjust, see what I mean?" Jeff said. "It's like part of a customer service." Then: "Okay. Now we want information out of you, mister. And you're going to be smart and tell us. It's simple. You've got stuff our client is interested in. You've got it in a hiding place. You're going to tell us where that hiding place is. That's all."

I groaned faintly, as much to stall him as anything else. He didn't stall easy. And he was suddenly grabbing me under the armpits and dragging me to my feet like a rag doll. "Too slow, sucker," he said with no change of tone. And he let me have a shot in the gut that touched my spine and turned everything inside me into poisoned jelly.

I tried not to yell in pain because I had to start out, at least, as if I wouldn't be a pushover for them. Maybe it was the wrong tactic. Maybe I should have let myself look like the pantywaist I felt like right from the start. Anyhow he let me fall on my face to the floor where I began to gag and fight to hold down all the food and drink I had had at Tail O' The Cock what seemed a long time ago right now. It wasn't easy. But I handled it. I was desperate not to lie in my own vomit in front of these two. Just desperate enough. I managed to say, "Who sent you?" as if I was really pretty tough and not afraid of what was to come.

The smaller, barrel-chested guy gave me a kick in the ribs, high and hard, and he said, "Don't test it, sucker. You'll get picked up with a sponge."

I didn't say anything and tried to catch my breath, which was still eluding me like floating feathers I couldn't quite grab hold of. Jeff stood me up, grasping me by the front of my shirt. He gave me another one in the belly, not as hard this time but still awful because it extended the pain of the first blow and didn't give me a chance to recover. My middle is in fair condition and I had tensed for the punch. But that big fist hurt like hell.

I sagged but didn't want to go down again for some dumb reason I couldn't fathom, and he held me up anyway with his powerful hands under my armpits. And he looked into my face, the smeared features behind the nylon like a nightmare, the mouth moving like a sick shadow. "Don't put yourself through this, sucker," he said, the voice raspy, and tougher now than it had been. "It gets worse. And it could be permanent. I told you. In ways you never dreamed. Babe is a kicker. That's his best number. First I put the sucker on the floor so he's crawling around looking for his mother's womb to hide in, if he can crawl at all. And then Babe does the rest. He knows how and where. Pretty soon the subject looks like a slab of calf's liver that a lot of people have jumped up and down on." He suddenly smashed me in the face with both fists and I felt my brains shake and my teeth rattle as I fell flat on my back. "Be reasonable," he said.

I started to get up like a fighter who wanted to beat the count of ten, and Jeff and Babe let me. I was dizzy and sick and unsteady and I was sure one of my teeth was loosened, blood dripping from my mouth, my lips puffed from one of the punches. I had been hit five times including the shot that had knocked me cold to start things off. I couldn't have licked a strong woman, or even a not-so-strong one. But I went for these two Jibboneys, don't ask me why, and I threw as good a right hand as I was capable of toward Jeff's chin. It was none too good and it skidded off his jaw harmlessly and left me sick with embarrassment.

He buckled me with another punch in the belly but didn't let me go down. He spun me and pushed me toward Babe, who was waiting with a timed punch on the jaw, an exquisite, dynamic uppercut that came at me with brutal contempt. I felt it land and my head snapped back and for the second time that night everything went black. He had flattened me with one punch. I realized it when I came to in what was probably less than half a minute. Not good for the brain cells.

"Come on, mister," Jeff was saying as my eyes squeezed open and panic seized me, not at the thought that they would kill me but that they would leave me crippled for life. "Talk. Where's the stuff? Come on, before it's too late and you're feeling sorry. You don't want to eat through a tube for the next six months or maybe all your life. You don't want your tongue to stop working right because your brain don't send messages anymore the way it's supposed to . . ."

"I don't know," I groaned and just lay there, trying to make myself survive, to hold out somehow. There were a hundred reasons why. And now these two pieces of scum were going to ruin every one of them just by giving me a beating. Nothing doing, I told myself. I had to take whatever they had and go all the way to the edge with them. "I don't know . . ."

"What don't you know, sucker?" Babe said and kicked me easily in the testes. Easily is all it takes in that area.

I let my eyes close and I just lay there as if it didn't matter suddenly. I couldn't fool anyone. "Come on, sucker," Jeff said, poking me with his foot as if I were a lazy dog that needed prodding. "Don't screw around like this," he said in a strangely pleading voice. "Why lose your ass? It's only money in the long run."

I tried to move my lips into a sneer. "I guess I'm just middle-class, Jeff . . ."

"Let me stomp him," Babe said.

Everything hurt far beyond simple hurting, everything throbbing and burning like fever spots. My jaw felt as if it might have been fractured, the swelling already great, and my body was numb with the punishment they had inflicted. I was on the verge of begging and pleading for mercy and swearing that I didn't know what they were talking about. "You may as well shoot me and get it over with," I managed to say, not moving. "This isn't going to get you anything . . ."

"No?" Jeff said, unimpressed.

"No," I answered. I had gone in an opposite direction. I must have been nuts. "You're going to wear yourselves out."

"Looking for special treatment, huh?" Jeff said. "Okay, baby, if that's what you want."

They started to pick me up, not gently, and I said, "I've got a partner who could whip you both at the same time . . ."

"Yeah?" Jeff said. "Too bad he ain't here right now." And he drubbed me in the ribs four or five times while Babe held me from behind, and I knew he had cracked something. It was awful and I sagged in Babe's grasp. "Yeah, too bad."

Babe dropped me to my hands and knees and kicked me hard at the base of the spine and sent me sprawling on my face. "Fuck both of you," I said, and I think by then I was not in my right mind.

I just lay there waiting for what came next, halfway between life and death it felt. But nothing happened and I didn't pass out. I realized that though they were beating me unmercifully just as they had promised, they were doing it skillfully, gauging just how much I could take. Babe's knockout punch had been a mistake they didn't want to make again. They needed me conscious so I could feel what was being done to me. I was acting tough and suicidal because I thought it might make them stop what they were doing and check back with whoever the boss of the operation was. Maybe I could even have made some kind of a deal. My head was so full of gauze anything seemed possible. But it was a wrong tack. They picked me up and worked on me some more, Jeff ramming lefts and rights at just the right speed into my ribs and belly, Babe kicking me in different places the same way when I went down. It was a brief session and I wound up face down, panting for breath with an open mouth from which blood and spittle came to dampen the coarse floor-cover, still feeling the pain I thought would have begun to disappear by now.

Jeff was down on one knee beside me again. He pulled my head back by the hair and said, "What is it, sucker? The money only? Is it that important that you'll take this to hang on to it?"

"I guess it must be," I said.

"Or is it some kind of pride? Yeah, pride. That's it. You figure you have to show what you're made of, is that it, pal?"

"I guess maybe that's it too," I said.

I said these things or something like them. But nothing came out straight or easy, all the words had trouble, and I couldn't put anything together without straining and breathing hard.

"You think everyone'll call you yellow for caving in, don't you, pal?" Jeff said. "But use your head. They won't think like that at all. Not when they see what you went through. They'll all say the sucker is tough and reliable. But everybody's only human, that's what they'll say . . ."

"Yeah? Did you ever look in the mirror?" I said.

"Okay," I heard Babe say behind me. "That's enough for me. Sit on him. We'll smoke a couple of cigarettes."

Jeff dug his knee into the small of my back and held me in a hammerlock that was tearing my arm out of its socket, and Babe put the lighted end of a cigarette into the arch of my right foot, his knees on the ankle of my left foot to keep me in place. Jeff was pushing the side of my face against the hempy floor-covering, one of his hands pressing down on my head with all his weight. Babe had my right leg bent at the knee and trapped in the crook of his left arm as if he had a headlock on someone, and with his right hand was doing all the damage. I tried everything but couldn't begin to buck them off of me. I had to yell under this kind of torture, I coldn't keep it inside. The smell of burnt flesh was unmistakable. I screamed in agony. I jerked and shuddered and suddenly that was that. I had gotten lucky and passed out.

36

THEY THREW a bucket of water on me. I could feel it but was ready to stay where I was. It took a second bucket of water to rouse me to the fullest appreciation of the work they had done on me. But there was something else. Worse in its way than the pain. I was being humiliated, made into a thing that these two could do with as they liked, play with, smear, wipe the floor with, and finally get to blubber and grovel. Taking all of this was a way of getting back at them, crazy as it sounds. All I could do was hold out until I either died or just called it off. The rage in me was its own kind of fever.

"You're in good shape for a guy your age, pal," Jeff said, looking down. "Or you used to be. What are you? About forty-three, forty-four? A little younger maybe."

Blood had crusted at the corners of my mouth and I touched it with my tongue. "You're going to kill me," I said, straining to say it, my jaw hurting on every word.

"Come on, why go through this?" Jeff said. "You can still recover and lead a nice normal life."

I didn't say anything and Jeff went on. "Here, we'll sit you up in a chair so you can be more comfortable, okay?" And they both dragged me into an armchair which didn't make me feel any better. Jeff leaned over me and Babe was behind him, and how much I wanted to see what was under those nylon stocking-masks. "Are you listening to me?" he said.

"I'm listening," I said.

"Are you listening good?"

I just made a little sound in my throat.

"Okay. You're the best we have seen, isn't that right, Babe?" Jeff said.

Babe grunted, then said, "Yeah, sure. He's a wonder."

"So you've got nothing to be ashamed of, pal," Jeff said.

"Can I ask a question?" I said painfully.

"Why not, pal? If it's short."

"You only get paid if you crack me?"

"Don't be so fucking bright, sucker," Babe said.

Jeff, the more amiable murderer, said, "Pal, we get paid no matter what. I told you before. The people who hire us know they are getting professionals. The way Heifetz plays a violin is the way we beat a man. No question about him cracking."

"But you wouldn't want to lose one," I said. "That's why you're after me like this."

"We never lose any," Jeff answered, still willing to talk. "We've done jobs for clients everywhere, people who know what's what and demand the best. We never lose any, pal."

I didn't say anything and Jeff said, "Now talk. And this is the last time I'll say it to you, sucker."

We were back to sucker and I knew he meant what he was saying. They were behind schedule and all the stops were about to come out. Some more beating, some more burning, some more of everything except worse. I couldn't stand the idea of another punch or a knee in the groin or whatever the routine would be. But I had one more shot at it and said, "You'd better call your client and tell him it's not working."

Babe came forward and Jeff let him at me. "That's the last of that shit with this guy," he growled, a brutal, unfeeling man with fists like frozen hams.

I tried to ward him off but he dragged me from the chair and began to beat me up and I was in no shape to avoid him. I collapsed to my knees and he grabbed my head and lifted his knee against my face and I felt something crack. Then he yanked me to my feet and held me by the shirt front and raked my belly with his free hand about five times. None of them was as good as his uppercut had been, not as good as Jeff's body-shots, and I supposed he had trouble with his punches downstairs. But they were good enough, and Jeff's voice came from behind him, "Careful, you'll put him away for good like that."

Babe flung me away from him and across the room as if I weighed a hundred and five pounds. I hit a wall and fell down. I couldn't take any more and I vomited and choked and couldn't catch my breath and couldn't talk. Babe came at me with a kick but at the last second was pulled back. "Wait a second, you'll croak this guy," Jeff whined impatiently. "He's ready, can't you see that? One more shot and he won't know who's president."

I couldn't stop heaving, convulsions ripping through me, my muscles on fire and pounding like a million pulses gone wild. I heard Jeff's voice again. "You're ready, ain't you, pal? I sure hope so for your sake." He sounded genuinely concerned for me.

"Yeah . . . Yeah, I'm ready," I said in a choking voice, my dignity gone, the life beaten out of me, the smart, experienced adult who liked all the right ties and jackets and Cole Porter and George Gershwin and who had been made a commissioned officer at twenty under fire in the war ground down into a quivering and helpless infant. "I'm ready . . ." I couldn't recognize my own voice and couldn't even hear it very well.

"That's good, pal," Jeff said, as if he were actually relieved. "Now you're being sensible. And you ain't got a thing to be ashamed of. I don't think I've seen two other guys as tough as you."

"Okay, monkey," Babe said, standing a few feet away from me as if I were too dirty to touch now. "Where is it?"

I told them. They had done to me exactly what they had said they would and I told them where it was. They had cracked me and I wanted to crawl into a hole and cover up my losses, my beating, and all my memories. These two guys had put me in that state of mind in just about half an hour.

"Okay, pal," Jeff said. "Babe will stay here with you until I call him on the phone and tell him you weren't jerking us. Which I don't think you are. Babe, help him up and let him get cleaned up in the bathroom if he wants to."

"Sure. Anything to make him happy."

I just lay there braced on one elbow waiting for the dry heaves to subside. I heard Jeff walk out of the place and then I heard a car start up. Then I heard myself groaning faintly.

37

I COULDN'T STAND up yet and I didn't want to try right away. But I moved on my hands and knees to put distance between me and where I had been sick on the floor. I was panting for breath and still feeling the heaves, even though not as bad as at first. Babe said, "It had better be like you say, sucker."

I didn't answer him but propped my back against the pedestal of the armchair. There was a bridge table and folding chairs also and a pullout sofa but nothing else in that room. I let my eyes drift while I sat there panting slowly so I could take in the place and maybe get some kind of a clue to where it was and who owned it. A folding shutter-door concealed what I was sure was a small stove and a kitchen sink. I assumed there was a bathroom in back of me. It was just a shack at the beach and maybe it belonged to no one at the moment. Maybe these two monkeys had broken into it because they knew it was vacant or maybe it belonged to a friend of theirs. It would take some doing to relocate the place. The atmosphere had no distinguishing features I was aware of, no special look or smell or sound. But I was suddenly sure these two had no intention of letting me walk out of that place or even crawl out alive. I don't know why.

I sat on the floor with my legs outstretched, my hands limp alongside my thighs, my back against the base of the armchair, my head almost lolling, my face smeared with blood and maybe tears, my mouth open for breath, and I looked up at the bastard in the nylon stocking mask standing in the center of the room, his hands at his sides as he stared at his handiwork. He said, "Ain't you a beautiful sight, sucker?"

I just kept gasping for breath, getting it back slowly but feeling very sick, everything throbbing. I looked at him.

"You got a wife or a girl friend, sucker? Or maybe one of each, huh? Wouldn't they like to get a look at you now. You'd make them puke. You'd make anyone puke."

I had had his number right from the start — the one whose only pleasure came in giving pain, the man who liked his work well enough to carry it around with him at all times. The other bum was strictly a professional, just as he had said. But this one, Babe the whipper, the head-puncher, the flesh-burner, and groin-kicker, liked his job enough to do it free of charge. I was sure of that now. Humiliation and physical agony inflicted on others was what made him tick. I just looked at him with my open mouth sucking air, the blood still trickling from what I knew to be a busted nose. And he wasn't going to let go. There was still some more to be done to me, if not physically, emotionally and psychologically, more fun to be had.

"How about it, sucker? You got a wife or some broad you're fucking?"

I didn't answer, just kept looking and feeling white-hot hate for what I saw. I wanted to get his nerves heated if I could. And when he said, "Have you?" I kept right on looking at him with my head tilted back and cocked to one side as if it were dangling there from nearly being knocked off.

"Don't want to talk about it, huh?" he said, and snorted. "That's okay. We saw you go into that apartment with a good-looking blond cunt when we were waiting for you. You doing it to her? If you are, you won't be doing it . . . for quite a while."

I saw he was tailing off because he wasn't getting anywhere with me and his mind couldn't make quick shifts. So I said to him, "And what do you do it with? A pig? Or is a pig too particular for that?"

He just stood there like a man made of stone, as if he couldn't believe his ears. I gave him another salvo. "Maybe that leaves you either your wife or your mother."

My tongue was thick but the message got through.

Babe slowly reached for his back pocket and pulled out a .38 revolver which he leveled loosely at me. "As soon as Jeff was going to call to say you were telling the truth I was going to put a slug right through your skull," he said with the dull rasp of hate in his voice. "But now it's not going to be that way . . ."

I had my answer. My suspicions were all too justified. The funny thing was I didn't care. Not that I wanted to die. But the thought didn't scare me. Not at that point, looking and feeling the way I did, a hundred and fifty-grand down the drain, a million dollars in diamonds for which I was responsible hijacked from me. My love of life was at a low ebb right at that moment. I just wanted to get this bastard to make a dumb move, any kind of a dumb move, even if it meant my curtain.

"First I'm going to let you have a bullet right in the nuts," he told me. "And I'm going to let you sit there until Jeff calls . . . just let you sit there and bleed."

"What if Jeff tells you I gave you a stall? That they're not there."

He shook the blurred face back and forth and said confidently, "You didn't, sucker. We know that. Waiting like this is just a technicality."

"They'll nail you," I said. "There's too much to boomerang on you, too many loose ends, too many leads you don't know anything about . . ."

"We're in the clear," he said. "There are other people with a motive. The drug pushers you killed. They could of done it. Their pals. They even sent threatening notes about it, we know that . . ."

"Who's in back of you?" I said thickly.

"Maybe I'll tell you just as you're croaking," he said.

"Fuck yourself," I said, to goad him. "Fuck your mother too. Fuck your whole family . . ."

I was hoping he would want to put his hands on me for that. He did. He took those two steps forward that I was gambling on. And the hate I felt was a momentary substitute for strength and energy, and I jerked forward with my last inch of guts and grabbed his ankle. It was an unexpected move and it worked.

I pulled his foot with a short, sudden tug and toppled him

backwards. Not all the way, just half way between falling and keeping his balance. He yelled the usual things at me and recovered quickly and rushed toward me where I still sat on the floor, his gun ready, his body crouched to fling itself on me, as if he was going to beat, strangle, and shoot me all at the same time. And that was when I went to the long-shot idea I had been entertaining for the past minute or two. And I reached back over my shoulder to the one lamp in the room, sitting on a low end table right next to the armchair I was braced against, not twelve inches away from my right ear. It had a billowing potter's base and a long stem, which I grabbed hold of as Babe was regaining his balance. I brought it down in an arc as I continued to sit where I was. And as I did the shade snapped off where the stem is connected to the finial. And I realized that I had grabbed it at the lampshade connection, much too high, and that the base had become a flying object rather than a club. Which hadn't been my plan.

It hit Babe and knocked the gun out of his hand. But it didn't hit him in the head and it hardly slowed him down. He was on me with a rush and the promise to tear out my guts. And I used what I had left. The lampshade.

I rammed it down over his head with absolutely no hope and as I did I was reminded of guys who put on lampshades to be the life of the party. I had heard about them but I had never seen one. And Babe was not that type. I couldn't believe it when he let out an air-splitting scream of pain and rocked back on his knees. I never expected that kind of result. It was a futile, laughable effort and I had known it. But agonized cries were coming out of him from under that lampshade as he hulked there on his knees and seemed to be carefully trying to remove the thing.

I was still bright enough to know that things had been turned around very suddenly for me. And I was strong and energetic enough to scramble for the fumble, as Don called this kind of break. On my hands and knees I got to that fallen .38 and scooped it up. Babe and I were now both on our knees about ten feet apart, and he was reduced to sharp rhythmically spaced cries of pain, like a coxswain's call. "Oh! Oh! Oh! Oh!" And he was slowly and carefully removing the lampshade from his head where it had been attached, I could see, by about two inches of a snapped rim-spoke that had pierced his right eye socket, from which blood was now streaming down his cheek, soaking the nylon that still covered his face, a bloody hole in it where once an eye had peered through.

He was turned toward me with the lampshade in his hands in front of him as if it were a box containing gifts, and he was spitting words of hate through his disbelief and shock, all the vile and numbing words that have been heard so often before. I looked at him and said, "You've got a run in your stocking, Babe." And holding the gun steady with both hands I shot him twice. Once in the chest, once in the head, fast. He went down hard and didn't move. I fell on my face and gasped for breath again.

I knew he was dead and I just lay there, glad I had killed him but knowing it was too late to matter. A forty-nine-year-old man beaten up on the floor of a strange house, his only chance for a decent chunk of dough out the window, his last chance for a cruise through purple passionflowers gone, his future behind him, doesn't figure to have much to feel hopeful about. And I didn't. And then I realized that I had a line to the outside, that there was a telephone somewhere.

I raised myself up on my hands and knees and it was not easy. I looked around in the now nearly dark room, the glow of a rose-filtered bulb coming from a wall bracket across the room. The phone was on the floor in a corner near the window which was covered by a lowered venetian blind. I could see it clearly enough even with only one eye, the other eye swollen shut. I struggled to get up and stay on my feet long enough to stagger past Babe's dead body. I reached the phone and went down on the floor with it and carefully dialed Don's number. My heart was beating faster with the hope that he was at home and then I remembered that it was very late and he had left us to go home to sleep hours before.

In the middle of the second ring his voice came through and I knew I had awakened him. "Hello . . ."

"Don, it's Jim . . ."

"Jim?"

"Yes."

"What's up?" Then: "You okay? You sound . . ."

"No, I'm not okay, I've been waylaid by a couple of strong-arm guys working for somebody who's after the jewelry," I said, talking as fast as I could through my discomfort. And then the tough part somehow was saying, "And they beat it out of me . . ."

"Jesus, are you very badly hurt?"

"Plenty, but I'll live. Now listen to me and then move faster than you ever did in your life, kid . . ."

"Sure, sure, go ahead, Jim, what is it?"

"One of the goons is dead. I shot him. But the other one is on his way to my post office box in Hollywood — the one on Wilcox. I keep it for emergencies. In it is a key to a TWA wall locker at L.A. International where I have had the jewelry stashed for the past week. You might be able to head the goon off because he's got a long drive from here in front of him . . ."

"Keep talking, Jim, I'm getting my pants on right now. What's the number of the box?"

"Two thirty-seven, and the combination is two to the left stopping at ten . . ."

"Yeah . . ."

"One to the right stopping at five . . . and then a full spin left stopping at zero. You got that?"

"Got it."

"There's just a chance if you break a few speed laws. He probably won't do that, so you might, just *might,* catch him or even get in ahead of him . . ."

"Right."

"Anyhow, it's worth a try. If you do, get the key out and run with it . . ."

"Should I go to the airport and get the stuff?"

"No, no, too risky. I want those Brinks guards to pick it up. Somebody's too close for comfort and they might know more than we think they do and it might lead them right to you. No. Soon as possible, mail the thing to Steven Elson at Coastal Manufacturers Trust and Savings. That's the safest move right now."

"Jim, where the hell are you?"

"I don't know. Somewhere at the beach, but it could be San Diego for all I could tell. Don't worry about that. I can use this phone and get help. Just you get going."

"I'm on my way."

"But look, if you happen to catch up with him at the box, watch yourself. He's big and vicious. Don't take chances. Get in back of him and watch his elbows."

"Don't worry."

I hung up and then picked up the receiver again and dialed the operator and said, "Operator, can you tell me where the prefix eight-two-three is located?"

"That's Mar Vista."

"Thank you. Would you connect me with the Mar Vista sheriff's station?"

38

I WAS OUT COLD by the time I got collected from that house, and I never knew a thing about the ambulance ride that got me to the Santa Monica Hospital where I finally found myself.

I woke up and it was dark except for a small night-light glowing softly on a rheostatic wall-switch. For an instant in my grogginess I thought I was back in the shack with that dull red glow. Then I remembered talking to the Mar Vista cops on the phone and giving them the number so they could trace my location and come and get me. I remembered nothing after that.

The blinds were drawn in the room and the door was closed, but the more awake I became the more I could perceive time. I could faintly make out a glimmer of daylight outside the window of the room. I must have been under for hours, maybe with a shot of something administered by a doctor.

I put my hand to my jaw. It was swollen but I could move it and I didn't think it was broken. The rest of my face had been cleaned up, naturally, and swabbed off, a bandage on my nose and one on my head, some sort of dressing behind my left ear held by adhesive that wound around my forehead and made a full circle to the back of my skull. The spot ached dullishly, more and more as I came awake. It was where I had taken the sap to begin with. They must have broken something back there, and here I was a hospital patient, sick, feverish, beat, down in the basement of life. And all the questions were starting to crowd in on me, the hows and the whys and the wherefores.

I began to stir. Fever and a cracked skull or not, I had to get into motion, find out who was where and what was happening. I raised myself a little so I could look for a signal bell, sore and aching but too anxious to care. I found it dangling behind me just inches from my reach. I pressed the button and could hear nothing. But within seconds a nurse came into the room. They had been waiting for me to show signs of life.

She turned the rheostat light higher and came toward me saying, "How do you feel?"

"Okay. Let some daylight into the room, will you?"

"Sure," she said and opened the venetian-blind slats, and I could see she was a quick-moving, chunky little redhead about thirty years old who was ready to do what she could to make me happy. "I'd like to take your temperature before we do anything else," she said, coming alongside the bed. "And then we'll have the doctor look at you."

"Give me a telephone," I said. "I've got some calls to make right away. What time is it?"

"Nine forty-five and try to take life a little easy for the moment, huh?"

"Don't sit on me, sister, I'm not five years old," I said. "I've got people to contact."

"And you've got some recovering to do. You might not have noticed but this isn't your living room or your favorite nightclub. Come on, be good and give me a reading."

I let her stick the thermometer in my mouth and she walked out of the room for a couple of minutes while I lay there. No phone was visible. She came back with a young doctor and she took the thermometer from me and read it as he said, "You've had a good going-over, sir."

"I admit it, doctor," I said, and I realized I could see him clearly out of only one eye, that my left eye was puffed up and almost completely shut.

"By person or persons unknown?" he asked.

"That's about it."

"A hundred and four-fifths," the nurse muttered to herself and then wrote it down on my chart.

"Let's take a look," the doctor said, gathering my covers down to the groin and lifting the hospital smock they had dressed me in. "Slight ecchymosis," he decided. "But not as bad as the facial area." He put his hands gently on me and found what he was looking for. "You're going to have to be strapped. That's a fractured asternal, I'm sure."

"I have a feeling I'm not going to die from any of this, doctor, and I would like to find out what's been going on in the last four or five hours, and I'd like to make a phone call or two."

"It's on the floor next to your bed and you can use it. But first let me do what I'm paid to do, Mr. Blaney," he said, and continued the poking and pressing routine — palpation, they call it — and he found plenty of tenderness. But he said, "You don't seem to have any internal injury and that makes you very lucky. Or tough. But you should be X-rayed. We set your nose, by the way. It was broken. That doesn't surprise you, I'm sure."

"No. Look, has anybody been here asking for me?"

"There were some policemen earlier," my nurse said. "And there's someone in the waiting room right now. Miss Perry."

"Oh, is she? And the policemen are all gone?"

"Except for a cop sitting in the hall," the doctor said. "How's that head feel?"

"Wonderful. How long has Miss Perry been here?"

"A couple of hours that I know of," the nurse said. "Ever since I came on. Want me to send her in now?"

I took a breath and the redhead seemed to read my mind and she said, "Don't let it bother you too much. She was in here while you were asleep and so nothing is going to come as too much of a shock to her."

"Okay."

"You have a doctor of your own, I assume," said the tall young man, all white and shiny in his high-neck hospital tunic.

"Well, in a way. But forget it for now, there's no reason to call him on my account. Was a Mr. Price here?"

"Maybe," the nurse said. "But not since I've been on. Would you like some toast and tea?"

"Coffee."

"Lay off the caffeine, at least for today, Mr. Blaney," the doctor said. "We're trying to calm your nerve-ends, not stimulate them. You're going to have to do some heavy relaxing over the next few days if you want to heal in half the time it will take you otherwise. You're pretty lucky as it is."

"Anybody can see that," I said.

"Should I send Miss Perry in?" the nurse said.

I sighed and it hurt the fractured asternal. "Yes, I suppose so," I said.

"Don't worry about it," Rusty the nurse said. "She's just glad you're alive."

"Keep him on the aspirin for the fever," the doctor said. "And start the proteolytic enzyme right now." He started to walk toward the doctor, adding, "And, oh, Miss Reynolds, tell Doctor Bradman to strap that ribcage right away. Let me know if there's anything you want, Mr. Blaney." And he was gone.

I said to Rusty, "Just put that phone on the table so I can reach it."

Then she left also and Bedelia came in. There were tears in her eyes as she came alongside the bed.

"It's okay," I said. "There's plenty to cry about, sweetheart, but not about my health."

"Funny. I don't give a damn about anything *but* your health right now," she said.

"Have you talked to Don?" I asked.

"Yes, he called me from here at about six o'clock this morning and I came over and met him . . ."

"You mean you've been here since — what? Seven o'clock?"

"What did you think I would do? Wait to hear from you sometime next week?"

"What did Don tell you?"

"It was too late," she said in just the tone of voice needed to say somebody had died on the operating table. She closed her eyes a moment and said, "Your box was empty."

I took my hand off the phone. "Then you've got the whole story, the whole beautiful piece of golden screwing," I said in a frustrated, rambling way, turning my head to one side on the pillow. "I thought I had a prayer because I had gotten loose within a few minutes after the goon took off for the post office . . ."

"Don will be back later," Bedelia said. "He was with the cops until eight o'clock. I told him to go home and get some sleep."

"That was it, was it?" I said, looking into those expressive, still moist blue eyes looking down at me. "That was all? . . ."

"Don't let it matter," she pleaded. "I know how it sounds, but it's only money, damn it. I only wish you hadn't taken *this* for it. I wish you had given it to them."

"I did give it to them, that's just the point," I said, sore with myself somehow.

"I mean right away," she said. "Or at least after the first punch or two when you could see what they meant to do. What good would it be if you were dead or in a wheelchair?"

"I had to defend it, didn't I?" I said. "We all worked like steeplejacks for that payoff. I had to try to hold on to it. I just couldn't take as much as I thought I could. And they got it out of me. And now someone else is probably already sitting with the stuff in his or her lap, waiting to be fenced in Hong Kong or somewhere for plenty while we hang from a clothesline being philosophical about the whole thing, huh? . . ."

She didn't say anything, just took my hand and held it gently. "But who?" I said, and screwed up my eyes trying to puzzle it out, the swollen one paining me for my trouble. "Which one of the little sweethearts killed two men and did this to me so he could get his hands on those rocks? Mrs. Colby and Ganner, after all the smart calls I was making on them? Or Merrilee and Craig? Well, she made a pitch to me up in Mariposa Beach, didn't she? And Haggard Colby once tried to fling me down a flight of stairs. Brotherly love is not his strong suit. He could very easily feel entitled to that jewelry. Or someone else. Ackerman, maybe . . ."

"I just keep thinking that I hope you're okay and in one piece," she said with a faint, mirthless smile. "And you keep thinking about the God-damned money."

"I keep thinking about a lot of things, sweetheart," I said, like someone who was either a little paranoid or who had the trickiest idea anyone ever had. "I keep thinking about all those damned fine cops who have been on the case . . . Not just about Ganner and Merrilee and the Colby brothers and people like that. I keep thinking about those cops too . . ."

She looked at me just the way I thought she would, suddenly very interested and a little bit perplexed. "That's right," I said. "I could name six of them right off hand who know all there is to know about that part of things. The diamond jewelry hidden away in a safe place. They all know about it from me directly . . . And that's been bothering me more and more since last night."

One of the interns, I supposed, came in to strap me, and I stopped talking.

Bedelia stood at the window while he did the job, and I said, "Think this will hold me together for a while yet, doc?"

He didn't crack a smile and said, "In your shape it would take the Wizard of Oz to do that."

The binding he did made me feel better, less busted up. I thanked him and as soon as he walked out I began bitching again. "So there goes the dough for Loretta's tuition, the boat ride for you and me, and my reputation — all in one package. And there will be a lot of suspicious lawyers and bankers, and maybe even private detectives and insurance investigators all over me because about a million bucks in diamonds that I was in charge of just happens to be missing."

"Suspicious of you?" she said. "After they see this beating you've had? They'd have to be insane."

"For what that stuff will bring a lot of people would take a beating. And have."

"A beating maybe, but not a pulverizing," she insisted. And then, "How crazy you were, darling."

"And I thought I was being very logical about the whole thing," I said.

Her soft smile was transmuted into a questioning frown. "But why the policemen?" she said, suddenly reminded.

"Because there isn't one chance in a thousand that amateurs hired those two guys," I said. "They talked just enough to convince me they're known only in special circles. To a Ganner, maybe, or some other crook or racketeer who would have a line on people like them. Or . . . a cop."

"Oh."

"They talked a lot about their professional standing and about hiring out only to clients who wanted the best in their particular line of work, that kind of junk," I said. "It's guesswork, I admit. But who else would know about people like them except other people with a connection somewhere? . . ."

"That pretty well lets out Colby's relatives, doesn't it?" she said.

"Not all the way, but some," I said. "I'd move Ganner's flag in a little closer to the center."

"So would Don. And he has some crazy idea about going back to

Vegas. I just remembered him saying something about it."

"They'd kill him this time."

"He says he knows a couple of people he could get to go along. I think he's insane. And I think it's insane even to think about any of it any more. It's over and there's nothing we can do about it."

Rusty came in with the tray of tea and toast and we stopped talking, of course. "I'd like you to take the aspirin and this little mint pill as soon as you finish your food," she said. "The mint pill has to go into you every two hours until tomorrow morning."

"What is it?"

"It reduces the edema."

"The swelling?"

"That's right. Do you need to void?"

"We all need to, nurse," I said.

"I mean at the moment," she came back, unruffled. "I have to have a specimen. But it's up to you — now or after you've eaten." She put a small specimen jar on the table next to me.

As she headed for the door I said, "How do you know I won't give you the wrong specimen? Maybe Miss Perry's."

She didn't reply and Bedelia laughed in shock. "Jim, how crude."

"Yeah," I said, starting to raise myself up to get out of bed. "Something about lying here like this brings that out in one. I'll hate myself when I'm back in my right mind again."

She started to laugh again and then was horrified to see me trying to get over the edge of the bed. "Jim, you can't get up," she said, rushing around to the side I was struggling on.

"Why not? She didn't say not to."

"She didn't take you for a moron."

"I'm under orders to pee for the lady," I said, slightly lightheaded through all the pain. "And I can't disobey."

"You're supposed to use the thingamabob over there," she said. "See? It looks like a perfect fit."

"It's all of about five feet into that bathroom," I said. "Just give me the right equipment and I'll get the job done."

"You're so weak right now that even I could keep you down if I wanted to," she said.

"I'll take you up on that sometime," I said, feeling a little rocky on my pins as I set my feet on the floor, a bandage buffering the burned one, and headed for the bathroom, grabbing that stupid hospital-smock to close the gap in back exposing my behind. "You'll have to bring me some pajamas," I said, and shut the bathroom door. Then I did what had to be done. My urine was red with blood.

I stood there and my legs shook a little. I gave the little jar its small percentage and then put it in the medicine chest. I didn't want Bedelia to get even a glimpse of it. I went back where she was waiting and got into bed. I began to eat the toast and drink the tea. Before I was done I swallowed the various pills and I said to her, "Listen, baby, there's no sense in your hanging around here right now . . ."

She kept her face blank and I added, "You can do something for me, in fact. Get my medical insurance policy out and let the agent know what's happened. His name is Harry Burns. Maybe you can pick up the forms from him and help me fill them out later on or tomorrow. It's in the accordion folder in the lower left-hand drawer in my desk."

"I know. I guess you're as washed out as you can be."

"Just a little. The pills do that."

That was the way I got rid of her. I was feeling old and angry and a little scared and I didn't want her around to be a witness to it. I finished the toast and tea without any zest and then lay there until Rusty came back and asked for the specimen. A nurse's aid took the tray and I told Rusty the specimen was in the medicine chest. She looked at me funny, of course, but when she came out with it in her hand she understood. "I just didn't want Miss Perry to get a look at it accidentally," I said.

"Don't worry about it," she said. "It's common enough after this kind of a beating. It's part of the trauma. You'll be all right in a few days."

"You don't see me shaking all over, do you?" I said.

"Oh, what a sweet disposition," she said benignly, and left me there to myself. I fell asleep then. It was a funny shift from the infantile bout of bathroom humor and the giddiness to the curdled feeling I now had even in my sleep.

39

I WAS AWAKE before Rusty came in to get the mint-flavored enzyme pill into me and said, "There's a policeman outside, a Lieutenant Wagner. But you don't need to see him unless you're up to it. We can keep him out."

"I'm glad I've got that choice. But send him in."

She had her hand on my forehead. "I think you're cooler. How about a lamb chop for lunch?"

"If you're the one to cook it," I said.

"Are you always this frisky or only after you've been beaten up? Here, swallow this."

Wagner came in, hatless, wearing a brown suit and tie, and that same matter-of-fact, undramatic manner of his looked different to me now than it had before. Now it was a possible cover-up. "Well, this puts you out of the running as far as the murders are concerned," he said.

"I never knew I was *in* the running," I said.

"Well, not up front maybe, but not really all the way out of it until now," he said, standing at the foot of the bed looking at me. "You're in the clear now."

"Fine. But what makes you so sure that whoever did this to me was necessarily the same one who killed Colby and Brooks?" I said.

That surprised him. But he answered, "There's a pattern. If

you buy the idea of the same murderer on both Colby and Brooks — and I do for all the reasons you yourself give for it — then the jewelry was his original motive in those two crimes. So why should we assume he wouldn't be quick to go after you once he knew you were the only key to getting his hands on it? Someone who commits two murders for profit has a big investment in it." He shrugged. "Why should we look for another party coming out of left field to do this?"

"Just asking, Lieutenant."

"Can you tell us anything about the people who did it? Such as what they said or anything they may have let drop that could lead us to who's behind them?"

"Did you make the guy I shot?"

"Oh, yeah. Sonny Temple. A hood out of Chicago — a hit-man and a strong-arm boy with just a couple of short-term convictions. No gang affiliation, just for hire. To do jobs like this one." He gestured vaguely in my direction. "His only known contact was Artie Buck Ryan — another of the same kind. No gang affiliation but plenty of contacts. For hire. Also out of Chicago. If the mob doesn't want a certain kind of job to come too close to home they hire a crazy like him. Stops at nothing. We think Ryan was the other guy with Sonny who worked on you." He paused and then said, "And here is what I really came up here to tell you. And it's a beaut."

"I'm ready."

"Okay. We found this same Artie Buck Ryan in an alley about a hundred feet off Hollywood Boulevard a little while ago with two slugs in him. He still had his ring and a wallet stuffed with hundred-dollar-bills. Probably dead about eight hours."

I grunted and said, "I'll be damned."

"Didn't expect to hear that, did you?"

"No."

"Can you add anything to what your partner told us?"

"Don?"

"Yes. He called us to find out if we had a report on you because he had no idea where you had called him from," Wagner said. "We had heard from Mar Vista by that time and we met him here at about three in the morning."

"You didn't get much sleep, did you?"

"I've had a few hours. I go on vacation next week anyway."

"Did he tell you about the key in the post office box?"

"Yes, he did."

"Well, then you've got it all. That's what happened. All I can add to it is that the bigger guy, who must have been Ryan, if you're right about it, bragged considerably about being a professional hired only by people who want the best. And at the moment I'm pissing blood just to prove how right he was."

"No names, huh?"

"They didn't get around to that," I said. "It looks like Ryan met his client with the key from my post office box or with the combination and location, and the client paid him off. Not too smart of Ryan. That part surprises me."

"Maybe he wasn't looking for it."

"Obviously. But why? Who's the client?" I looked right at Wagner from where I was propped up on my pillows. "It might not be the same one who murdered Colby and Brooks. It might be someone who got in on it only after it was out in the open."

"You're back to that again, are you?" He screwed up his forehead and looked bothered. "What are you trying to say?"

"That a pro of some kind hired Artie and Sonny — not a greedy uncle or a jealous business partner — a pro who just might or might not be the one who killed Colby and Brooks. That's all I'm saying at the moment, Lieutenant. Except that I'd be damned interested in that ballistics report."

"Ballistics?"

"You're going to check the slugs in Ryan against the ones that came out of Colby, aren't you?"

"Sure we are," he said, but I wasn't sure he had had it in mind until I mentioned it. Cops sometimes get so loaded down with details that the simplest matters escape their notice. "You must think we're dummies," he added with a forced smile.

"I'm one of your biggest boosters, Lieutenant, remember?" I said. "But I'll tell you something else. I'd be even more interested in the whereabouts of a half dozen policemen I could name at about one o'clock this morning. Which I assume is just about the time Artie was bumped off."

Wagner narrowed his eyes and in what was an angry voice for him, he said, "I think the beating went to your head, Blaney."

"That's very funny, Lieutenant."

"You know what I mean. You're taking potshots."

"Maybe. But I just lost myself a hundred-and-fifty-thousand-dollar fee the hard way. And that hasn't made a diplomat out of me."

I had nothing to lose with a hit-'em-in-the-face approach. He was right, it was potshots. And I'd have taken them at Saint Francis if he had been there, just to be sure I had left no stone unturned. Wagner sensed as much and he gave me a sour smile and said, "I'm not going to be offended, Blaney. I know how it is. And the theory isn't that crazy, to be honest. But it's *just* a theory and don't let it carry you away, if you're smart." He added in a cool voice, "Wild charges have a way of backfiring sometimes."

As he was walking toward the door I said, "You'll let me know about the ballistics, won't you?"

"Sure. I hope your head gets better."

I said, "Thanks," and I dozed a little bit after he left. I woke up when the door opened slowly and Don walked in. "I hope you feel better than you look," he said.

I said, "I think anybody would."

"They said you had no internal injuries but that you had some fever."

I put my hand up to forestall further conversation on the subject so I could concentrate all my strength on getting out of bed and getting to the bathroom. Don gave me a hand and I said, "Thanks. Just a quick leak."

I went into the bathroom and once again urinated blood.

When I came out and headed for the bed, Don said, "I think we were dead wrong, Jim. Ganner got back into it with both feet. It was just like Bedelia said. He can read. And he knew about the murder and that you were still the guy with the ice. Hell, it was all over the TV news and in the papers like an open invitation for him to take a crack at you."

"It was there for everybody."

"Sure. But none of the other people are that quick, that nuts, and that smart all at the same time, you know what I mean, Jim?"

"Maybe."

"I mean, this is no hysterical daughter or crazy brother. It's not their kind of thing because they don't know how it's done or who to go to."

"I'm with you on that," I said.

He shook his head. "Okay. You know this guy Eisenberg? The one who came to Vegas to deal with Ganner for the jewelry?"

"The fence."

"Well, he's in L.A. He runs a dump hotel on Seventh Street near Vermont. And I'll tell you what I've done. I hired Buddy Hughes to watch him. He was very effective for us before, remember?"

"Wait a minute, Don. Even if you're right, Eisenberg might not want to handle this stuff from Ganner now because he knows there's a murder involved."

"I think Ganner will either come to him or he'll go there. And I think we can get the stuff back the minute they meet because nobody'll be expecting it."

"Listen, Don, get yourself onto something else. The whereabouts between midnight and two a.m. last night of a list of cops I'm going to supply you with in a minute."

He stared at me in surprise. "Cops?"

"We agree on this thing up to a point. You say it's Ganner and I say it's a cop who screwed us out of our hard-earned money. And I've got some pretty good reasons for saying it."

Don looked at me attentively and waited to hear what I was getting at.

"First let me tell you that I think the only way to handle it is to talk to these particular cops pointblank and ask them directly to account for their moves. And if one of them is what I think he may be, you could be dead very fast. He'll lie first and then try to kill you before you can check up on his story."

"Isn't that the idea?"

"It's known as drawing enemy fire."

"Who do you have in mind, Jim?"

"I'll tell you who and why," I said. "Of the seven names, five are L.A., two are Mariposa Beach — that's Carrodas and Praxy. The others are Sergeants Birney and Saunders in Homicide; Sergeants Keely and Poulter in Narcotics. And our friend Lieutenant Wagner, who is already on guard because I put him there a little while ago." I nodded a little to emphasize it when I added, "There could be others. But these all know me by sight. And that's important to some extent because any one of them could point me out in a hurry. Not a big factor but something. Now the thing that makes me go for this is that there are so many of them and they all know about the jewelry from right up close. Number two, a cop, if he's a bad apple, could conceivably put an idea like this together very fast. He's familiar with the territory even if he's always been a straight cop and he wouldn't be timid about it. A cop, any cop, could get to an Artie Ryan and a Sonny Temple. As you just pointed out, civilians wouldn't know where to start to find people like that. They didn't exactly have an ad in the paper with a phone number and address. Number three, Artie Ryan is already dead. His client knocked him off as soon as the job was done. That damned well took a pro, from what I knew of Artie even under the stocking on his head . . ."

"Boy, that was fast."

"Now, there's one other interesting thing. I could say fascinating. And it almost rules Ganner out completely. Something you couldn't have known about until now because you weren't there."

"What's that?"

"After Ryan left me alone with Sonny, I told Sonny he couldn't get away with killing me. That was because he had already tipped off the fact they were going to do it, after all. They started off with stocking masks so I wouldn't suspect it and say, What the hell, why should I tell you anything at all? And then it came out. And I said to Sonny that there was too much in the whole case to lead right back to them and their client, whoever he was, if I was bumped off. And he said he knew there were other people with a strong motive for killing me. He knew about the dealer I had killed and said he knew that there were even threatening notes to prove a revenge motive on the part of the dealer's pals."

"He said that?"

"That's one thing that no one picked up in the newspapers or on TV because it had no relationship to anything; it was strictly an unknown item as far as the public was concerned. So obviously someone gave him that information to make him feel secure about killing me. Not that he wasn't a professional killer. But he might have had qualms about this one for certain reasons, he and Artie both. So he was told not to worry, the cops would be looking in another direction altogether for my killer."

"So that made him happier."

"Yes. Now *three cops* on our list actually *saw* the notes I received. Carrodas, Keely, and Poulter. In fact, the notes were left with Keely and Poulter for lab tests. So you can see what I'm driving at."

"I sure do."

"It's all circumstantial, and it might lead us nowhere. But it's all we've got. The blab about the notes is the strongest part of the whole idea. After that you can make it up for yourself and some of it works pretty well. Cops are just people. And even nuns go bad."

He shook his head. "I'll get moving on it." He got up from the straight-back chair he had been straddling front-to-back and said, "Listen, is there anything I can get for you?"

"No, I don't think so," I said, and then I had an afterthought. "Yeah, there is something, as a matter of fact."

"What?"

"Bring me my thirty-eight, will you?"

He looked at me funny and I added, "I know it sounds a little nutty. But just in case."

"It doesn't sound nutty to me. I'll take care of it."

"The one in the office."

He started for the door and I added, "Oh, and take Buddy Hughes with you on this . . . If you think you can trust him."

"He's okay," Don said, and walked out.

I lay there worrying for a while until my lunch tray arrived. I ate about half of what was there and then went back to sleep. There was very little else to do when you felt this tired.

40

In the afternoon Bedelia came back with the insurance forms, but I was in no mood or condition to bother with them, and we talked for a time and then were silent while she read a magazine and I listened to the radio she had also brought along. There was a TV set in the room and I didn't want to look at it just then. I dozed a little and after a while Rusty came in to push her enzyme pill and aspirins and to take my temperature. It was just a hundred, down four-fifths. "You don't have to hang around here, sweetheart," I said to Bedelia at around five o'clock. "Why don't you leave?"

"To go where and do what?" she said.

"All I'm going to do is sleep, darling. I'm not on my deathbed. I feel like an idiot lying here in a stupor with you just sitting there . . . I'll be livelier tomorrow. I couldn't be *less* lively than I am today anyhow. Look, why don't you go to a movie? Call your friend Gay, she's a nice straight kid, and go to see something. There were a couple of things around that weren't bad. Go ahead and do that for me. Meet her and have a hamburger or something and get your mind off me . . ."

"Oh, sure . . ."

"Give it a try. Call her now. Or call somebody else if you like."

"Okay."

She telephoned Gay and they talked for a couple of minutes and I was only vaguely aware of what was being said. When she hung up she said, "She's correcting test-papers tonight. So so much for that. But I'll go, if it will make you happier."

"I'll be better tomorrow, sweetheart."

She kissed me and left. I felt like hell and I just couldn't take having her in the room like that with me half-dead with medication and looking seventy years old. At least I *felt* seventy years old and fading fast. All I wanted to do was sleep. And except for the wake-ups by the night nurse for the enzyme pill I slept better than a roomful of babies until morning. And then I felt a lot better than I had been feeling. My fever was gone.

Bedelia came by just after lunch and I was sitting up and in a slightly different frame of mind than I had been in the day before. We even played gin and watched some daytime TV with the game shows and all of that and I wasn't feeling too bad. "Darling, you look much better today," she said.

"It's those pills," I said. "They take the swelling down just as advertised."

Rusty came in and said, "You're scheduled for an I.V.P. tomorrow morning at eight o'clock."

"I.V.P.? What kind of a pee is that?"

"It stands for intravenous pyelogram. Kidney X-ray to you."

"Oh." It depressed me somehow and I caught sight of Bedelia listening with wide attentive eyes as Rusty said, "You mustn't take in anything after dinner tonight — no solids or liquids. You won't take in anything in the morning either until the pyelogram is completed."

"You can count on me," I said lightly but was feeling let down.

When Rusty had left us alone Bedelia said, "Is anything wrong?"

"You mean beside the fact we never got to the purple passionflowers? Not a hell of a lot, sweetheart."

She nervously washed a deck of cards and put them aside. "I mean with you," she said. "I haven't talked to the doctor so I don't know."

"I'm fine."

"Why are they taking a kidney X-ray?"

"They like to take pictures. Nothing's wrong. That is, with me. Outside of that I can't think of anything that's right." I shook my head. "If only I hadn't been off guard when I walked out to my car . . ."

"How were you to guess at anything like that?"

"I was too complacent," I lamented. "Too ready to celebrate and load up on wine and whiskey. If I had been thinking I'd have had the sense to know we were going through a crucial period until I turned the diamonds over to the bank. What made me forget the fundamentals? I don't know. But I did. Otherwise I'd have looked around before getting into the car. They can't take you by surprise if you're waiting for them. When you know the whereabouts of a million dollars' worth of jewelry you have to assume that there are people who will kill you to get it. And that's what I was forgetting. And that's why I'm lying here like this and everything is in pieces . . ."

"Jim, darling, don't blame yourself this way," Bedelia said, getting up and standing next to me where I sat up in bed. "It's not like you . . ."

"Overnight a whole lot about me has changed forever. I never thought I couldn't take care of myself in any situation. I always thought I was in control of what happened to me. I had a four-star setup right in my hands and I blew it. I'll never see the same guy in the mirror again."

"You can't help feeling depressed now," she said. "Who could be any other way? But you'll feel different after you're up and around, you'll see."

"Everything is out of sync," I went on, almost unable to stop singing the blues once I had begun. A hospital will do that to you, at least it did it to me. "It's like you and me, love. I always said to myself, now that I'm about to become impotent and doddering I go ahead and meet up with a gorgeous young tomato like this." I laughed a little to take the sting out of it.

She sighed deeply and closed her eyes.

"I'm only sorry about our boat ride," I said. "It would have been swell."

"It's not the end of the world. Maybe we can take it sometime later on anyway."

"Sure. We can save up for it. What do you think it will take? About five years?" I added quickly, "Just kidding."

"No, you're not," she said almost grimly.

It was five o'clock by then and Don walked into the room. We all sort of looked at each other. Nobody was too happy and it was showing. "I talked to Sergeant Birney and Sergeant Saunders," Don said. "And they were none too polite with their answers."

I tried to high-sign Don but it was no use. Bedelia looked at both of us. "What kind of questions did you ask them?" she said.

"I asked them where they were at one in the morning two nights ago," Don answered her directly.

She looked at us as if we were both nuts. "Are you going to do the same thing with any other policemen?" she said. "What will that get you?"

"Well, maybe one of them will show his hand," Don said.

"You mean and maybe try to kill you," she said. "That's the only way he would show his hand if he's guilty. Is that what you're counting on?"

"We don't know exactly what we're counting on," Don answered. "But we might hit pay dirt because Jim is convinced one of these cops is the guy who hijacked the diamonds and I pretty much go along with that." He shrugged and looked at me.

"Go ahead, if you've any more to say," I said. "She's got the picture now."

"A guilty party who is told he's under suspicion is likelier to tip his hand than one who thinks he's in the clear. That is, he might get desperate. That's all we're counting on. Or that's what we're hoping for."

She shook her head like an expert who had been asked a technical question. "It's almost childish," she said. "And it's dangerous. If there's any real ground for the suspicion you should take it to someone higher up."

"Like who? Someone in the department who will automatically cover up for department members?" Don said.

"Not if there's concrete evidence, Don," she said wisely. "There's murder and grand theft involved. That's different, I would think, from other things."

"Well, why don't we drop it," I said. "It's making me tired. But don't worry about it, Bedelia. Nobody's going to try to kill us. They'll only have to look at us to start laughing their heads off."

She didn't say anything and just picked up her purse and went down the hall to freshen up. As soon as she was gone I said, "She's right. It *is* a lousy idea. We can keep trying. But all you can get out of it is a shot-in-the-dark hit on the right guy and then hope he will in some way expose himself."

"Or try to kill us," Don said, and put my .38 in my hand.

I looked at it and checked the cylinder automatically and put it in the nightstand drawer next to the bed. The stand was for the patient's personal effects and no one ever inspected it. "No, he's not even going to try to do that," I said, disgusted. "Why should he? All he has to do is let things cool off."

Don gave me a faintly superior look and said, "Why did he try to kill you to begin with? That was what he had in mind when he hired those two goons. You said so yourself."

I thought about it and said, "Well, maybe that was then and this is now. Maybe he doesn't need me dead now."

"Does that make sense?"

"I don't know," I said and let out a deeply inhaled breath. Then I added, "He *did* want me killed at that moment all right. There's no doubt of that." It still hurt to frown or squint but I did a little of each and took things further. "And he wanted the two goons dead eventually too. Otherwise he wouldn't have hit Artie Ryan the minute he finished doing business with him. The question is, how did he intend to get Sonny Temple?"

"Maybe sombody else killed Ryan."

"Never. But I think what happened as far as I was concerned is simple. If I had been killed right then and there no one would have known for sure there was a theft. I wouldn't have been around to say what happened."

"Well sure, there was a ready-made motive for your murder. They could have left you in a ditch and let people think that the friends of the guys you shot took their vengeance."

"Yeah," I drawled slowly, something bothering me. "But was it worth it? I don't know. Maybe it would have helped him. In fact, he wouldn't even have needed to move the jewelry from its hiding place if I were dead." I added ironically, "And maybe he *didn't* until he heard I *was*n't dead . . . But I don't know."

"Oh, he damned well moved it all right," Don said. "He must have been ten seconds in front of me all the way. And when I saw that your p.o. box was empty I beat it out to the airport like a shot. Christ, I wasn't going to leave *that* possibility unchecked. What the hell else did I have to do anyway? I was wide awake by then."

"He must have been going like hell."

"When I got there the TWA locker wasn't in use. If it had been I'd have staked it out until hell froze over. But the stuff *was* moved right away."

I stared sourly into space. "Yeah, well maybe it was just in the cards this way . . ."

"I figure the stuff will get broken up before it's fenced, don't you, Jim?"

I didn't answer and Bedelia came back into the room and said that I had begun to look tired. I said that in fact I *was* tired, but that life was like that when you got old and battered and bruised — not only by somebody's fists and feet, but by all the shocks and jolts that come when you least expect them.

Bedelia said, "How sad you sound, darling," a little catch in her voice. "Is it because of anything you've been told by the doctor? . . ."

"Is there something wrong, Jim?" Don asked.

"He's being X-rayed tomorrow morning for kidney damage," Bedelia said. "Miss Reynolds just told me."

"Oh, Jesus," Don muttered.

"That's not what's bothering me right now," I said. "It's something else."

They both seemed hardly aware of the fact that I had reached over and opened my nightstand drawer and removed from it the .38 Don had brought me. "I never thought I would have this in my hand this fast, if ever," I said. "Or for this reason." I looked at Don and said, "Empty your pockets, Don," aiming the gun right at him. "And don't palm anything."

41

BEDELIA looked thunderstruck and Don was no less than that and both of them stood there frozen stiff.

"Jim . . ." Don said my name and stopped. It was as if the breath had been kicked out of him. "What is this? Some kind of a rib?"

"Put everything in your pockets right on the table, Don, and then I'm going to tell you why I know you killed Colby and Brooks and Artie Ryan and tried to kill me to get your hands on the big bundle of diamonds."

Bedelia was wide-eyed. "Jim, am I going crazy?" she said.

"He did it all, sweetheart," I said, torn between rage and disappointment. It was as if a brother had turned out to be a Nazi spy during the war. "He almost got away with it and we'd never have known. And then finally he'd have killed me because he had to. That was part of it, wasn't it, Don?"

"Jim, I . . ."

I leveled the gun, just propped-up high enough through my pain and fatigue and my sore back where the banged-up kidney was, to have a controlled shot at him. "Don't count on the condition I'm in, Don," I said. "I'd have two through your skull if I wanted to before you could get at me. And you wouldn't want Bedelia in on anything like that, would you?" I squinted with the one good eye at him and added, "Or would you give a damn at that?"

"Jim, I don't understand," Bedelia said. "Don is your friend. This can't be real."

"It is real, Bedelia," I said. "You're going to be telephoning the police in a minute, that's how real."

By now Don was just looking at me, not with any particular emotion but with less shock and fake surprise at what was going on, no more of that can-this-really-be-happening look. "You made a couple of fundamental mistakes, Don," I went on. "One was killing Artie Ryan. You did kill him, didn't you, Don?"

"Jim, you're making a pretty big mistake of your own," he said, and there was the slightest catch in his manly western drawl, a touch of anger now in his eyes. "And I don't think we can ever be friends again. Not after this."

"Okay, Don. I'll just lay it out and let you listen and you can tell me where my mistakes are. Whoever hired Artie Ryan and Sonny Temple might have planned to get rid of them all right and with every good reason. But he wasn't going to be stupid enough to knock off Artie and not Sonny at the same time." I shook my head and kept the gun leveled. "Because that would have tipped Sonny off in very short order, and he'd have known just what to expect, and the client wouldn't be the smart, tough pro we know he is. Isn't that right, Don? Except that Sonny was already dead himself by then, wasn't he? He was dead because I had shot him. And who knew that I had shot him, Don? Nobody except you. Because I had told you on the phone. Nobody else had any idea — none of those cops we've been so suspicious of, for instance. If one of them had been the client, he'd never have killed Artie when they met because he'd have been afraid of Sonny. He'd have had to get them together. And he wouldn't have known where Sonny was by then because if I had been bumped off on schedule Sonny would have gone from the shack to meet Artie somewhere probably unknown to anyone but them. So he'd have had to wait. Just as *you* figured to do before you knew Sonny was dead. But I had done part of the job for you. And me you could get to later, right?"

I glanced at Bedelia who was stock-still and horrified by what she was seeing and hearing. I went on. "But that wasn't the big one, Don . . ."

He looked at me without expression at the moment, a big, athletic all-American image, neat, clean, groomed. "Empty out your pockets," I said again. "Turn out the linings."

He knew I wasn't kidding and that stalling wouldn't buy anything. And he did as I said while I trained the gun on him. "Now back up," I ordered. "Okay, that's far enough."

I fished one of the keys out of the change and various other items he had deposited on the nightstand. I held it up. It was a wall-locker key with a number cut clearly into the tab-head. "This, I'll lay odds, opens the door on the Colby jewelry," I said. "I figured you might have done that, Don — taken the jewels from one locker and put them in another. Why not? Why take them away from the airport? You needed somewhere to keep them until you were ready to pick them up and convert them into all that dough they're worth. Especially in today's market. And everything would have been jake. But your tongue skidded a little bit, Don, just enough to tell me everything. Because how could you have gone to the locker when I never told you where it was?"

"You *did* tell me," he insisted, as if it would overturn my case against him.

"Not the number," I said. "You said the locker was empty when you got out to the airport. How could you have known that when all I said was that it was a wall-locker at TWA? How could you have known which one if you hadn't seen the number on the key itself which I mailed to my p.o. box? I couldn't have told you the TWA number because I didn't know it. I still don't. If I had, I'd have told you to go directly to the airport and nab anyone who went to it. There are a tremendous number of lockers in that area. You knew which one it was because you already had the key on you. But you overdid things just now, Don, just the way you did that morning when you asked Wagner twice about how the body got into the elevator shaft, as if it baffled you. It was a conscious attempt to cover yourself up a little bit more. I didn't think anything of it at the time. But now I know what it was. And it wasn't necessary. No more than telling me how conscientious you were about going to the airport was. But for just one treacherous little split-second you forgot how you came to know the location of the locker, and that it wasn't through me. And that's the smoking gun in your hand as far as I'm concerned, Don."

"Am I hearing you right?" he said, parts of his face arranging themselves into a thinly disguised anger I had never seen before.

"You know you are. You probably met Ryan somewhere in Hollywood, let him give you the post office box combination — the one I had already given you on the plane — just to go through the motions with him, knocked him off, dropped him in the alleyway, picked up the key, and . . . that was that. When you got out to my locker you shifted the jewelry to another locker of your own. And this has to be the key to that locker, Don. This is what public-locker keys look like. I know that much."

"Jim, I don't know what to say," Don said. "I hear you but I don't believe it. I have to chalk it off to your condition, the way you must be feeling both mentally and physically."

"Don, you're not going to be bush on top of everything else, are you?" I said.

"Jim, maybe Don is right," Bedelia said, hating to believe any of it. "I mean, couldn't this all be a series of strange quirky coincidences that really don't prove anything? . . ."

"You'd like it to be that way, sweetheart, and so would I," I said, never taking my eyes off Don now as he stood there with almost nothing left but the instinct to stay cool. It didn't work because the eyes were fixed and tense. "But it's not that way, damn it, and he knows it."

"Jim, none of that would stand up in court, you know that," Don said. "It's circumstantial. It doesn't prove anything . . ."

"Only to me, Don, only to me. And that's what counts. I don't give a damn whether you ever get into court or not. But you will. Because I've got to tell the cops, Don. There's no way I can duck that. And what's going to hang you is ballistics. The slugs that went into either Colby or Ryan are going to be traced to one of your guns. I'm sure you didn't get rid of them because replacing them would have attracted attention to you. And as long as you weren't under suspicion for anything, you were safe. But that's all it will take now. They may never get you on Brooks's murder, but they won't have to."

"Don, is it true?" Bedelia said with pleading eyes.

He looked at her in a strangely expressionless way and she was starting to get the shocking message. I said, "You fit all the same angles any cop does, Don. And even a little better. Because you knew more about me than any cop did. None of them ever visited Bedelia or ever had any reason to know where she lived. Or knew that I would take her home the other night. And yet Sonny and Artie were waiting at her place — waiting because they knew we'd show up. So someone who knew our habits and routine intimately had to have sent them. Someone with all kinds of experience in criminal investigation and with contacts with all kinds of criminals. Like Sonny and Artie. You fit that description pretty well, Don."

Bedelia had sunk into the chair alongside of my bed. I glanced at her and went on. "Of course, this is all hindsight, because none of it ever crossed my mind until a few minutes ago. And now it won't let go. I couldn't kick any of it out if I wanted to. And neither can you, can you, Don?"

The collapse was slow but sure. He didn't talk at first and you could tell right away he was through denying anything. "I didn't want to kill you, Jim," he finally said. "I swear to God that hurting you was something I didn't want to do. You've got to believe that . . ."

"Oh, Don," Bedelia groaned.

"I needed that money, Jim," Don said, "more than I needed to breathe almost. And there wasn't anything I wouldn't have done to get it . . ."

Bedelia looked at him with disgust I had never seen in her eyes for anything or anyone in all the time I knew her, not even for Ganner.

"I know you needed it, Don," I said. "And I think I know what for. For Jean."

He shook his head. "That's it, Jim," he said. "She's in trouble with the business, the half-a-million dollar kind of trouble. She can't meet notes that are due and she can't get loans on anything."

"I know," I said. "And it's tough for a boy to see his mom in trouble, but all those dead men, regardless of their lowness of character, had no responsibility in her predicament. If they had, I'd have said, do what had to be done. And when it came to me . . ." I laughed faintly. "Well, you tell me."

"I didn't sleep easy over that, Jim, you've got to believe that."

"Oh, how terrible for you," Bedelia said contemptuously.

"It's true," Don said in a strangely hurt and pleading way. "I didn't want this to happen."

"No, Don," I said. "You didn't want this to happen. You had something else in mind — my body in a ditch with a half dozen slugs in it, so it would look like the drug crowd did the job. Just as you said before, there was a built-in motive for my murder right off the bat."

"Look, Jim. I just wanted the jewelry, nothing else. All I had in mind was the robbery."

"To begin with. But you knew I would put two and two together if all of a sudden Jean's fortunes took a miraculous upswing. And you couldn't take that chance. I was going to have to go, no two ways about it."

Bedelia made a choked groaning sound, her eyes filled with absolute loathing. "You're not human," she said through clenched teeth.

"Sure, he's human," I said. "He's a killer and a thief. And since when isn't that human? He loves his mother. He even loves us in his way, don't you, Don?"

"Hell, Jim, don't make light of me," he said resentfully.

I said, "Call the police downtown, Bedelia, and ask for Wagner or somebody working with him."

"I know you've got to do that, Jim, and I'm not sore at you for it," Don said. Then, "Bedelia . . ."

"Don't talk to me," she said with such coldness and intolerance that it was like the slash of a whip across his face. "The sight of you makes me feel filthy."

His head seemed to jerk and he looked as if he had gone into a trance. As Bedelia picked up the phone on the side of the bed separating her from him, I said, "The gang vengeance thing was perfect as a motive. Weeks and weeks had gone by since the shooting in the parking lot. And no one had made a move against me. So you decided that you would. It may have been a nonexistent gang. But who would be able to prove that? Especially if the death-threat notes were established beforehand. So you wrote them yourself — two of them — and signed them Slow Death. If I'm wrong, go ahead and say so."

"You're smart, Jim, smarter than hell," he said, still in that strange trancelike state.

"What you didn't count on was that there *was* a gang that wanted vengeance and that they had their own way of doing things — much more painful, more subtle than just knocking me off. And they got to Jan with the heroin. So there we were with two sets of vengeance and written evidence documenting them both. And they badly contradicted each other, at least in my mind. It didn't put a crimp in your plans, but you decided to let it ride.

My murder could still look like gang vengeance later on."

He said nothing and I went on. "And when Colby wasn't in town after we got back from Vegas, the delay was made to order for you. But you needed a confederate and you already had one. You had gotten to know Brooks and his grievances just well enough during your investigation of Mrs. Colby's disappearance in the very beginning. I remember your mentioning it to me. If ever there was a ripe banana this guy was it. You're very impressive and persuasive, Don. And you made him promises about how easy it would be and no one would get hurt, didn't you? But it didn't work out that way and someone did get hurt and you knew he was the type to panic about something like that. You're too good a detective, Don, not to know all the unconcealed habits of somebody you're working on. And when Brooks came down to the pool that morning, there you were with all the steps worked out in advance. Neat, clean, quick, even ingenious. Brooks had had his last swim. But he had served his purpose. Without him you wouldn't have known where the rendezvous point was or had anyone to drive you out there so you could wait in ambush without a car. And now that you didn't have to worry about Brooks you could get back on the track and go after me in a straight line and with no splits in the loot this time. Actually it even turned out better than you had hoped . . ."

"Jim, you've got it all worked out in your mind right down to the letter," Don said, looking right at me now. "But I don't think I'm going to stick around to listen to it."

Bedelia had not yet called the police but stopped to listen, and Don said, "One thing you've got to be able to do in life is know when you're a loser, Jim, and not argue about it. Well, that's me. And there's no court of appeal . . ."

I watched him carefully as he suddenly sauntered a couple of steps in front of the bed and I shifted the line of my aim with him. "Hold it, Don, and don't do anything foolish," I warned him.

"I won't, Jim," he said. "Foolish would be to hang around and let the nails get hammered into me."

"Oh, see yourself *that* way, do you?"

"Oh, don't misunderstand. I might deserve it but my mother doesn't. She's innocent and the least I can do for her is make a quick exit. So I'm walking out of here, Jim, right through that door."

"Don't, Don . . ."

"There's only one way you're going to stop me, Jim," he said calmly. "Right through the head, Jim, that's all I ask."

"Don't be crazy," I said.

"Crazy is the other way," he said. "One thing that never scared me, Jim, was the thought of dying."

He looked at Bedelia whose eyes were riveted on him. He started moving toward the door. "Go ahead, Jim," he said. "Otherwise I disappear through that door."

"All I have to do is wing you, Don."

"You wouldn't really do that, would you, Jim? Let them take me and drag it all out. You wouldn't let them do that."

"I'm not going to kill you, Don," I said. "One more step and I'll put one in your leg, I promise you that. I'm not sentimental about you, Don, get that straight right now."

He got it straight and stopped in his tracks. He just looked at me and shrugged a little, and Bedelia asked for the police.

Don walked back across the front of my bed and stopped where he had been standing originally. I followed him with the gun and he seemed to have changed his mind about things. But I knew he hadn't. "Okay, Jim," he said and paced a few steps toward the window. "What would you do if I pulled out my gun and started shooting right now?"

"Don't, Don," was all I could think of, and I heard Bedelia give a little start in the middle of her conversation with the switchboard at Parker Center.

"But what if I did?" he said, his back to the window, looking at me with a new easygoing expression on his handsome face.

"I'd have to shoot you, but not in the head," I said. "And what would you have gained?"

"Why don't you shoot yourself if it means that much to you?" Bedelia said with uncompromising cruelty.

He smiled sadly. "It's tough to hurt people you love. And it's tough to love people and watch them hate you . . ."

We watched him turn his back on us to stare out of the window and Bedelia handed the phone to me. It was Wagner on the other end and I kept pointing the gun at Don's back as I said to Wagner, "I'm holding a gun on Don Price as I talk to you because he did the three murders . . . The three *murders,* wake up, for Christ's sake, I talk plain enough. Yes, he admits it — Artie Ryan too, that's right. So get over here will you, I'd rather not wait too long, all right? . . ."

Don remained standing with his back turned, hearing every word, and he raised the window to let in some fresh air. Cool breezes came in from the late afternoon skies and Bedelia said, "There's a draft on Jim," coldly.

Don looked over his shoulder and said, "You can shut the window after I leave, Bedelia."

He sat on the windowsill and swung his legs over to the outside and pushed himself off into space and out of our sight. My room was nine stories above a cement courtyard. Bedelia gasped and cried out as if she had been hit in the stomach by Artie or Sonny.

42

AT ABOUT EIGHT O'CLOCK the hospital cracked down and insisted that I be left alone, and the doctor chased Wagner and the cops and the man from the D.A.'s office, who was there to find out if a crime had been committed, and gave me a Seconal to insure some sleep. I didn't want it but I took it anyhow and said good night to Bedelia.

Her face was washed clean of its usual glow, a shocked chalky look to her skin. Neither of us mentioned the fact that the Colby diamonds were back in my hands, and she went home. I had given the police plenty of preliminary material, and now everybody would take days to figure out a legal disposition to place on the matter and then hold an inquest, which I would not attend but for which I would give a deposition to the coroner's assistant and a recording secretary. But basically the thing uppermost in my mind as I drifted off to sleep was what I faced the next morning.

It took place at eight a.m. and I was wheeled to the X-ray room in a chair and I felt a hundred years old. The process is embarrassing because you're helpless lying there on a table with only a sheet draping your pubis in the most precarious way while a female technician injects you and takes her pictures of the dye inside of you. The indignity was minor but noticeable. A cold and impassive, long-faced brunette with her hair tied in a bun did the job on me, and when it was over they let me put back my hospital smock and bathrobe and they started to wheel me out of the place. I caught one of the doctors walking out of one of the examination rooms and I recognized him and I said, "When do I get the results of this humiliating experience, doc?"

"Why should you call it that?" he said seriously.

I didn't have an answer and he said, "I can tell you now there's a touch of nephritis there that's going to require treatment. But to what extent I can't say until I study the plates further." Then he looked at me carefully all of a sudden. "You've been through plenty, haven't you? I hope things will be a little quieter for you from now on."

"I appreciate your kind thoughts, doctor."

A male nurse wheeled me away and up we went in the elevator, about half a dozen people standing, me sitting in the chair. We got off at my floor and as he wheeled me down the corridor Bedelia was waiting outside my room, looking toward me questioningly. She looked as blond and beautiful as ever but she looked at me with a smile that seemed faint and eyes no longer the way they had always been. She wore a black dress and it made me uneasy, becoming as it was, because it had an air of mourning, not just for Don certainly, but for herself, for me, for all of us. I wanted to cut its effect. I looked up from the wheelchair and said, "Want to wrestle?"

She gave it the flick of a smile and said, "Are you okay?"

"Sure."

I got into bed and Rusty hovered over me, propping up the pillows, turning down the corners, and pouring the enzyme pill, now taken only three times a day, into my hand and giving me a glass of water. "Take this and I'll get you your breakfast," she said.

"I thought these were so magical that I'd be back to my former handsome self by now," I said, edgy more than funny about it.

"Can you do anything but complain?" she said. "Your fever is gone, you have a beautiful visitor, and everybody on the floor loves you. What more can a man ask for?"

It was as if nothing out of the ordinary had happened the day before. But of course outside of that room the place was buzzing with it, a thousand-to-one on that. "I ask for very little, Miss Reynolds," I said.

"I know. You're known as Saint James, the martyr of Santa Monica Hospital. No less."

She swept out of the room and Bedelia and I were left to ourselves in a way we had never been before.

"Did they tell you anything?" she asked.

"Nothing final," I said.

She grabbed herself by the elbows across her waist nervously and took a deep breath and paced a few feet toward the window. "I still can't believe it," she said. "It's like a nightmare. Or as if I've gone insane."

"I've got a little of the same feeling, but I'm fighting it," I said.

Evidently the breakfast tray was right outside and Rusty walked back in with it, eggs, toast, and coffee, and orange juice from a concentrate can, and it looked like dinner at Perino's to me. I shouldn't have felt that way at all but I did. Rusty said, "If I were you, I'd bar all visitors today. You need rest."

"Isn't that up to the doctor?" Bedelia said.

"I don't mean you, I mean policemen and all that kind of thing," Rusty said. "Yes, the doctor can put a restriction on visitors. But the hospital would prefer the patient to authorize it on his own in a case of this kind."

"Okay, no visitors and no calls from cops," I agreed, and sipped the orange juice. "And no reporters, by the way."

"A Mr. Steven Elson called while you were in X-ray," Rusty said.

"I'll talk to him, Jim," Bedelia said. "I'll give him a call in a little while. Don't tax yourself with that."

I didn't argue the point and Rusty nodded and went out. "Did you have breakfast?" I asked.

"Yes," she said and paced a few feet, nervous, still shaken. "I only feel sorry for Jean."

"Yes, that's going to be very rough."

"I suppose she's already been told by the police."

"Yes, positively. And it must be all over the news too."

"I keep wondering if I should call her, but . . ."

"Not me," I said. "There's no way to smooth over anything like this and nothing I could do to help her. What could I say? 'I'm sorry your son, who was a multiple-murderer and had me beaten up, jumped out of a window when faced with exposure and arrest'?" I shook my head. "In fact, I'm not even sure she won't wind up hating me anyway. People are like that. Especially doting mothers."

"Oh, do you think she would be that unfair?"

"When you get next to the bone, love, nobody's fair about anything," I said. I ate my eggs and said, "I don't know what the hell made me this hungry. I'm eating like a pregnant woman."

"When will they have a report on the X-ray?" Bedelia said.

"Don't worry about it."

"I won't, as soon as I know it's okay."

"It's not much, I'm sure. Just a little bruise."

"Enough to put blood in your urine," she said, and then again became not exactly angry but cold and outraged. "How *could* he?" she said, remembering. "How could he look us in the face day after day? My God, it's so obvious it's trite. You can't say anything about it that wouldn't be trite. The way he stepped all over friendship and trust . . ." Her face was unforgiving.

"To save his mother, you have to remember that," I said.

"From what? Having to sell an overelaborate house and be reduced to living like the rest of us? No, that doesn't help it any."

"You have to give up all those feelings sooner or later, darling," I said. "You can't go on with the bitterness because it doesn't change a thing."

"You're an original, darling. You haven't uttered a word of anger *or* bitterness about it."

She looked at me with loving eyes and I said what I knew I had to say eventually. "Why should I? All he did was have me beaten up and half-killed for a million dollars' worth of diamond jewelry . . . I never *slept* with him."

Her eyes opened up and I could hear a sharp intake of breath. It was something that could never be unsaid and I knew that nothing was ever going to be the same again. "If I had," I went on with it, "I might have felt different — deceived and humiliated just the way you do."

She just looked at me and couldn't talk yet.

"You do, don't you?" I said. "Because you didn't know what was going on inside of him when you were giving yourself to him. It's okay, sweetheart, I could tell the minute I saw the way you reacted to him yesterday."

"Jim . . ."

"It's okay."

"Jim . . ."

"Take it easy."

Her face flushed and her mouth grew distended and her eyes took on a hot, shiny, embarrassed look, pain in all of it, pain she was trying to hold down. "Oh, Jim," she said in a strained voice, her eyes filled with tears. "What have I done to us? . . ."

I didn't have an immediate answer and I looked away for just an instant and she said, "Was it *that* obvious?"

"Not until yesterday. Not until you said you felt filthy." I shook my head. "When a woman says something like that it can only refer to one thing. And you were saying it about Don."

She lowered her head in an acquiescent way and murmured, "Yes . . ."

"Then I remembered other little things you don't pay attention to at the time they happen, just as I did with Don himself. For instance, you said you spent all day last Friday with your friend, Gay. But the other night when you were talking to her on the phone I realized she's a school teacher. And unless she was sick or something she'd have to be in school on an ordinary Friday. So you just used her name without thinking in order to cover up where you had really been that day. And I can guess now where that was. And with whom. Want to correct me?"

"No . . . That was one of the times . . ."

"Maybe I knew it right at that very moment. But I didn't let it come through. And now I think back to a funny feeling I had when I left the two of you alone in Vegas that day because he didn't answer his phone but you answered yours. The feeling lasted about three seconds."

She raised her head to look at me and confessed. "Yes . . . We were together. Another of the very few times . . ."

"But I'm not enraged about it or anything like it," I said. "I want you to know that right off."

"I'd rather you tried to kill me than say something like that."

"Why?"

"Because I love you . . ."

"I know that."

"I could never love another man the way I love you," she said. "But I began to love Don too in another way — almost sisterly, strange as that may sound. Because until yesterday in that terrible and, yes, humiliating, moment, I thought he was the only loyal and loving person in my life besides you. I found out about a year ago how lonely he was and how he felt about me, or said he did. I didn't know what to do. And neither did he. I thought it was tormenting him. And maybe at the time it was . . ."

I watched her closely and I still loved her but knew it was all over no matter what she said, and for all the reasons I had given myself long before now.

"And then you went away to San Francisco when your mother died and you had to settle her affairs . . ."

"Yes," I said.

"It was then for the first time. I won't try to explain it, but I had absolutely no desire when we did it. I know it will sound terrible, but I did it to make him happy. Oh, I was lonely, as lonely as he was. Because I couldn't hold on to reality during those four days. I couldn't believe you would ever come back to me. I've always felt that way whenever I've been away from you for more than a day. That was part of it. But I was not on fire for him and he knew it. And it was only the once, Jim, and never again. Until you began to talk about the inevitable end of our being together. It was almost as if you were reconciling me to being passed on to someone else because you were convinced you were too old for me. You even said so in so many words to Don himself. And he told it to me as if it would make our times together less guilty." She shook her head. "I thought he loved me. And I thought I loved him in some sort of a strange, almost incestuous way . . . But I always loved you in spite of it, Jim. And I always will love you . . ." She smiled, wet-eyed, and said, "Trite. But true . . ."

"That's right, sweetheart. But you're going to need someone else," I said, "just as I've always told you you would."

"Because of Don?" she demanded quietly.

"It tells me you need a lot more than I can give, sweetheart," I said.

"You're hurt, I know," she said. "Your pride is wounded, but it shouldn't be, darling . . ."

"Maybe, sweetheart. But I understand. And there was nothing incestuous about it. The cold fact is that Don would have had you eventually on a regular basis. And why not? There was only one hitch. He turned out to be a triple-murderer with a mother fixation. That was the difference, nothing else. So there will be someone else — there will *have* to be . . ."

"Jim . . ."

"I can't see myself being whatever it is you think I am to you at the same time somebody else is being what I no longer *can* be. It's not the part I want to play in *any*one's life. And that's the way I would wind up, sweetheart. I'd have to. It wouldn't be fair to you any other way. That's what I've been getting at all the time."

"Jim, you're not calling it a day with me, are you?"

She was still a little tearful and I wondered to myself fleetingly if I had some sneaking enjoyment of her tears and of the fact that I could make her feel this way, and the idea made me a little bit ashamed of myself. But just a little bit.

"Darling," I said. "You made love to Don because you liked it. Not because you started out feeling sorry for him or any of the other things you told yourself it was all about. You're young and passionate and oozing with sex and you haven't reached your peak yet. And someday you're going to be very glad you're not chained to an old agreement without much to recommend it except sentimental memories and sympathy."

I stopped talking, felt tired, and I watched something come over her that wasn't familiar to me, like the disappointment and pleading in the eyes of a young child that suddenly turns into hard realization and acceptance. And in a voice I hadn't heard her use before she said, "All right, Jim . . . Maybe you've finally convinced me . . ."

It was unexpected. But I took it. "You don't owe me anything, darling," was the way I put it.

She picked up her shoulder-strap purse and stood there in the black dress, her eyes a glistening blue, her lips a little dry at the moment, the blond hair short and vibrant as new wheat in the sunshine, and she said, "You're getting even, Jim. You don't even know it, but that's what you're doing. You're hurt and you want to hurt back. You want me to feel some of the pain . . ."

"Don't say that, sweetheart."

"I've got to say it." She began to walk toward the door. "And I've got to leave now, darling. There's no place for me to sit, stand, or lie down, and I've got to leave . . ."

"Look, Bedelia . . ."
"Whatever's left of me I've got to try to save. And maybe I can."
That was the last thing she said and then was gone.

43

AFTER THAT THE DAYS didn't go by easily but I got better slowly, the more obvious abrasions and contusions fading, the edema just about gone by the end of the first week. When I got the money from the Colby estate, to skip over the tedious details, I called Rita and asked her to come by the hospital. By then I was up and walking in the corridor, or sitting in my robe and playing solitaire, or gin rummy with an ambulatory fellow-patient who had been assigned to the bed that had been empty next to me for the first four or five days. He took a powder when Rita arrived, tall, trim, a marvelous-looking forty-five-year-old in a wide-brimmed straw hat that enshadowed her face with middle-aged allure. She had already been to see me once the week before because Bedelia had actually called her to tell her what had happened and where I could be found. "Your girl is obviously the gallant type," she had said at the time.

Now she stood next to where I was sitting at the edge of the bed and said, "Oh, Jim, you look so much better."

"I'm glad to hear that," I said.

"Loretta wanted to come but I didn't want her to see you. It's tough enough on mistresses and ex-wives to have to look at it," she said.

"I've ended up with an iffy kidney, but I'm fine otherwise," I said. "I should be out of here in four or five days — a grand total of two weeks."

"You should go on a cruise somewhere," she said. "Just sit on the sundeck of a ship and let stewards bring you drinks and sandwiches and live the lush life."

"I had considered it," I said.

"Steve and I did that last year. Just a two-week thing up along the coast to British Columbia." She grew thoughtful and said, "You and I never did that. We should have."

"I guess we should have," I said.

"Well, now you can do it with whoever. You'll get your strength back more slowly that way, but I suppose you won't mind."

"Oh, cut it out," I said gently, and I took an envelope from the nightstand and handed it to her. "Here. This is for Loretta. Take it out; you can look at it."

The flap was merely inserted and Rita removed from inside the check I had made out to Loretta for ten thousand dollars. Her face grew very still and her eyes verged on tears that never came. "You *are* a superdaddy, aren't you?" she said.

"I'm nothing," I said. "The kid is *so* bright, *so* sweet, and *so* good that we're lucky to even know her. What's the money? My pockets are stuffed."

"For you and your lucky lady. I'm jealous as hell, but I'm glad for you."

"Well, skip being jealous," I said. "There is no lucky lady. She's gone. It had to happen and it did."

Rita was really surprised. "I won't pry. But wasn't this a weird time for it?"

"Half the time is weird and the other half is lousy. There is no right time for anything, love, don't you know that yet? But I don't want to talk about it particularly. We both did our best, just the way you and I did. What about Jan?"

"A lot about Jan," she said, gliding easily into the change of subject. "I've seen her. I've seen Strelli too."

I looked into her eyes under the hat brim and couldn't believe what she had said. "He said that I could look through every mug shot in the police files of all the cities in the country and never find him because he has no record."

I didn't say anything, just waited.

"The man you killed *was* his brother, just as you suspected. He tried to get back at you. He knows he was wrong . . ."

"Where is he? Where did you see him?" I asked her in a hard but quiet voice, feeling more rage and emotion than I ever felt about what Don did to me.

"Don't get excited, Jim," she said in a wise, just-as-quiet voice. "He isn't the same boy today that he was two months ago. He's changed. He couldn't help himself. And thank God. Because now Jan is clean. She never was a true addict. Be grateful for that. Anyhow, I had a feeling about it all the time — that is, after Jan left home the second time and called from outside L.A. I mentioned it to you."

"Mentioned what?"

"That maybe he had fallen in love with her. And I was right."

"Oh, Christ, Rita . . ."

"That's just what happened, Jim, like it or not. And Strelli is as helpless, if you think about it, as we are. He never anticipated anything like that, needless to say. Well, it happened. And it changed him from a boy full of hate and anger to a loving and — well, I won't go too far with a characterization or a character reference. But I think it's safe to say there's been a transformation. He's madly in love with her, Jim, believe that or not in this day of swingers and easy sex and group gropes and what not."

I didn't say anything, just looked at her.

"I've seen it and I know," she said. "I met them at Disneyland, of all places, and had lunch with them. Strelli has a job waiting for him with a commercial-art house in New York. He's an art school graduate . . ."

"That's just marvelous," I said tonelessly.

She said sagely, "It is what it is, Jim."

I spread my palms upturned in acceptance and said nothing.

"They're going to be married — quickly and quietly."

Then I shook my head ironically and let out a deep breath.

"It may have begun like something on a police blotter," she said. "But it's ended up like something in Faith Baldwin." She laughed. "Well, for God's sake. Disneyland!"

44

I MAILED A CHECK for ten thousand dollars to Bedelia just before I left the hospital. I wanted her to have it and I put in a note saying that she had more than earned it and I signed Love with my name. A day or two after I was back in my apartment the check came back to me in the mail. There was a note with it that said, "Dear Jim, I don't think I'm worth this kind of a tip. My salary took care of everything adequately and anything else cannot be given a monetary value. Bedelia."

I walked with a cane for a few weeks after I came home. I stayed pretty much to myself, watched a few high school baseball games in the big recreational area across the street from my apartment building, wondered what I would do with all that dough that had been dropped in my lap, looked at TV, read the newspaper every day and also a book about how the Allies cracked the German code during the war. I attended Loretta's high school graduation, an event from which I got more satisfaction than anything I could remember in a long time. I think about six weeks went by before I telephoned Bedelia, not less than that anyhow. A young man answered, said only, "Hello," and I waited for just a few seconds before I hung up.